AUBREY TAYLOR

You Left us in Georgia

Contents

To my precious Sugar Club,
who gave me the confidence to share Bishop with the world.
ifykyk

This novel contains topics of self-harm and suicide.

Take breaks, get some water, and snuggle your loved ones, pets, and stuffed animals.

Be kind to yourself, being a human being is tough.

if it's still in your mind,
it's worth taking the risk.

1

I shook the sleep from my body. The smell of day-old whiskey wafted from the sheets and into my nose. *I need a shower,* I thought. I flipped the sheet back off of me and stumbled from the bed. The cotton shorts I had thrown on before I drunkenly had fallen asleep were stuck to my thighs in the Georgian heat.

I grabbed my phone off the table in the kitchen and made my way to the bathroom. Flicking the light on and I backed off quickly with a hiss. Lights and hangovers did not mix, I shut my eyes for a minute letting the wave of pain and nausea roll through me before sitting down on the toilet to go pee.

I turned my phone on, the sheer white light from the screen blinding me. *Why is everything so damn bright?* I huffed as my phone vibrated for almost a minute straight and an onslaught of texts, missed calls, and notifications from *Instagram.*

"What did I do now?" I sighed, most of the missed calls and texts were from Natalie, a few from Willa, and three very alarming voice messages from Nicholas.

"Nora! I hope to god you got home okay, you disappeared from the bar without a word and Willa has no idea where you would have gone." Nicholas's voice mimicked the sound of a cat's nails on a chalkboard early in the morning. *"I told Josh you were going*

to take the day off tomorrow but you need to call someone to let them know you're okay. I didn't know he was going to get brought up last night, I'm such an idiot for bringing her along. I should have known she would..."

The message ended abruptly. I chuckled, that's right. I had left the bar last night in a trance of whiskey and rage. It felt like rage but I knew better than anyone it wasn't, it was sadness, it was an empty feeling that twisted and turned until it had become a rage. Nicholas had brought *her* to the bar. He had invited that wench, Kate.

Kate wasn't the worst human I had ever encountered but she certainly made it hard to like her. We had gone to school together when we were younger, we spent every summer until we were twenty-three at the beach houses their families owned. Bartley owned the biggest house on the block, freshly built, and loomed over everything in judgment. Kate was Bishop's younger sister. On the other end of the lane was the Roberts's house, Sean their only son, was an American dream human being. Respectful, kind, the kind of guy that girls dream of. We spent every summer together. As we grew older we turned into our own people but I had no idea how Kate had turned so toxic.

I called Natalie, the phone barely rang once before she picked up, "Oh dear god," she breathed into the phone, she was on a run. "Can you never do that again?"

"I'm sorry I was feeling claustrophobic," I leaned over, pushed the curtain out of my way, and turned the shower on.

"That's no excuse to bolt, Willa called me freaking out!" Nat sighed, the sounds of the park around her filling the silence in the phone call.

2

"I'm fine, I'll call Willa." I sighed and stripped out of the shorts and sports bra I was wearing.

"I have a question for you," Nat stopped breathing hard and waited for me to tell her to continue.

"If this is about coming home for the summer, you can forget it." I snapped. It didn't matter how many times she asked me, I wasn't going to go back there. I couldn't.

"Come on, I convinced Ben that it would be fun. You have to come. Mom misses you, and dad really liked the idea but didn't think I could get you to come. I need you there. You need some time away from everything to relax." She begged, I had never once heard my sister beg me for anything.

"Dad's right, you aren't going to get me to come. The beach house isn't relaxing for me. It's emotional torture." I growled this time, absolutely pissed off she was even asking this of me.

"He won't be there. Sean is coming, and Uncle Curtis." she paused, and I could hear the frustration in her voice. The need for me to be there was loud and clear as she spoke again, "it'll be like old times."

"The old times hold a lot of crappy memories, Nat." I bit my tongue from saying anything else stupid. "I need to shower, I have to get to work."

I hung up on her, throwing the cell phone on the counter and letting the warm water clean me of last night's alcohol. I shampoo all the smoke and grime from my hair, and the dark makeup I had worn comes off with the face cloth.

Just as the headache began to subside my phone rang from the counter, I wrapped a towel around myself and climbed out. *For fuck sake will everyone just leave me alone for five minutes?* "Hello? Oh, god Hi Josh," I said, realizing the number.

"Hey, Nick said you would be out today but could I trouble

you to go do a couple pickups? Nothing crazy, just a few things we need to do prints over the weekend. Mr. Matthews says the bass and the cello are both ready to be picked up. " He asked, I had planned on going in despite the kind planning of Nicholas seeing my hangover ahead of time.

"Yeah," I sighed into the phone as I threw the towel over the shower rod and left the bathroom. I moved around my small studio apartment, shuffling things out of the way as I walked back to the closet, "Hey Josh," I said, about to regret my decision. "There's some family stuff going on this summer, how badly do you need me in the house to do my job? My sister wants me to join them for a couple of weeks max."

Josh laughed, I half expected him to say no. If he did then I would have had a decent excuse for Natalie about why I couldn't join them. "Honestly, summer is slow for events. We only have the big garden event at the end of August, can you be back for that? Everything else I really just need your ears and eyes over the laptop."

"Alright, that's..." I paused, shaking my head in disbelief. "Awesome, just what I wanted to hear. I'll drop those things off later today and grab my work folders. Thanks, Josh."

"No worries Nora, I'll text you the addresses for pick-ups. You work too hard, enjoy the time off." He said before hanging up. Everyone kept saying to me, but it never resonated the way they wanted. Relaxing didn't come easy when your heart was breaking with every passing moment. And as easily as I was able to forget him, he slipped back into my thoughts without even having to pop the lock on the door.

He hadn't called in months, before that I hadn't seen him for almost a year and a half. He had contracts in Japan he had to handle, and meetings in New Zealand he couldn't afford to miss. He could afford to walk away from me, but not that, not his money and his company.

He was always so closed off about everything he did, every meeting and phone call. It drove me nuts but when he looked at me with eyes that glimmered like the sea after a storm I forgot everything. I forgot all the fights, all the screaming and arguing because I knew he loved me more than he ever said out loud but it just wasn't enough.

I could feel the bile rising in my throat, tearing through me. I ran back to the bathroom and vomited over and over until my stomach was empty. This was the worst idea I had ever had. I cleaned myself off, pulling a clean white blouse on and buttoning the pearl buttons up to just above my breasts, and slid into a pair of tight black jeans. I shoved my feet into a pair of thick-soled black boots and grabbed my small green bag from the hook beside the kitchen.

The heat would be the death of me in Atlanta. It was so sticky and hot that even fresh out of the shower I could feel myself melting. I made quick work of the pickups, sliding the repaired instruments into the trunk of my car. For the last three years, I had been putting my event coordinator and graphics degree to the test working for Josh Fasen. He ran one of the largest entertainment companies in Atlanta. He specializes in planning events for large orchestra functions. Our largest event of the year was the Garden Gala in August and the rooftop New Years' party he threw for some of the most famous and rich in Georgia.

I was the head of the department, or what I affectionately called "The lead of keeping Josh from losing his shit." I was paid more than I deserved, it all going into savings funds so one day I could live far away from any city in peace and quiet.

Alone in the woods with my violin and a pack of cats that acted like guard dogs.

"Hey!" Nicholas met me in the parking lot with a trolley to help carry the boxes up to the fifth-floor offices. "How are you feeling?" He was dressed in a deep burgundy polo that matched his dark complexion, he had sunglasses on to cover his own hangover.

"I should punch you in the throat for bringing her last night," I snarled at him, "you're such an asshole."

"I know," he flashes a wide smile at me, he lifts his sunglasses and winks one of his chocolate brown eyes. Nick was Josh's younger brother. The troublemaker. No matter what leash Josh tried to keep his brother on, Nicholas found a to slip the lead and get lost. "I am sorry."

"Sure you are, be careful with that." I nudge him as he pulls the cello from the trunk and slings it over his shoulder. "I'm leaving for the summer tomorrow, I'm going with Nat down to Tybee."

The look on his face said it all, "That's a terrible idea." It came out as more of a laugh than shock when the words left his lips. "Don't all the beach houses sit on the same stretch of land out there?" He asked, pressing the button on the elevator. "The Bartley house is one of them isn't it?"

"Oh you betcha," I groaned, rolling my head around on my neck. I was suddenly feeling very tense.

"How long has it been since you've been back there?" He asked.

"Since the summer dad got sick," I answered solemnly.

"The *summer*?" Nick stopped short of entering the office. He put his hand on my arm and removed his sunglasses fully to stare at me in disbelief, "like the summer he left?"

6

"Yeah Nick, the summer since Bishop left."

2

"Do you really need all of this?" Ben eyed up the amount of bags I dropped at his feet. "The washing machine at the beach house works, you know."

"Shut up Ben," I laughed, climbing into the back seat of the jeep. Natalie had her nose in a book while she waited but she set down when I shut my door.

"Are you doing okay? You seem nervous," she said and I titled my head to the left, "sorry yeah, it'll be fun I promise."

"Promise? Seems like a tall order, even for you Nat." I shook my head and pulled my dirty old sketchbook from my bag. It would be a long four hours to the house. The notebook would keep my attention and stop me from thinking about all the anxiety rushing into my brain.

It was making my skin itchy and I felt feverish. I scratched the pencil across the page in harsh lines, smudging and fixing but never erasing. Letting all the feelings flow freely onto the paper like free therapy. Ben looked back at me every once and a while as he drove, his face concerned and tight. He always looked like that, stern but his eyes were soft and welcoming.

Ben was a degree-certified therapist, and the reason I started sketching was that he suggested I keep a diary. I had a terrible time with words. It's why I played music because even when

I couldn't speak the music was there to fill the space. "Stop hovering and keep your eyes on the road."

He shook his head but kept checking in anyways until we pulled into a gas station restaurant for lunch. I hauled the notebook with me, the only thing keeping me from yelling and crying was that scratching noise the pencil made. The closer we got to Tybee, the more unhinged I became. I could feel myself losing whatever control I had formed over the last years. The lack of contact had been good for us, we hadn't been together since Bishop left but every time the phone rang and it was his number on the screen I answered. It had been like a bad habit I couldn't quit. The phone rang, and I answered. It didn't matter what time difference there was, *I answered.*

Ben had suggested the full cut-off. At first, I had agreed but like a two-pack-a-day smoker, I answered the phone the very next day. Most times, Bishop would call and not say a single word. He would just lay on the other end of the phone and let the sound of my heart shattering fill the silence around us. It was a bad, broken record.

It was only when Nat answered one day. She lost her mind on me claiming that I was letting him have control over my life. That was when Ben forced me to get a new phone number, one Bishop didn't have. I cried for a month after. It was the worst withdrawal I had ever experienced. So I filled the silence, filled the empty space that he had left with booze and bars. Natalie didn't like it but at least I wasn't on the verge of self-harm anymore. That's all that really mattered. *We don't wanna have to babysit you anymore Nora, we have lives too.*

I was a burden at that point. I realized I had become the same thing to Bishop. He only called to keep me from killing myself. That's the moment it clicked, that he didn't care about my feelings anymore. He was protecting himself from the soul-crushing guilt he would have gone through if I had done something extreme.

I had come close one night, teetering on the edge of a ten-story office building. The snow had fallen so beautifully that day. It never snowed in Georgia. All I could think of in my drunken stupor was how graceful I would look when they found me. *I would be a snow angel.*

I couldn't do it though, the image of my dad and mom stopped me short. Toes curled over the freezing cold metal sliding that bordered the rooftop, I slid back and cried for hours. I would have frozen to death if Nick and Willa hadn't traced my phone and come to get me. That was the end of my freedom, that was the day Natalie lost her mind and I changed mine.

I would no longer burden anyone.

I was better now, I felt better now. I took therapy once a week with a therapist Ben had referred me to across the hall from his office and I only went to the bar twice a week. It was a compromise for not becoming an alcoholic.

"What are you drawing?" Ben asked, I hadn't even realized I had sat down let alone flipped open my book and continued drawing. I looked down, shaking my head and slammed the book shut. "It's okay to draw him," he said lightly, looking to where Natalie went to the bathroom. She would have disagreed.

"Nat doesn't understand that for you to let go, you need to think about him sometimes. It's okay to do that. Your skills have improved greatly since the last time you showed me your book. May I see?" He holds his hand out to me.

"Don't let her see," I said. "Please," his soft brown eyes connect with mine as I slide the book to his fingertips.

"This is a new one," he raised an eyebrow looking up at me from an angle.

"After I cut him off, I couldn't stop. It's the only thing stopping me from going insane." I swallowed hard and watched him flip open the front page to the new notebook. He flipped carefully through pages of the same image. The same beautiful dark hair, scribbled and smudged. The same painfully sad eyes. Every single page was marred the same way.

"These are excruciatingly exquisite Nora." He sounded shocked. "This trip will be good for you, it's time to reclaim your home."

He looked at me, a look of sympathy crossed his face but flutters away and leaves a sense of pride. A smile formed on his lips. "I'm proud of you."

"Proud of her for what?" Nat slides into the booth next to me.

"Doctor and Client confidentiality." Ben teased, flicking Nat's nose with a finger and sneakily sliding the book back to me. I tucked it into my bag and waited for the waitress to come to serve us.

Natalie and Ben had been inseparable for a century. I couldn't remember far enough back to a day when they weren't together. Ben had grown up down the street from us, and our parents used to bring him to the beach house every summer. He was an only child and his parents were doctors that worked crazy hours.

I don't even think they ever realized he was gone most summers.

Natalie had been the popular girl, the one everyone wanted to spend time with during the summers. Ben was older than us, but he spent his days with his nose in books and surfing. He didn't care about the people she hung out with but he was always watching. She just never noticed. I remembered the day she realized she was in love with him, it was like watching fireworks explode inside a very small room. Intense and terrifying all at once.

She was fifteen and had gone out, dressed in a black slip dress and a bathing suit. Kate was throwing a bonfire at the end of the street. They ended up surfing out to one of the small sandy islands and partying there. Natalie lost her phone and got separated from the group, she had drunk too much. She fell asleep against a tree and almost froze to death because she was wet.

Ben had looked for her all night, screaming up and down the streets on his shitty bicycle until he found her. Blue-lipped and shaking. I watched him slam through the wicker mesh front door and wake the entire house up as he set her on the couch. I wrapped blankets around her until she woke up, confused and completely unaware of how she got home.

Natalie hadn't said a word to him, I had never seen him so angry.

In the morning she crept from bed after my parents had gone to work but Ben was waiting for her in the kitchen. His eyes were still alight from the night before, the rage was still simmering.

"What were you thinking?" He asked her, more calmly than I had expected. I tried to mind my own business as I shoved cheerios in my mouth. "You could have died."

"Don't be dramatic, I fell asleep. I'm fine." I knew instantly this was not the right choice of words. Natalie brushed past him and opened the fridge to grab a water bottle.

"You're fine because I found you, I brought you home and Nora

warmed you up so you could go to bed. You're alive and untouched because we cared enough to come to find you. Kate didn't seem to give a fuck where you were when I called her. She didn't even realize you had come to the party, let alone left drunk and alone!"
Ben was screaming at that point.

Natalie didn't back down, she squared her shoulders. Her soft red hair fell around her face in luscious waves and her green eyes were wet with tears. "Why do you care, Ben?

"Why do I care?" He shook his head, his curly brown mop of hair moving gently. "You are the only thing I care about and you wander around with no self-preservation Natalie! I spend my summers watching out for you so you don't kill yourself, or drink yourself to death. I would do anything with you, all day if you just asked."

"Then why don't you?" That was as close to an apology Ben would get from her, a submission to his needs and wants. She had been submitting ever since.

"Will you surf with me today?" He asked and she followed.

"Order me a sandwich," Ben said, tapping the menu and wandering off to the bathroom.

"I called dad, he's excited to see you. Uncle Curtis gets in from the airport this afternoon, he's bringing his girlfriend." Natalie groaned, the waitress collected our orders and sauntered away.

"Which one is that?" I asked, and she only shrugged in response. "I don't even remember his old girlfriend."

"It was Kate..." Nat laughed wildly. My mouth dropped open, "you haven't been around for almost three years. She leached off of him for a whole year, he would take her on trips and buy her clothes. It was awful."

"I'm glad I missed that she's like ten years younger than him," I rolled my eyes and checked my phone for messages. I had two missed calls from an unknown number, I scowled at them and deleted the notifications.

"It's okay," the waitress set the food down in front of us and Nat shoved a handful of french fries in her mouth. "She's not coming, at least I didn't invite her."

We finished our food, all of us full beyond repair and we climbed back in the jeep. "I'll drive." I offered and Ben nodded, opening the passenger door for Nat to climb in. He fell asleep within five minutes back on the road. He snored the rest of the way to the beach house, the smell of salt water hit my nose like a cruel reminder that this was my home and I could never run away from it.

The beach house looked exactly the same, towering over the jeep. Two stories of teal chipped paint, and pale white shutters framed each of the six windows that let the light into the front of the house. The back was still encased in a large, white-painted deck with stairs that led down through the dense bush and trees to the beach.

"Welcome home, Nori," Ben laughed, unpacking the trunk. I hadn't heard that name in years, I turned to him with a scowl and took a deep breath. I didn't feel at home.

3

I stood outside the house, one hand tightly gripped on my bag. My hand is shoved inside of it gripped tightly to the notebook within. "Don't stand there forever."

Ben sighed before the wicker door slammed shut behind him. I could feel my teeth grinding together, the way my muscles tensed, and the way my heart felt sick but I still couldn't move. I could hear Natalie laughing with my mother inside, I could feel the tears threatening to fall but I wiped them away.

"Yes mom, she's here." I heard Nat say from inside and wait for the onslaught of questions but mom said nothing, not a word. She crashed into me, her arms engulfing me in the tightest, warmest hug I'd ever experienced.

I sunk into it like it was a warm bath and let her nuzzle her nose into my hair. "Oh, I missed you so much it hurts." She mused as she pulled back to examine my face. "You are so beautiful, you haven't aged a day." Kissing me gently on the cheek before rubbing her nose against mine, "thank you for coming."

"Ben thinks it'll be good for me," I said defeated, her hands pressed to my face. She looked older, her red strands of hair tucked into a bun they were graying around the roots. Her face was covered in new lines I hadn't seen before and her eyes were graying from their typical forest green.

"It will be, come on inside with you. Dad will be home soon." There was a hesitation in her voice, a tone that didn't sit quite right with me but I followed nonetheless.

The house smelled the same. Saltwater mixed with the smells of tequila, grapefruit, and lime. It was my favorite smell in the world because it meant summertime. It meant, surfing and bonfires on the beach. It meant short shorts in the day and thick sweaters in the evening. I had missed it more than I cared to admit.

Mom hadn't moved a single piece of furniture. The old white sofa sat against the tall banister stairs in the living room, a long wicker coffee table filling the space between the couch and the TV. Two old, reclining chairs sat on opposite ends covered in old knitted blankets in ugly colors that belonged in the seventies.

The kitchen island was still a nasty sea blue color and the white counter had seen better days. The honey-colored cabinets were a stark contrast against the dark blue walls. The stairs curved, a small platform a few steps up then led to the bedrooms and bathroom that occupied the upper levels. The room I shared with Natalie was up there, and so was the room Ben had used and my parent's room. There was a guest room on the main floor that Uncle Curtis usually used. Nothing had changed. It was oddly comforting for me, to know that even after all the time spent away no one had moved a single inch. Time stood still in Tybee and for that I was thankful.

"Well, well, well… if it isn't Stitch in the flesh." A familiar voice made a smile creep up on my face, a smile I had forgotten existed until that very moment.

16

"Ponyboy Curtis!" I laughed, Sean stood in the frame of the back door, wearing a dark red t-shirt with his arms folded across his chest. We had read the Outsiders in grade eight, and there was something about the undying goodness of Ponyboy that made me think of Sean.

For a second, standing there in the doorway, I saw the boy I used to know, short cropped blonde hair that stuck up in every direction. A clean-shaven jaw and the bluest eyes you'd ever seen. He was scrawny back then, but now he was broad and had gained at least thirty pounds of muscle. His hair was longer and darker, it flipped over on the top and laid back against the top. His jaw had widened and had a thick covering of dirty blonde hair. I stopped thinking that this meeting, like this, might be awkward but he didn't hesitate.

He took three long strides toward me and wrapped me up in his arms without pause or thought. I rested against him and let the smell of banana wax and cologne take me over. He ran a hand through my hair, holding tight, and took a deep breath in, "I'm really here, you can let go."

I said it out loud but he takes a full thirty seconds before he finally does, "I'm sorry it's just been so long since you've been here," he stared at me for a long time, his hands still on my arms.

"Really, really here…" I said again. I placed my hands on his biceps and made a face, "you're bulking up again."

Sean just laughed, shaking his head, and walked back into the kitchen to help my mom unpack the groceries that littered the island. "Curtis said his girlfriend is a vegetarian," my mom rolled her eyes, tossing vegetables into the sink to wash them.

I just laughed with a shrug, I didn't care either way. She wouldn't last long, no one ever did with Curtis. He was too childish, he was a hard worker but his spare time was spent jet-setting around the world. He didn't want to start a family, I didn't blame him. Having a family was hard. It was the same story every time, he dated a girl for six months, they had fun he'd introduce them to the family and within the month she'd be gone. Mom always said bringing them home to meet the family was just asking for trouble. It was a curse because not weeks later the girl would expect a ring. It was comical.

I set my bag down, slipped not one but four notebooks from the inside, and went out on the back deck. I kicked off my shoes and wandered down the stairs. A long winding path led to the tree house our dad built us when we were younger. It was a miracle the thing was still sturdy. I tested my weight on one of the old ladder rungs before I pulled myself up. I slid the notebooks along the floor, using my now free hands to hoist myself inside. It smelt of dust and evergreen trees inside. Empty beer bottles littered the corner, every single one had missed the trash can. The gas-operated lamp still flickered on with a click of the lighter that sat beside it. I hold it up, shining the light on the four walls of the old tree house. Each one was plastered with photos of us from the ages of five throughout the years.

I ran my fingers softly over the old photos, cracked and weathered each one a memory of what this place used to be for me. Natalie huddled into the arms of Ben, Sean in his football jersey, and even Kate made an appearance. The two of us wrapped in each other arms with giant smiles on our painted faces, she was supposed to be a tiger and I had chosen a butterfly. The heat had melted the paint and we just looked a mess.

As we got older the pictures became lonely, solo photos

of Kate spinning in small dresses and beers in both hands. Natalie is in the bathroom fixing her hair in the mirror. Ben is alone on the dock, his face in a book and headphones in his ears. Sean sitting on a surfboard just offshore. There were tons of me, each one from a distance and dark in color.

I touched one of myself sleeping, blankets pulled up over my shoulders, and my red hair tangled in the ruffles of the old pillow my face was pressed into. Bishop had taken every single one of these on his old Polaroid. He took every photo of us all that summer. A sad reflection of how far we wandered from one another. The ones of myself hurt, and a dull throb rippled through me. All of the ones of Bishop were gone, I had burned them. Their ashes still occupied the trash can in the tree house, that was the last time anyone had been up there. The day he left, I lost my mind and destroyed every single piece of evidence that he existed.

The photos of us tangled together, the ones of us from homecoming, every single photo of him wet and sandy after spending the morning surfing with Sean and Ben. They were gone.

I set the notebooks on the old weathered couch that we had fought to get into the tree house, we had used pulleys and every ounce of strength we had to get it in there piece by piece. It had seen better days. I tugged at the corners of the messy sketches and tore each one carefully from the notebook. I created a small pile of them until they were all removed from the books.

I slowly and surely tacked each sketch to the wall of the tree house, soon the wall was back to normal. Littered with photos of Bishop between the photos of the rest of us yet again. I left the empty books in the trash can with the ashes and climbed down carefully from the tree house. The bottom rung cracks under my weight but holds on until I am safely back on the ground.

I took my time walking back to the house, the sun was slowly setting in the sky and mom had turned the backlights on so I could find my way back. Dad had strung tiny bulbs along the trees leading all the way down the beach one year after Nat broke her arm while walking in the dark. The lights were soft and created a warm glow through the trees all the way back up to the base of the stairs.

I climbed them slowly, I wanted out of these hot clothes. The Grey T-shirt I had worn that morning was drenched in sweat and the leggings weren't much better. I could hear Uncle Curtis laughing from inside the house and picked up my pace, I hadn't seen him in so long and it was wonderful to hear him. But as I turn the corner to the house I see that Sean looms nervously at the top of the stairs.

"Let's go for a walk," he said. He avoided my gaze and held his arm across the top of the deck blocking my way up to the house.

"What's wrong?" I asked, a sinking feeling growing in my stomach. "I want to see dad, and Curtis."

I try to push past him but he stops me, he's too strong for me to shove away. He's so tense, every muscle in his body is rigid and tight around me. "Please Nora, don't.

Bishop stood on the other side of the counter, talking with my mother. His hands shoved into the pockets of his dark petticoat, he looked up to the window and his blue eyes cut into me like hundreds of tiny shards of glass.

The world spun so fast that I suffered whiplash.

"Why is he here," I managed to whisper, Sean just holding

me in place. I don't know if I'm even standing on my own anymore. "Why is he here!!" I yelled as Natalie pushed the screen door open on the backdoor. Her eyes were full of regret.

"Let me talk to her," she said and Sean finally let go of me. I stumbled for a second, he held his hand out if I needed it but I pushed him off.

"Did you know he was coming?" I asked simply. My eyes wrenched away from Bishop, and onto her. "Well?" I can hear myself scream but it doesn't register how loud I am until Nat flinches.

"Curtis brought Kate, apparently they're seeing each other again." Nat shook her head. Her eyes are sympathetic. "Kate invited Bishop," she mumbled, but it was clear as day as the words slipped out of her mouth. "I guess when she saw you the other day she called him, and told him about the family all coming home."

"The calls," I groaned, ripping my phone from my back pocket. I had missed three more unknown number calls since I had checked at the dinner. "He was calling me all day, I wonder what he has to say." I pushed Sean away from me and stormed into the house, throwing the phone on the counter so hard the screen shattered.

I wanted to ask him so many things but the words froze in my throat. Every inch of my body shook, my hands rattled against my side and my heart. His dark brown hair was shorter, pushed back off his face, but it still looked just as soft as I remembered. My fingers ached to run through it. I watched as his tongue flicked across his bottom lip and dragged it under his teeth. His whole jaw tensing with the motion, I wanted to scream at him but I couldn't find a single word mean enough to call him.

He hadn't changed a bit, his sharp, angled jaw still covered in dark scruffy hair and his lips still the softest shade of pink. His blue eyes watched me as I took him in, his strong neck and broad shoulders hid under his fancy jacket.

I turned, looking at dad. His weathered face looked back with the utmost sympathy in his old gray eyes. He sighed and opened his arms to me. I took the chance and crashed into him, hugging him so tightly that I heard him groan under the weight.

"I didn't know until I got to the airport," he whispered in my ear, his breath warm against my face. "He came in on the same flight as Curtis."

"It stings," I mumbled back. Ben stood against the back counter, his arms over his chest. He was the only one who didn't look at me like I was going to break. He nodded and gave me a soft smile of encouragement. I could do this, even though it was heartbreaking.

"I know sweetheart." He rubbed my back and let me go.

"Uncle," I said through clenched teeth, he smiled pathetically at me. He looked older, tattoos covered both his arms now and he carried heavy bags under his eyes. "Kate, lovely to see you again. Strange you didn't mention you were coming when I saw you on Friday, or that you were seeing Curtis…again."

"I did mention it, Nora," Kate replied, her hand playing with the collar of Curtis's button-down shirt. "You were too drunk to notice, you didn't even know about the trip. Don't you remember why you ran away?"

Nat hissed from the doorway, causing Kate to roll her eyes. "Curtis and I are going to stay down the street, mind if I borrow the car?" My dad threw her the keys without a blink, the faster she vacated the better.

"Dinner will be ready in half an hour," Mom mentioned as Curtis shooed Kate from the house. Bishop doesn't budge, he doesn't say a single word. He just stared at me, his cold blue eyes never leaving my body.

"I'm going to go for a walk," I said, a growl left on my lips as Sean tried to follow. "Alone."

4

I slumped down onto the old dirty couch and rested my head against the back of it. The smell of rain wafted through the open windows of the tree house, relaxing all my senses enough to let my guard down. The tears followed on swift wings as every emotion hit me at once.

I don't know how long I sat there crying, but I hadn't realized he was standing there until the floorboard beneath him creaked in protest to the weight.

"Go the hell away," I growl through clenched teeth without even opening my eyes. I couldn't handle seeing him, standing there looking at me with sad eyes and his painfully handsome face. I grabbed an empty bottle from the ground on my left and chucked it. I hear it smash against the wall and shatter to the floor.

"Nora," my name comes out husky and dark on his lips, a warning to watch what I do next and I cannot help but open my eyes. I sat up, resting my hands on the dirty couch and looking at him.

"Bishop," I responded, the use of his middle name broke something in him. All the tension in his face slipped but only for a moment before he regained his control and froze his features over again.

"You blocked my cell number?" He asked, his hand coming up to rub his scruffy jawline.

"You found the new one easily enough," I said. The conversation was hard, all I wanted to do was cry.

"So that's it? You all of a sudden don't need me anymore?" He growled.

"I haven't needed you for years. I've wanted you, craved you, dreamed about you." I said calmly, my blood boiled under my skin, I was so warm and uncomfortable. "You don't get to blame me for this," I grind my teeth, motioning my hand from my chest toward him and back again. "Distance between us."

"I owe you an apology," He said finally, it sounded like it was painful to say it and I laughed because it was the only thing that kept me from crying again.

"For what Bishop?" I raised my eyebrows at him. I chucked another bottle at him, he stepped to the right and knelt down on the floor careful not to sit in any glass.

"For leaving you," he said coldly. "I should have never left you, not with everything that was going on, not ever."

"Well you did," I snapped. "I was falling apart, piece by piece that summer. I was becoming nothing but a shell of myself so stressed out and scared I couldn't function. You decided it was too much to see me like that, and you walked out."

"I asked you to come, begged you to come with me to Tokyo." He shut his eyes and groaned, his hair falling to his face. He looked up at me through the heavy dark strands of brown hair and I could see even in the dim light of the tree house, water brimmed those beautiful glass eyes.

"Did you though? Is that how you remember it? Dad was sick, we didn't know if he'd live past August, everyone was leaving for college and I was left there to help mom take care of him. I sacrificed everything and you ran away because you were scared." I went to grab another bottle but his hand covered my own on the floor and he shook his head softly for me not to.

"I'm sorry Nora," it came out as a whine, a pleading noise that was meant to gain sympathy but I had never been so angry with him.

"Why come back?" I asked one more question as he stood to leave.

"You wouldn't answer my calls," he said. "The drawings are haunting." He stopped before climbing down the ladder.

That's the point, I think to myself. I stared up at the photos that plastered the walls like paint and wanted to puke. I had put them there to heal myself, to close the crater that had formed inside of me. It was torture, sitting for hours drawing those sketches over and over. The pain in his eyes when he left me that day burned into me like branding on my skin. Every time I closed my eyes for the last three years all I saw were those horrible blue eyes.

Everything was too loud, the rain was too loud, and the sound of my heart beating in my chest was too loud. I took to the walls, ripping down every last photo that was stuck there. The faces floated to the floor like snow as I ripped them to shreds. I screamed, as loud as I could until there was no breath left in my lungs. I picked up the remaining bottles, throwing them against the walls just to hear something else than my own thoughts.

The lantern exploded, the gas catching on fire and spreading along the couch. It all caught so quickly I didn't have time to put it out. The fire licked at the wall behind the couch, the old and beaten wood catching so easily it might as well be covered in gasoline too. I watched as the photos went up in flames, burning to ash and turning to nothing.

I struggled with the latch, ripping it open and sliding out onto the ladder. The rain had made it so wet that my foot slipped but my grip held and I steadied myself. I took a deep breath and continued down, "Nora!" I heard Bishop scream from the path, the tree house was lit up like a Christmas tree.

I heard the crack before I fell, the rung that had cracked earlier gave out underneath me. My grip slipped and I plummeted to the ground. The last thing I remembered was darkness as the tree house started to shift in the tree above me and the sound of Bishop screaming for me to move.

My eyes fluttered open, my whole body was throbbing in pain.

My eyes fluttered closed, Bishop was there I could hear him breathing. Right by my side.

My eyes fluttered open, and he stared down at me, cradled in his arms as he fought to climb the wet path back to the house in the rain.

My eyes fluttered close, "hey stay with me Nori, come back." I smiled, I missed the soft tone of his voice and the rush it gave my heart.

······

The sounds of hospital machines woke me. The steady beeping of my heartbeat outside of my body rang in my ears.

Pain rolled over me in a wave, I felt the nausea climbing and before I could stop myself I rolled over so I could puke into a pan beside me.

My eyes adjusted to the room slower than I would have liked, impatient to find out what happened. Dad sits in the chair next to me, a grim scowl across his sleeping face. "Dad?" I groaned, my throat dry and covered in puke.

I needed water.

"Hey sweetheart," he sat up and rubbed the sleep from his face. He handed me the glass and I reached for it but a sharp pain screamed through my shoulder. "Let me help," he offered, bringing the straw to my chapped lips.

"You broke your arm," he said grimly and set the water down on the table.

"How long have I been here," I feel like I've been laying in this bed for months. Every bone and muscle in my body was stiff and grumpy with me.

"Three years," he rubbed my leg gently.

"What?" I sat up and yelped in pain.

"I'm joking," he laughed and I wanted to punch him but he smiled at me. The anger dissipated and I requested more water. "It's been three days."

"I burned the tree house down," I bit my lip.

"Oh I know sweetheart," he shook his head. "You're lucky you weren't still in it when it fell out of the tree."

Mom entered the room, a thankful look on her face upon seeing me sitting up and chatting with dad. She showered my face with kisses and backed up, she had a bag of clean clothes and a few books. "The doctor said he'd be in any minute."

Right on cue the doctor knocked twice and entered the room with a clipboard in tow. "Nice to see you awake and lucid Ms. Quinn." He flipped the pages over. "Broken arm, that will need physiotherapy."

"It's my violin hand," I said, swallowing the defeat in my voice. "Will I still be able to play?"

"Once the cast comes off in a month or two we'll be able to judge the damage better. For now, no you won't be able to play. You inhaled a lot of smoke, and you hit your head extremely hard when you fell. There was some bleeding but it seems to have fixed itself and the swelling is all but gone." He explained setting the clipboard on the bed and he flashed a light in my eyes.

"You'll be able to go home today, but no burning anymore buildings down while you're in them, Nora." He warned.

Mom pulled clothes from the bag and set them on the bed for me. "I had to bring one of Sean's sweaters, we didn't have any that would fit over your cast at the house." She held up a giant-looking dark blue hoodie.

"Like scrawny Sean, that would be a tent on him," I said, she looked at me over the hoodie in confusion but shook her head and ignored what I had said helping me get dressed.

"Let's get you home," Dad said, giving mom a concerned look as he called for the nurse to start the discharge papers.

5

The drive home is long, but it gives me a chance to wrap my head around what happened. I didn't mean to burn down the tree house. The thoughts in my head are tangled and confused. Sean's sweater hangs from me loosely, the red fabric soft against my sore skin.

I want to ask mom questions, and figure out why I feel out of place but I know she would worry so I keep my mouth shut. We pull up to the beach house, the weather is dark and gloomy. Clouds hang low in the sky threatening rain, it makes everything smell so clean. There is a slight smell of burnt wood in the air. I wonder how bad the damage is to the tree house.

Nat waits by the front door, her deep crimson hair flips around in the wind and snags on the gray hoodie she wears. "How are you feeling?" She asks as I climb from the car, almost losing my balance. I stumble back and hit my elbow on the door.

"I was fine until that, fuck me," I rub the sore spot and walk through the open door. Uncle Curtis stands with a strange yet familiar, snobby-looking blonde woman in the kitchen. They are fussing with raw vegetables, arguing over the best way to cut them.

Everything else seems to be normal, Ben sits at the dining room table his fingers moving across a keyboard rapidly and his glasses are pushed down on his nose. Natalie helps me upstairs to my room and tucks me into the bed.

"How bad is the damage?" I ask her cautiously about the tree house.

"It's gone, lucky the rain dealt with the fire pretty quick. Only a few trees caught on fire. Bishop has been down there all day clearing the path from all the destruction. He's been acting weird." She says and I nod but keep quiet.

"I'll go get you some water, just rest." She kisses my forehead and disappears down the hall. I climb from the bed, finding my footing I move to peer out the small upstairs window.

Near the beach I can see the empty space where trees are missing now, I had fucked up royally.

"Hey, Nora. You're supposed to be in bed," I turn to see Sean, a large and muscular version of him, but him nonetheless. He startles me as he steps forward, "what's wrong?" his hand still stretched to me.

"I think I'm missing time," I admit easily to him. "The last time I remember seeing you...you were thirty pounds lighter and you certainly didn't have a beard."

The look on his face is pure shock, he steps forward this time. I don't flinch as he leads me to the edge of the bed and sits with me. "I saw you for Christmas not seven months ago," he says but I didn't remember that. "You bought me the sweater you're wearing," I look down and rub the fabric between my fingers.

"Sean," his name comes out a muffled whimper as he wraps his arms around me. "Who is the woman in the kitchen with uncle?" I ask, scared of the answer.

"Kate?" He asks. "We've known her since we were sixteen Nora," he seems more concerned now. "You just turned twenty-three."

"You don't remember her at all?" Sean stares at me for a moment and nods his head slightly in understanding. "Did you let your mom know? The doctor?"

"I wasn't sure until we got home, I thought mom was being funny when she had given me your sweater. Ben's hair is turning gray, and Curtis looks happier than I've ever seen him. Natalie looked like she was ready to vomit all over me and then she mentioned some man named Bishop." I say, Sean's whole body tenses, and the arm he has laid around me squeezes tighter.

"You don't remember Bishop?" He looks down at me, waiting for an answer.

"I'm losing my fucking mind." I shoot up from my seat and start to pace around the tiny beach room.

"Stay here," Sean says, standing as he towers over me. His face is tense and he won't make eye contact.

I wait for what feels like hours before Ben walks into my room, his glasses are tucked into the pocket of his gray button-up shirt and his hands are shoved into the pockets of his board shorts. He studies me for a second, "Sean said you're missing time, how far back do you remember Nora?"

"I remember we celebrated Sean's fifteenth birthday at the pier, and I remember the Christmas after that you spent with us because your mom was working, and Natalie got into ballet school that year." I recite exactly what I can remember, no more, no less.

"You're missing eight years Nora," the words tumble out of his mouth, he sounds more confused than I do.

32

"I knew you were acting weird," Mom stands in the doorway now, her hands on her hips. "We will go back to the doctor tomorrow." She stomps away and we all take a collective sigh as she disappears down the stairs.

"Come on. There's nothing we can do about your head today. I've read some things on exposure therapy that might help and keeping you locked in your room isn't one of the tips." Ben tugs at my sweater and wraps his arm around my shoulders. "Let's go sit on the deck before it rains."

Ben leads me downstairs and out the back door, he grabs a blanket from the couch and lays it over my feet. The ocean waves crash against the beach making the most calming noise against the rush of intrusive thoughts my brain is being bombarded by.

Ben types away at his computer, I am grateful for his silence. "Hey," Natalie brings out a cup of water and a bag of chips, setting them down on the table beside me. "Eat something. Mom told me you can't remember anything."

"I remember you losing the top to your bathing suit after you tried to show off for Ben in the surfing contest when you were fourteen," I laugh, taking a long drink of water.

"Very good," Ben winks at Natalie. A laugh left his lips, "I remember that day almost as well."

"Both of you shut up," Nat smacks his outstretched legs. "I have something I want to talk to you about. Since you can't remember anything it's probably the best time."

"We invited everyone here this summer because we're getting married here instead of on New Year as we planned." She says, but the pieces don't all fit together until Ben leans over, a soft twinkle in his warm brown eyes.

"We're engaged," he whispers and I smile.

"Why are you moving the wedding then?" I ask, my heart was filled with joy that they were. I may not remember most of how they got to this point but I sure was glad they were here.

"I am pregnant," Natalie says, her face is on the verge of crying but a smile forms on her lips.

"I'm going to be an Aunt?" I say, letting the blanket slide to the floor as I sit forward to grab her shaking hands. "Oh god, I'm going to be the worst Aunt ever!"

"Good, then you're just as terrified as me." She stares at me baffled.

"Also smooth, waiting until I can't remember a single moment about my past to tell me the biggest secret ever. Classy," I sneer with a smile on my face. The stairs creak causing me to turn to investigate.

A tall, extremely handsome, and barely clothed man stands cleaning his ash-covered hands with a rag. His jeans hang low on his hips showing off a very visible hardened pelvic muscle. His chest glistened with sweat and his hair was pushed back off his face in dark waves. He stares at me with soft blue eyes but there's a hollow look to them that I can't figure out.

Sean steps in front of him, blocking my view of the very pretty man.

"Hold on," Sean puts his hand up, stopping him from all the way up onto the deck. He lowers his voice, speaking in hushed tones. "Somethings wrong. She's missing pieces of her memory."

A painful look crosses the man's face, this must be Bishop. He had the same look on his face that Natalie did when she spoke of Bishop, and that Sean did when I said I didn't remember who he was. A sorrowful look that terrifies me.

34

"What does that mean Roberts?" He speaks and the sound of his voice sends chills down my spine, I sit up to listen better and Ben gives me a disapproving look.

"She doesn't have a damn clue who you are, Bishop, or what you did," Sean growls under his breath, I can barely hear what he says but a stunned and confused look crosses his blue eyes briefly. "Stay away from her until we figure out how to get her thinking straight again. You understand me."

"Fuck off Sean," Bishop pushes past him and wanders into the house.

6

"Nora, don't." Sean grabs my wrist and tilts his head to the side. "It's not worth the conversation," he says but I pull from his grip gently and slide into the house.

"It's worth it to me," I say, and he just nods his head.

"Just be careful," he warns. I give him a soft smile in return and close the door behind me.

"Where did Bishop go?" I ask, my dad looks up from his newspaper and points to the stairs.

I slowly move up the steps, carefully as each plant of my foot on the old wood hurts my bones a little more than the last. I can hear the shower running so I go sit on the edge of my unmade bed.

I play with the corners of the window sill, picking the paint chips off one by one until I can see the old wood underneath the ugly yellow color. "You cried when Natalie did that," the sound of his husky voice snaps me from my thoughts.

"You were supposed to pick the color together and she got the yellow paint without asking one day." He stands with a cream-colored towel wrapped around his hips. The same sharp muscles are visible even more so now, dark hair peeks out from the top of the tower and is dark even in contrast to the tanned color of his skin.

"You tried to convince me to scrape it off for you but I'm a bit more afraid of Natalie than I was you at the time." Everything about him is comforting, mesmerizing, and familiar. His hair is wet and falls against his forehead, it sticks to the back of his neck.

"I don't remember that," I swallow hard.

"Yeah, so I've heard." He says.

"Why does everyone call me Nori?" I ask a simple question to start. He seems so rigid, the muscles along his shoulders and chest are tight. He takes slow calculated breaths as he moves further into the room.

"I don't call you that," he says, a simple reply to a simple question.

"Why not?" I raise my eyebrows.

"I have other names for you, less appropriate ones." His lip twitches when he says it and something inside of me begins to warm. "How many years are you missing Nora?"

"They say about eight, I don't remember anything between Sean's fifteen birthday up until I woke up in the hospital. The doctor says I hit my head really hard when I fell. I can't even remember why I was in the tree." I admit with a sad smile.

"You were upset and when you get upset, that's where you go to hide." He says it so quietly. I look up from my lap and meet his eyes, they're so sad all the time.

"Why was I upset, why was I in the tree house, Bishop?" I'm scared to ask, fear creeps up my spine and into my soul. It's crushing and it takes me a minute to regain my breath.

"I wasn't supposed to be here this summer," he's being honest with me. "I was told not to come by more than one person but your *dad* called me," he stops so suddenly I can hear the sound of his heart beating in the silence. He sighs and rubs his hand along the back of his neck. "It doesn't matter Nora, you can't remember anything I did. It's all gone. The good with the bad."

My arm throbs in my cast and I scrunch my nose up until the feeling passes.

"Where does it hurt?" He's kneeling in front of me when the stars clear from my eyes. His hands were on my knees waiting for an answer. His bright blue eyes stare up at me from this angle and I can see every tiny difference in the colors that swirl around in his iris.

"It's just my arm, it's fine," I say and he jerks back and my knees feel cold without his hands.

"What do you need Nora?" He asks. He sits on the bed across from me still wearing nothing but a towel. My brain is distracted by every movement he makes.

"Why was Sean so upset with you?" I ask.

"He's just being protective," Bishop sighs, he shakes his hair loose and runs both hands through it until it's pushed back off his face again.

"Why?" I feel like a broken record. Why this, why that but it's the only thing I could say.

"We have a rough history, it hasn't always been the best and as of late, it came to a head. He's just making sure you don't blindly fall back in love with me." The honesty is refreshing but confusing all at once.

"You seem quite sure of yourself," and he did. He speaks so confidently yet it never gives me the answer I need, the answer I crave from him. *Why the hell is everyone so nervous about you?* I want to ask.

"Were we together? You talk about me like I was some kind

of love-sick puppy dog. But you look at me like I am the most dangerous thing in the room. It's extremely confusing," he doesn't retreat this time. He leans forward on his knees and smiles. It's so soft I might have missed it if I wasn't paying close attention. But it was gentle, and like he hadn't meant to do it disappeared.

"We were." He says, his tongue running over his lip nervously. "I was the puppy, you were this ball of energy and light that I couldn't help but follow everywhere you went. I am also the danger." He stops.

"Don't stop," I say to him. I need more.

"You were never safe with me around. I can't control myself and no matter how much I tried to distance myself," he swallows hard. A cold look flashes across his face.

"There's too much to the story to tell you," he's back to stone, his jaw twitching as he watches me. "Too much you're better off never knowing."

"I wish I knew. I wish I hadn't been in that stupid tree house or fallen so hard. I wish I could remember you," I say frustration lacing my words.

"No, you don't." It's all but a whisper when it leaves his lips.

Before I can answer, the second wave of pain tickles my arm until it becomes a full-blown muscle spasm. Bishop moves over to me, careful not to touch me but watches me closely as the pain subsides. He hands me the water on the table, waiting for me to finish before he takes it back.

His hand brushes against mine and he all but hisses. "Why do you seem terrified to touch me?"

"I am anything but terrified to touch you, Nora."

The words warm my core, and I try to keep myself from fidgeting on the bed.

His eyes are wild and curious as he inches forward. He closes the distance between us. "I'm terrified that if I touch you, I won't know how to stop. I know every inch of your body. I know every freckle," he cups my face and runs his thumb against my cheek. "I know every mole, blemish, and scar. I know every curve that makes your body so hard to resist."

I watch his Adam's apple bob in his throat as he comes inches from my parted mouth. "If you could remember anything right now would be a good time because I'm having a very hard time not taking advantage of this," his jaw tenses as he bites his lip. His hand trails slowly down my neck.

"Ben said that exposure to things I know could help jog my memory," I say sitting so still I think I might explode if he moves any closer. I can smell the soap, the sage that drips from his wet body. "All I know right now is that I know nothing about you. That can't be a bad thing can it?" I ask.

"Nora," he pauses, dragging out my name in agony. "It's the worst thing."

"Can you try?" I ask, "try to help me remember. It looks to me that we both need help," I say but it comes out so slow.

"What exactly do I need help with?" He asks.

"You came here this summer looking for forgiveness, I don't know for what but you at least owe it to me to let me try," I say, I bring my hand up and lift his chin to meet my gaze.

"Don't move," is all he says before he stands moving to the door, his fingers wrap around the rung of the old chair that sits in the corner and he shoves it under the door knob.

I watch all of the muscles in his back ripple as he makes sure the door can't be opened.

"You taught me that," he says, turning around and tightening the knot on his towel. He moves across the room, grabbing the large free-standing mirror and turning it so I could see myself sitting on the bed. "Your mom refused to put a lock on the door after she caught Nat and Ben up here one night. It really put a wrench in our plans but you always found a way to be a troublemaker."

He moves so slowly I wanna yell at him to walk quicker, to come back and put his hand back on my neck as he had before. I don't know what this feeling is but it's so raw it hurts.

"This scar," he climbs behind me on the bed, careful not to shift my weight or touch me with anything but his finger. He ran along a small, jagged bump just along my shoulder. "You got from a chain link fence sneaking into the community pool."

"And this one," he moved my hair off my face without touching me. His finger presses to a long scar behind my ear, trailing it down past my ear to my nape. "You got it from a parrot who bit you on the pier while you were trying to take a photo with it."

"Now you have matching ones," he runs his finger along the bandage that curves from the base of my earlobe to the back of my skull. Twelve stitches from the fall, even thinking about the wound, makes the gash throb in pain.

He pulls the collar of my sweater loose around my shoulder and kisses a small cluster of scars that stain the skin. I forget the pain almost instantly. He stares at me in the mirror, his blue eyes glimmering as his lips press to my warm skin. "These are from a BB gun," he whispers.

He removes his lips from my skin and it leaves a cold spot where they had been. His hand snakes around, his fingers tugging at the hem of the sweater until they are underneath and against my stomach. He lifted the fabric until I could see my stomach in the mirror, the flesh pale compared to the rest of me.

"This is the second biggest scar," he says softly, his breath warm on my neck. "You fell climbing up on the boardwalk, you dropped almost five feet to the beach. You didn't break a single bone, but you…" he presses his fingers along the scar. "You landed on a piece of driftwood, you needed thirteen stitches that time."

"Was I ever not in a cast or bleeding?" I ask and he chuckles into the nape of my neck.

I go to turn to look at him but he stops me, "I said don't move," he instructions, "focus on the mirror."

He shifts forward, trailing his hands along the top of my pants. His fingers dangerously close he tucks them in the band and pulls the fabric from my hip. A small ugly scar digs into my underwear line. He runs his finger so slow this time, my breath hitches as he touches the soft skin so delicately. "This one is my fault," he said. His voice broke a touch.

"What happened?" I ask because unlike the others he doesn't tell.

"Later," he slides off the bed, kneeling in front of me he uses both hands to move my hips until I'm standing. He undoes the button of my pants with ease, and carefully slides them from my hips. He pulls them all the way down until they're completely off and he throws them in a heap away from us.

I stand before him in nothing but the pair of dark blue underwear covering me. He runs his hand between my legs, pushing my legs apart with gentle touches. "This is the biggest one," he says. His face is terrified when he looks up at me, "this one is also my fault." He presses his lips to it and my entire body feels like it's on fire with his head between my legs.

I grimace, my hands finding his hair I pull him away. I fight with the rising sensation between my legs and force him to look at me. "Tell me what happened. Even if it's hard Bishop."

7

H e sits back, his hands leaving my body abruptly. I kneel down and sit in front of him with my legs crossed. My body protests with every moment but I want to see his face, his eyes, and all the sadness that's there.

"We got in an accident," he says. His voice is so agonizingly soft, like velvet against my ears. A huff of air leaves his lips and he sounds like he's crying. "We hit a truck on the back roads, you fractured your femur and dislocated your pelvis. It was four months in the hospital."

"Accidents happen," I say cupping his chin with my hand, rubbing my fingers in the scuff along his jaw. It felt natural to touch him in such an intimate way, to feel him in my grasp. "I sounded like a handful."

"I was drunk," he is crying, tears streaming from his eyes. "The worst part of it all is that you still didn't walk away. You didn't blame me or hate me for it. You took care of my guilt while dealing with all that pain. Don't you see Nora, it's better that you don't remember us. We were tragic, and you have this fresh start. You get to start over without the pain. It's life's way of telling me it's my turn to carry the burden."

"And if I don't want you to?" I ask.

"You don't get a choice in this, not this time." He says, I go to respond but the doorknob rattles violently.

"Nora?" Sean's voice floats through the door sounding panicked.

"Coming," I say, moving to stand from the floor. A small whimper leaves my lips and Bishop leans forward to help. The towel catches on his foot and when he stands with his hands under my forearms he's completely naked.

A giggle leaves my lips at the sight of him fully exposed, he was tanned all over and everything about what he was covering was exceptional. Part of me knew that I had seen a man's penis before but there was a small, unknown immature part of me that couldn't contain herself.

"Was that a giggle Nora?" he takes the sound as a challenge and slides a little closer. I can feel everything as he presses into me, his hands firmly grasping my elbows.

"Are you alright?" Sean's voice startles me and I swallow the feeling to lean forward and take Bishop's lips into mine.

"Put your towel on," I whisper, he takes this as a challenge too. The sadness in his eyes faded and was replaced with a playful look. "I'm going to let him in regardless."

"It's nothing Roberts hasn't walked in on before," he whispers back, husky and begging to be kissed he licks his bottom lip again.

"Well let's not make him suffer more than once shall we?" I say with a raised eyebrow.

"He has a habit of it, it's already happened more than once." He growls but lets go of me finally.

I walk over and remove the chair, opening it just as Bishop fixes the towel back over himself. "What the fuck Bishop?" Sean growls looking over him, and then back to me. "Where are your pants?"

I look down with a laugh, completely forgetting I wasn't wearing them until he points it out. Bishop brushes past me and hands them to me without even looking at Sean. "Do you need help getting them back on?" He asks.

I try not to look at the disapproving glare Sean is giving me over his shoulder, but it's all I can see as Bishop takes it upon himself to do it anyways. Kneeling down he picks up one foot at a time and slides my legs back into the tight pants. I can feel my face flush with color as he stands up and runs his finger along my underwear line. He takes the button in his fingers and does the pants up.

Sean clears his throat behind us. Bishop turns, for a moment I think they may argue. They both seem ready to, shoulders pinned back. "Don't worry, I was reminding her how awful a person I am." Bishop rolls his pretty blue eyes and his eyebrows knit together as he comes shoulder to shoulder with Sean.

"Come on, Bishop. You know that's not what I meant earlier," he drives to justify his words but Bishop just walks away, his footsteps fading down the stairs to the guest room. "What the hell was that all about?"

"He was showing me all the scars on my body," I say with a smile. "I'm not a china doll Sean."

"You are right now. You very much are a china doll." He crosses his arms and sighs, "I'm sorry. I just want you to be careful. You may not remember how many times I drove through the night to keep you alive, to keep you from hurting yourself or worse but I remember every single time, every single drive Nora. He broke you and I refuse to glue the pieces back together again."

"I'll be careful," I say, the conversation beforehand had given me no indication of what happened. Sean seems raddled, Bishop seems cagey and I am left not knowing what or who to believe. "I just want to know who I am."

"I can help you with that if you let me?" Sean smiles.

"Does it involve food?" I ask, returning the smile.

"Oddly enough it does." He raises a finger and flicks my nose with it. "Come on."

"I need this sweater off, it's too hot," I say.

Sean laughs and comes into the room. He digs through my bag, pulling out a t-shirt and a tank top. He holds them up for me to pick, I nod to the t-shirt. He sets it on the bed and helps me wiggle from the oversize sweater leaving me in my sports bra. He pulls the shirt over my head, pulls the caught hair out gently, and winks at me.

"I'm assuming you've done that before too," I laugh.

"You'd be surprised how many times a person can puke on themselves," he says with a smile but there's no teasing tone to his voice. He's watched me go through something so hard, a time I can't even begin to remember. "Let's go," he says resting a finger under my chin. "We have french fries to eat."

The diner was empty except for a small family eating in the back booth and a few truckers at the cherry red bar. Donna's hadn't changed, at least not that I can remember. It's still small, with bar stools and cracked red leather seats. The overhead stained glass lights still swing in the breeze of the open bay windows that circle the restaurant.

The menus are covered in plastic and the cups the waitress serves the water in are old red shiny plastic ones. I take a sip of mine as the waitress sets a basket of fries in front of us. "Why are we here?"

"Ah sweet Nora, if anything is going to jog your memory

it's these fries." I hate the hopeful look on his face. I can't bear to tell him that the only thing I can think of is the gentle touches left on my skin by Bishop's fingers not an hour before. That his touch brought back feelings. There are no memories, nothing comes to mind but the way my body reacts to Bishop is natural. It's a known reaction, my body had danced that dance with him before.

I grab two fries in my fingers, the salt is abrasive on my skin but he nudges my hand toward my mouth. "We were sitting in this restaurant, at this exact booth the day we met Bishop." I tilt my head suspiciously at him, not putting the fries in my mouth long enough to glare at him. "Don't give me that look, we were friends once, me and Bishop. The three of us were inseparable. He didn't just abandon you—" he stops and looks down with a huff. Saying too much.

"What does that mean? Abandoned us?" Sean groans and leans on his elbows across the table from me.

"I'm not the most unbiased player in the story that needs to be told." He shakes his head, "Wait until you see the doctor tomorrow. See what he says and if he suggests telling you stories then ask your dad what happened. He'll be the most honest with you, he was there on the front lines when it all happened. Now eat the fry."

The crunchy fries feel good on my tongue, the salt coating it enough that I need a drink of water to wash them down. "These are awful…" I choke on the water.

"Oh yeah, we never came here for the food. It was just a fun meeting spot and they didn't care if we brought in flasks of booze." Sean laughs but something about the smell of the diner, combined with the boyish laugh drifting over me mixed with the smell of hot oil and the warm breeze on my face triggers something.

"I don't think Nat will ever live that down," Sean nudges her in the ribs. Natalie and Ben sit crammed on the other side of the booth. Nat isn't laughing but Ben's face is bright red.

I shake my head and drink down more of my vanilla milkshake. It's the only good thing about this diner. Natalie had just embarrassed herself terribly. Every summer the town held surfing competitions for the local kids. This year Nat thought she would be brave and enter. We all knew it was to impress Ben. He and Sean had been winning in their age groups for years, but none of us had said a thing.

Natalie wasn't the type to be discouraged anyways.

"I knew I should have worn a wet suit." Nat rolls her eyes and continues to stab her salad aimlessly.

"We all told you to," Ben quips.

"Shut up Benjamin," she hisses. He just laughs at her, his eyes trail the shape of the side of her face. I don't think there was ever a time that he hadn't been madly in love with my sister.

I think of Sean so close beside me, his lanky body leaning back against the booth. His leg is up in the booth pressed against my back with his arm splayed across it lazily. His fingers brush my shoulder in circles as we eat a talk.

Sean was pretty, truly. It's the best word I can think of when I look at him. Every feature is painfully pretty. I turn my head, lips still on my straw, and look at him. He's got a cheeky grin on his face, his laughter is infectious. His hand grips his chest as he giggles at Natalie still. I could love Sean. The way Ben loves Nat.

I swallow the mouthful of vanilla shake. I could love Sean if he wasn't my best friend I think. Maybe though I hadn't started to see boys like that. Maybe I just had to wait a little longer and I'll know exactly what it feels like to be in love. Then there would be no question.

"Nori, truth or dare." Ben sits up and stares at me.

"Truth," I say, pushing the empty glass away from me.

"Lame, we know everything about you." Nat rolls her eyes. Not everything it seems.

"It's not called, dare or dare." I shake my head and Sean shifts behind me, he sits upright with both hands on the table.

"Maybe it should be," he suggests. "We know each other too well and picking truth is a crutch."

"You can't make new rules," I tilt my head to look at him properly. The smile that forms on his lips is cheeky, it's wide and so full of life.

"It's my birthday, and I'll change the rules if I want to. You're the youngest now, you don't get a say." Sean flicks my nose.

"Your birthday was a week ago," I complain.

"And what did you buy me?" He asks. I just groan, "nothing because you hate me, so this is my gift. A game of dare and dare."

"You know you can just call it 'Dare' right?" Ben shakes his head. His dark wavy hair is so long it's beginning to curl around his ears.

"It's more dramatic with two," Sean flashes his hands in the air mimicking fireworks. "Alright Nora, dare or dare?"

"God I hate you," I sneer. "Dare. And no ketchup, please. That was awful last time."

The bell over the door rings and a young girl with dark hair and big blue eyes saunters in. We can hear her complaints from the booth about how awful the diner is. I repress a laugh, still waiting for Sean to give me a challenge.

"Something easy, I dare you..." he pauses as a boy walks in behind the girl. The same dark hair, and blue eyes. They were the new kids that had moved into the giant beach house at the end of the street.

50

We had been trying to get sneak peeks of them all week but every time we got close with our bikes the movers shooed us away.

"I dare you to go break up with the new kid," a mischievous grin forms on his face.

"What are you talking about?" I shift uncomfortably as I watch the kids sit in a booth at the opposite end of the restaurant.

"Go over, make a scene. Pretend you're breaking up with him." Natalie laughs at him.

"That's cruel!" I say.

"I will throw you in the freezing cold morning water tomorrow if you don't accept the dare Nora, you know the rules." I could still feel the icy temperature of the water under my skin from the last time I denied a dare.

I slide out from the booth, fixing my tank top and shorts as I walk over to their booth. The girl had gotten up to use the restroom and the boy was sitting alone with his nose in a menu.

"Must be nice," I say. He drops the menu and his eyes connect with mine. So blue I forget to breathe.

Sean, Nat, and Ben hang off the back of our booth watching intently. "Did you need something?" The kid asks. He's not much older than us, his face still holds baby fat and a softness to it that I've never seen on older boys.

"I want to know how you can sit here and pretend I don't exist after what you did to me." I sit down, sliding into the booth with ease.

"Do I know you?" He whispers. Something about the way he acts is childish and free. A spark ignites within me.

"I have a confession," I whisper so only he can hear before yelling more obscene things. "This is a dare and I really don't wanna take a morning swim tomorrow. Just follow my lead."

"Anywhere." He says with such certainty and intensity I'm not

sure he's just talking about the dare anymore. It catches me off guard and I freeze, not sure what to say. He takes the reins, standing up and out of the booth, "how could I possibly resist that man, look at him!"

He points directly at Sean whose face lights up bright red. "I'm sorry but I have to end this. I'm in love with him and I can't deny it any longer."

His theatrics have the entire restaurant giggling but he shakes his head at me, "fight back," he laughs under his breath.

I stand up bringing a cup of water with me, square my shoulders, and grab the waist of his shorts. I don't take my eyes off of his as I dump the ice water down his pants.

I walk away before he can say anything more but a rabid gasp. "We should go," I burst into laughter as the boy's sister returned from the bathroom in hysterics. We file quickly out of the restaurant and ride as fast as we can home on our bikes.

Later that night we're all tangled in each other on the large couch watching a scary movie. The house is quiet except for the occasional scream from us at a jump scare. An exceptionally timed knock at the door causes us all to turn around and look at it.

"Well answer it," Nat pushes Ben's shoulder.

"Oh hell no," he says, tucking down into the couch.

"Chickens, all of you," I sigh, throwing my blankets off and walking over to the door.

I cautiously swing it open, "I never got your name," he says. He's wearing clean clothes and stands with his hands in his pockets.

"It's Nora." I am very aware that everyone is watching us.

"I'm Bishop," he says tilting his head to see the TV.

"Do you like scary movies, Bishop?" I ask welcoming him in.

"Hey, Nora!" Sean waves his hand in my face, "Jesus you zoned out badly there. You okay?"

"Yeah, I think the fries worked." I am baffled. He flashes a proud grin at me.

"Of course they did. So what did you remember?" He asks carefully.

"I remember a very pivotal game of, Dare and Dare." I laugh and his eyes go wide.

8

I sit at the island while mom busies herself preparing dinner. She sets the bag of potatoes on the counter and goes back to the fridge. "I made an appointment with the doctor tomorrow. Hopefully, he can give us an idea of how long-term this memory loss is."

She's mostly talking to herself, she's nervous and fidgeting with everything around her. I stand up, leaning over the island, and slide the potatoes closer. I grab the paring knife and stare at my cast for a moment. I fumble with myself trying to figure out a way to hold the potato and peel it. I position it on the counter and rest my cast along the side of it, curling the exposed fingers around it. It doesn't feel especially nice but I manage to hang on as I run the knife along the skin.

It lasts all of two peels before the potato shoots out of my grasp and lands on the floor. "Fuck," I groan, resting my forehead on the cool counter.

"Here," Bishop's voice forces me to lift my head. He's wearing a tight maroon shirt and jeans as he slides onto the stool next to me. He holds the potato, and takes my hand in his gripping my fingers around the knife and helping me peel the potatoes.

"Thank you," I say. I remove my hand from his. The gesture

is kind but I can't get over the feeling that I won't be playing the violin anytime soon.

I give him the knife and watch as he peels the rest of the potatoes and places them in a pot for my mom. "Thank you, Bishop," she presses her hand to his face and smiles at him.

"Mom likes you?" I laugh as he sits back down. No one is around to hear me ask beside her.

"Sometimes," he says, looking at her from across the island. "Sometimes she wants to kill me but she never turns her back on me."

"Are you ever going to explain yourself? The mystery that shrouds you like a black cloud," I ask.

"You'll remember eventually, I'll take every day I get without the burden of the bad memories. Then when you go back to hating me, maybe it won't hurt so badly." He says it without breaking eye contact. Mom stops moving around the kitchen and is watching us.

"Seems like a cop-out," I call him on his bullshit. "Save yourself the pain from explaining, have a few days of me fawning over you and then we go back to whatever mess made me light the tree house on fire." I raise my eyebrow at him and he just shakes his head. Dark strands of hair fall loose on his face.

"It's a shame the attitude wasn't forgotten with the memories." Bishop teases. "How about after dinner I show you something."

"Your continuous efforts to distract me from reality are adorable," I say, nudging his side with my elbow.

"Did you hear that Marianne? She thinks I'm adorable." My mom just laughs at him. There's a constrained light to his eyes, he's forcing a smile and his hands shake on the countertop.

I swallow hard, why did life hand me this man if I wasn't allowed to remember him?

After dinner, Ben and Bishop help to clean the kitchen while I stand in the bathroom mirror trying to fix my hair so it covers the nasty stitches at the back of my head. They're sore and look disgusting.

"You look beautiful, " Bishop moves behind me. He uses his hands to brush out the ends of my hair, taking it gently into a ponytail and pulling it back off of my face. "Much better."

"You're good at that, " I say, touching the stitches before he has a chance to cover them with a bandage. He presses the clean white covering to my skin. He backs away taking a few walks with my hair in his fingertips before letting go completely and standing in the doorway.

He looks at me solemnly but only for a moment before his eyes glaze back to the Hard icy blue color they usually are. He's pulled a neat clean leather jacket over his polo shirt. He looks handsome in the shiny black leather. I try to smile, but nerves eat away at me and grab my jacket from the door knob.

He helps me into it, my cast sticks in the sleeve but he shimmy's it forward until my hand pops out the other side. I grimace at the pain as my fingers come out the other side, he pulls my hand in his, bringing it up slowly to his lips and placing a soft kiss on each knuckle.

"This is a good surprise, don't be nervous." He smiles but it's forced and shaky.

"I'm not the only nervous one," I say with a laugh.

"If we don't get out of here before Roberts sees us then we might have trouble so move your ass, Darling." He winks and shoos me out of the bathroom. I follow him down the stairs, mom and dad sit on the couch together reading books.

"Be careful," my dad says without looking up from the book. "And Bartley," we stop at the door. "Helmets."

"Yes sir," he says, closing the door behind us. A motorcycle sits on the road before us. It's slim and black with the most gorgeous chrome accents. He leads me over and places a stylish black helmet over my head carefully. "Is that pressing on your stitches?" He asks and I shake my head.

He helps me swing onto the bike, my legs straddling the back part. "What the hell are you doing Bishop?" Sean's voice is agitated.

"Taking Nora to see something important," he says. His features have gone rigid and his shoulders are pinned back as he turns to come chest to chest with Sean. "Not everything needs to involve you, Roberts."

"Is that what you think? I'm jealous? This isn't some sick fear of missing out. I don't want her on that bike," Sean steps forward, he's in a black shirt and his hair is wet. He must have come back from surfing when he heard us leaving.

"Then why are you out here acting like a jealous little kid?" Bishop asks him.

"The last time she got on that bike she almost died," Sean growls.

"I don't drink anymore," he replies "I haven't since that night. I'm not that kid anymore Roberts and I'm sick of you acting like it."

"You're only saying that because she doesn't remember that kid. You're exactly the same. This little trip is selfish, putting her on the bike is for you. Not her." Sean points at me.

"I love being talked about like I'm not here," I say with a sigh. "Can we go now? I'll be okay Sean."

"Take this," he pushes past Bishop and hands me a cell phone.

"Call if you need a ride home. The password is your birthday." I bite my lip but take the phone and slip it into my jacket pocket.

"You're a drama queen Roberts," Bishop climbs on the bike and turns the engine on before Sean can get another word in.

I grip tightly to Bishop, and the fingers on my good hand dig into the leather as tightly as they can. "It's okay, I won't let you fall." He says over the sound of the motorcycle. He takes off slowly, giving me time to adjust before we are driving down the highway in the darkness.

The air on my face feels so good, it's light and fresh with rain as he moves the bike around corners and bends. I close my eyes and I feel like I'm flying. I can smell the warm scents of his cologne mixing with the fresh leather and the smell of the forest around us.

Before long he rolls the bike to a stop, the parking lot around is empty but we're standing in a marina. He climbs from the bike, his hands are sweaty and he's so nervous he shakes a bit as he slides me off the bike.

"I can swim right?" I ask him and he just shakes his head.

"No swimming tonight, but yes you can swim. You can surf really well too. I'd say better than most of us actually." He pulls my helmet off, fixing my ponytail, he checks to make sure my stitches are intact and takes my hand softly into his. We walk along the pier, between the boats, and under the stairs.

His heavy black boots make the wooden planks creak, I stop and see what he's looking at. A modest size sailboat, it's painted white and has the words, Cameron, on the side of it.

58

I smile, "why is my middle name written on that boat?"

"Well, you wouldn't let me name the boat Nora so I had to settle," he runs his hand along it. "We were going to sail this everywhere. You wanted to see the world," he unhooks the small rope closes the boat's lip off, and steps onto it.

He takes my hand and helps me up onto the deck of the boat. Gorgeous wood details almost all of it, running down the length to the wheel and main deck of the boat. There's a small set of stairs that leads into the underneath. I can only assume there's a cabin down there, with a bed and a small kitchen.

"You bought this for us?" I ask turning to see him walking towards the ropes that tied the boat to the dock. He nods his head gently, "Why? This boat is a beautiful Bishop, it had to be expensive."

"It was, but I have money to spend. It was worth it." He pushes the boat from the dock, comes back to me, and leads me to a small arrangement of blankets just beyond the wheel. "Sit here," he holds my hand as I clumsily sit on the blankets.

He guides the boat out as I sit taking in how breathtaking he looks. The wind brushed against his face and soft hair. His eyes seem to glimmer under the moonlight and they're even bluer than the water. They hold so many secrets, ones I wish I could remember.

"What do you do for work?" I ask him and he tenses.

"I'm the black sheep of the Bartley family business," he groans. "I'm the lawyer, I make everything go away when Kate or anyone else causes problems."

"How long have you been doing that?" I ask, he's so ashamed of his life. Hiding all these parts of him, I wonder if I knew what he did before I forgot everything.

"A long time," he drops an anchor into the lake pulling the sailboat to a halt. He sits across from me and hands me a water bottle from the bucket beside him. "You hated it," he admits, "but you always answered the phone. I live in Tokyo right now, it's close to our Asian investors and my father."

"Are we still…" I stop.

He looks up, his eyes are wet and sorrowful. "No," he says.

"But you still call?" I ask.

"I still call." His jaw tenses. "I didn't bring you out here to talk to you about this," he says. He's being short with me now as he stands. He runs a hand through his hair nervously, "I never got to show you this boat," he swallows.

"We had always talked about it," he explains. "Last summer I was here dealing with lawyers from a company we're dissolving. I came out here and stared at the water for hours, wishing I was on it with you. It was the first time I had really let what happened between us take control of my emotions. I called my assistant from the dock and made him find me a salesman."

"While we're here now," I say hoping he'll look at me again.

"I'm here, you're *not you*, it's not the same. Not really. I thought maybe showing you this would help you but Roberts was right. This was selfish." He takes his jacket off and sets it down, turning back to me. "I guess I haven't changed," he sighs.

"You don't strike me as the selfish type Bishop," I say. He looks at me and shakes his head gently moving towards me briskly as he kneels in front of me.

"That's the thing Nora, you don't know me." He says it, pain laces the words. His eyes are devastatingly sad. He runs a thumb along my bottom lip, taking his time pressing his skin to mine.

I open my eyes, and he's staring back at me. "Nora, baby you gotta get up."

I groan rolling over to cover my face with the blankets. "Mm nope, your dad has an appointment and you offered to take him. You gotta get up."

I feel his hands creep up and into the blankets, his fingers trailing my skin. Up my thighs, over my hips and they sink into the soft fabric of my underwear. I can feel his erection twitch against my butt, I instinctively push against him.

He rolls me over so I am facing him, and he kisses me. A kiss that starts out soft but as it always did turns rough and heavy. He grips my hair and plunders my mouth in hot, drugged moments. I press my naked chest to him, we are silent as he strokes me and places soft kisses on my cheeks, nose, lips, and closed eyes.

I only wake fully as he takes me onto him, my body so wet I easily accept it. He runs a hand over my hair, grabbing it firmly at my nape. He uses it like a handle to tilt my face up to him. His jaw clenched, he watches me with possessive eyes, he's kissing me again before I can tell him I need to get ready to go.

"No noise, your parents are awake downstairs." He smiles a very troublesome smile, I'm in so much trouble. He tucks into me, takes my nipple in his mouth, and slams into me again. He pounds into me so hard, and fast that it wrenches a whimper from my lips. A whimper that forms into the very long version of his name.

"Bishop," but he silences me with another kiss. He straightens, very slowly pushing my leg up, and thrusts into me hard with more of the same motion. I watch a cold smile form on his lips as he is rewarded with another elated gasp.

He stopped thrusting, his hand coming around and kneading at my ass, I begged for more pressing myself against him but he only withdrew further. "Please," I beg.

He moves back against me, diving roughly into me again. So hard and fast, again and again for a long moment before wrenching out of me again. I make a noise of distress when he pulls out.

"You're being a jerk," I moan and he laughs.

"Maybe you should have gotten out of bed," he smiles a sinister smile and strokes my lips with his finger.

"Well get the punishment over with," I lick his finger, and then kiss his lips dragging his bottom lip between my teeth roughly. "I have places to be."

He pounds into me without warning, one hand pulling my hair and the other rubs at my ass. He brings me over the edge, and then again without mercy. I am completely undone as he lets himself come with a loud groan, grinding deep inside of me. The hand in my hair moves to my chin, he grips it gently as he watches my release.

He gives me one swift kiss before pulling out of me, he climbs off of the bed leaving me laying there to watch his naked form move to the bedroom door and remove the chair holding it in place. He pulls on my arms, raising me from the bed. He pulls me against him, and kisses me deeply, a soft romantic kiss.

"I love you, Nora," he whispers.

"How many times did we uh—" I stopped. I can feel my face flush red, and Bishop raises an eyebrow at me not realizing what I just remembered. "Have sex in my parent's house?" I ask.

"Including weekends?" he teases.

9

"Are you ready to go?" Sean stands in the doorway, arms crossed. His face is clean shaven and his eyes sparkle in the dim light of my room. Mom ended up getting a call the night before and was going to miss my appointment. Sean had graciously offered to drive me instead.

"Yeah, I need to brush my hair though," I say. I instinctively go to grab the brush with my broken hand and groan.

"Here," he moves behind me so quietly for such a big man, he leans over and takes the brush from me. He runs it through my hair softly and smiles staring down at me. "I love your hair," he says. "It's always been so soft, and thick."

"I wish right now I could shave it all off." I sigh, "not being able to pull it back in this heat is horrible."

"Lucky for you," he says taking the hair between his fingers he braids it slowly down. His fingers brush along the side of my face as he takes the strands into the braid. "I learned how to french braid the first time you broke your arm for that exact reason." He takes an elastic off the table and wraps it around the air.

"How did I get so lucky?" I ask and he winks at me.

"I have no idea," He stands back, and when he puts his hands in his pockets his shoulders and biceps grow in size and I have

YOU LEFT US IN GEORGIA

a time thinking about much else. "I have to apologize, I don't have a cool motorcycle to take you on."

We walk outside and he holds the door open to a black *Silverado*, helping me inside with one hand. He shuts the door and wanders around to the driver's side. The music floods the cab when he rolls the engine to a start.

The drive to the hospital feels just as long as the drive back home. The view is much better with Sean in the driver's seat. He's wearing dark sunglasses that suit his face, and now with the scruff gone I can see how nicely the curves of his jaw compliment him.

"When did you get so old?" I reach out and graze my fingers along the jaw, it's smooth under my fingers.

"You got old with me Nora," he tenses at my touch, "you'll remember eventually, you may not have come home all these years but I came to you. It's been hard watching you spiral but the last year has been so good."

"I don't feel sad right now Sean, I feel confused and a little lost in time but I feel happy," I say retracting my hand. He looks at me briefly taking his eyes off the road to look at mine.

"You've been happy, we've been happy." He doesn't say anything else as he pulls into the hospital parking lot and turns off the engine. "I'm sorry that was uncalled for. You can't help how your emotions are affecting you right now. It's been really nice to see you so carefree, I'll admit that."

"I'm calling Sean, you shouldn't even be out right now." Nick scowls at me as I set the empty highball glass on the bar. *"You're out of control Nora."*

"Quite the opposite Nick, I am perfectly in control now." It had been three weeks since I cut him off.

"This is what you call control?" He asks, his dark brown eyes

full of judgment. "You just fought a guy outside for calling you, sweetheart."

"Okay," I turn to face him fully now on the bar stool, "That guy deserved a good punch," I shift the bag of ice on my knuckles. They were sore and would be swollen in the morning. "Control is selective, I use the booze to control how I feel about the world around me when I'm sober, Nicholas."

"Well I still called Sean an hour ago so," he nods to the door of the pub.

"You said you're going to call him, not that you had! I thought I had a chance to bargain. That was sneaky Nick..." I turn around, my shoulders tight, and see Sean standing in a full suit staring at me. He must have driven straight from work, he was still wearing his work clothes. "Tattle-tail."

"I had to Nora, you had a really rough night and he's the only one you ever listen to when you're like this besides Natalie." He sighs.

"And she's so sick of me she didn't pick up the phone when you tried her," I step off the stool and trip over my own two feet. I correct myself before walking towards the door, Sean hands me my jacket and opens the door for me.

"You were at work," I say tensely as we walk to his truck.

"I was," he says, opening the truck door and waiting for me to get inside. He stops before closing the door and comes to eye level with me. "Why do you do this to yourself?"

"It was a work event Sean," I grab the handle and close it myself as he's forced to back away. The world spins as he drives us across Atlanta to my apartment, he takes my waist and leads me to the stairs. He pulls his keys out and unlocks the door with his spare, leading us into the darkness.

He lets go of me and starts lighting the candles that scatter throughout the apartment with his lighter until the soft warm glow I love so much is throughout. I sink into the bed and kick my shoes off. They clatter against the hardwood and tumble to a stop.

Sean grabs two beers from the fridge and sets them on the table, stripping his dress jacket off his sculpted shoulders, and removing his gun belt from his hips he throws it on the wicker chair to his left. He disappears into the bathroom, coming back with a cloth and rubbing alcohol. He sits on the bed, giving me room to slide closer to him. I hook one leg around his back and hip letting the other rest over his knee.

He presses into me for a moment, just sitting here in silence. He takes my hand firmly in his and presses the cloth to my raw knuckles. I hiss, trying to pull my hand away but he tilts his head, his blue eyes so serious.

"What happened?" He asks, finishing up and handing me a beer. He lifts his arm so I can tuck myself into the neat groves of his toned body. My shoulder fitting perfectly under him, I take a long breath and look up at him trying not to pick the label off my beer.

"Can you not pull a good cop routine on me right now?" I ask. "Bring me home, clean my hand but I don't want to talk about him."

"How did he know you were going to be there Nora?" He looks down at me, concern flashes across his face.

"It was a warning," I bite my lip, "He wanted me to know that I can't just cut him off, that he can do whatever he wants and I'm never allowed to forget him."

He rubs the top of my head with his hand, setting his beer down. He drags his hand down my side, using his strength to move me into his lap fully with only one arm. I wrap my arms around his middle, my fingernails dig into his back and I let myself sob into his chest.

66

"I'm sorry, work's been so intense lately with homicide. I haven't been able to keep proper tabs on where he is. This is my fault, Nora." Sean squeezes both arms around me, bringing me even closer than before. The fabric of his white dress shirt is so soft against my sore face.

"I should have just let him keep calling, it's my fault. I cut him off." Sean pulls us back, falling into the soft gray comforter behind us. I slide myself over and rest my head against him, bringing my leg up across his hips. "I'm sorry you had to drive all the way to pick me up again, this is the last time I promise," I look up at him, but his eyes are closed and he's facing the ceiling.

"I'll always come, Nora," he says in a whisper, "regardless of what you think I don't drive an hour each way because I have to, or because you're sad. I come because I want to be here more than anywhere else, ever." He runs a hand along my hair, when he finally looks at me there is such a fire in his blue eyes.

I move slowly, bringing my lips to his and for the first time in eighteen years, I am granted the chance to know exactly how he tastes. The kiss is slow at first, cautious in our movements with one another until it becomes wild and hungry.

He slides a hand between us, buttoning the pants I wore and dipping into my underwear in one motion. "Is this okay?" he asks before going further, I nod without taking my eyes off him. He dips lower, moving his thumb in soft circles over my clit, he circles painfully slowly as I work on unbuttoning his pants. He takes a moment to shed them completely, laying back against the bed and bringing me forward to him. I rest my legs over his hips, his erection pressing against his boxers.

I take my time with each button until I can strip the dress shirt from his arms. I run my hands over his chest and up to his shoulders. Feeling every muscle as I go, I cup his face in my hands pressing a *fumbled kiss to his soft lips.*

He takes me like that, with little circles of his hips pressing up into me alongside his smooth thumb and his skin under my hands. Finally, he grabs my hips firmly and thrusts into me until I quiver around him. He nearly bucks me off his length before yanking me back down and continuing to use quick thrusts to bring me over the edge. I whimpered against his skin as he pushed my hips into him and released a rough moan from his lips.

He lifts me roughly in his arms, and my legs wrap around his hips as he carries us to the bathroom still intertwined at the hips. He strips the rest of my clothes from me, leaving them in a messy heap on the floor. Not drawing anything out he pushes me against the shower wall letting the steamy water roll over us. He buries himself against my core, as I grip his perfect blonde hair now wet and slick in my hands. He drove into me hard, sending a whimper tumbling from my lips.

He kissed me softly, traveling his tongue into my mouth as he drove into me. "God, Nora," he says, driving into me. I try to respond but words didn't seem to be enough to describe how good I felt as he pounded all words out of me. I come again, gasping into his mouth as he grunts and shutters against me. He looks at me through the downpour of water, wanting to look at what his pleasure had done to me.

A loud banging noise at the front door interrupted whatever Sean was about to say, his mouth hanging open, he ran his hands through his hair and pushed it off his face. He reaches around me, shuts the water off, and hands me a towel. He kisses my neck, and even though more loud knocking he takes his time to dry every inch of my body.

Whoever is at the door is persistent, Sean pulls his boxers on and grabs his gun from the chair. "Put that down," I say, wrapping myself in my dark green robe I pad across the floor in bare feet to the front door. "It's probably Willa, when she gets drunk she shows up here."

"That doesn't sound like Willa to me," he isn't wrong, the banging is loud enough to be a strong male but I don't let it bother me. My body is still reeling from the orgasms that Sean had given me not minutes beforehand.

I open the door slowly and all time stops, Bishop stands with his hand raised to knock again. "You can come out Sean, I know you're here." He doesn't even look at me, he keeps his eye line above my head and stares into my apartment. "Your truck is out front, and it's a little late for a game of scrabble between old friends."

He pushes into my apartment but I put my hand out, it touches him but like I am a hot iron rod he hisses and pulls back. "Stay out of my home Bishop," I say. I can feel myself shaking but my voice is strong. "Where's your date?"

He swallows hard, Sean moves in silent footsteps as though he wasn't a massive human. I barely hear him as his hand comes to my back. "She's in the car," he says, he still won't look at me.

"Then go take her home Bishop, I don't need you here." The feeling of Sean's hand on my back steadies me, I can only hope that this won't make me cry.

"No, you have everything you need, don't you?" When he finally looks at me it feels like the world is on fire, his blue eyes are so intense on mine I can feel my legs giving way.

"Go home Bishop," I say again before closing the door.

"Sean," I say as he opens the passenger door for me. He looks at me waiting, begging for me to say something. The same look he gave me in my memory, hopeful and curious. My heart aches for a moment. "Why didn't you tell me?"

I can tell by the look on his face he knows what I mean,

"You'll have to be more specific Nora," he steps forward and brushes a loose strand of hair from my collarbone. The feeling of his fingers on my skin feels so different now.

"If I don't get my memories back if I don't remember... were you ever going to tell me that we were together?" I clench my jaw.

His jaw twitches, and he leans against the truck door with a heavy sigh, "It was once," he said. "Recently, we never got to find out what it meant."

"Why did you tell me the last time we saw each other was Christmas?" I ask, angry now.

"Nora you stopped answering my calls too," he shakes his head, "I just thought maybe if I didn't tell you then you wouldn't have to be ashamed of what we did anymore. Like I could erase it finally, and we could be us again?"

"Isn't that up to me to decide?" I ask, "I'm such a different person right now, I just wanna know how I turned into someone so ugly."

"No, no," Sean places a hand on my face, "you aren't the ugly one here. It's Bishop, it's me. We've been pulling you around like a toy we didn't want to share for so long that we created the emotional walls you put up to guard ourselves against us. Our crimes were that we just loved you so much and we were too selfish to let you be happy."

"Have you seen him since that night?" I raise my eyebrow at him.

"I have, more than once." He answers with his head down, "let's go talk to the doctor, and after I'll take you home. I think you need to have a conversation with your dad."

70

10

"So from the scans it looks like you have minor damage to your hippocampus, that will affect your long-term memory. As the swelling goes down, you'll most likely regain a lot of these memories." The doctor points to images suspended in the light.

"Is there anything I can do to speed it up?" I ask nervously, Sean shifts in his seat beside me, his knee rubbing against mine in support.

"Unfortunately, not much. This kind of injury is more of a waiting game. You'll start to regain those lost years sometimes, one at a time and sometimes in a massive dump. That can be overwhelming so try not to find yourself alone anywhere." He sighs, "I do have good news though, the break in your arm isn't nearly as bad as we previously thought. The new x-rays we got this morning show more of a minor fracture. We were concerned about having to perform surgery to reset some bones but it all looks amazing."

"So how long do I need the cast?" I ask.

"Three more weeks, then we can switch you to a removable brace. You're probably already sick of not bathing properly, hey?" The doctor flashes a smile at me. "I will have Shelly schedule you for an appointment in two weeks to see how you're feeling, we'll take new x-rays and go from there."

"Thanks, Doc," Sean says as he leaves the room. We walk through the hospital in silence. It's not until we're back in the car that he asks, "you alright?"

"Yeah, actually. It's nice to know the memory loss isn't permanent." I say to him, but in reality, I'm terrified. Everything that has happened over the last few days has been alien but comfortable. "I know I should be grateful that it'll return, but it's been so nice to get to know you both without whatever weight was holding us all down before. I know that when my memory comes back it'll hurt but I'll have all these new memories too," I stop, my eyes drifting to the floor. "Does that make me selfish? For me to want to have these feelings?"

Sean places a finger under my chin and pulls my eyes to meet his, "When your memory starts coming back we'll all be here for you. I promise, no matter what feelings return with them."

"I was happy," I say quietly, and he tilts his head. "I don't remember why I was so upset in the first place, but when I saw you standing at the door of that pub. I was happy."

A smile grows on his face as he listens, "Was it like that every time?" His smile drops and I know I've said the wrong thing. "Were you always saving me from my own drunken stupor?"

"Not always, it was more common though after," he stops, biting his lip. "After Bishop left, he would make these phone calls—"

"I know, he told me." Sean looks surprised that Bishop would admit that to me.

"Ben told you that in order to move on from what happened between the two of you that you needed to cut him off completely." He explains, and he takes my hand in his hand over the console. "It took some convincing but we got you a new phone and that was the end of it. Something changed in you then, and you snapped. The last couple of months you've been self-medicating with booze."

"And the night you came to get me?" I ask, hopeful that I hadn't reached the limit of what he would tell me just yet.

"He took it upon himself to show up at the work event you had planned. It was a huge night for you, it was one of the first jobs you hosted alone. He had no right being there, Nick Fasen—" he pauses to look at me again, "A friend you met in college, he tried to bring you home but you refused."

"I sound like a terror, I'm sorry I put you all through that." I groan.

"You weren't yourself, don't get too down about it." He brings my hand to his lips and places a kiss on it.

"I need to know more Sean," I pull my hand back and sigh. He shakes his head gently but turns the engine over on the truck.

"That's a conversation for your dad."

"Don't move," my dad's voice rose up to the stairs where I was crouched listening to the conversation. Sean and Bishop stand outside, I can see them clearly where they stand on the porch as far away from each other as they can. "Explain yourselves," my dad barks.

Bishop's eye is bruised, nasty pinkish purple color forms along his cheekbones. Sean wipes the blood from his split lip, both sitting silently under the wraith of my father's glare. "You boys, come into my house. You spend every summer here, you surf off my beach and you eat my food. You're always respectful, now is not the time to be quiet."

"We were playing volleyball," Bishop says first, his voice is full

*of gravel and he licks his bottom lip. "Sean here is a sore loser,"
the words come out and Sean closes the distance between the two
of them. My dad barely has time to come between them, shoving
them back to their ends of the sidewalk.*

*"He pushed me, on purpose to prove a point. He's been pushing
my buttons all week trying to get me to fight him and I finally did."
Sean groans, shifting his weight on the couch. "I'm only sorry I
didn't hit him harder."*

*"Sean Grant Roberts," My mother scoffs from the kitchen island,
I can't see her from where I am hidden listening to them fight but I
know that voice anywhere.*

*"Sorry ma'am," he nods his head slightly. When he raises it his
eyes catch mine through the screen door, I know he can see me
sitting on the stairs. His jaw tenses because he knows that the fight
between him and Bishop, was his fault. He had instigated it on the
beach, completely unprovoked.*

*It has always been easier to blame things on Bishop, he's stoic and
only speaks when no one is listening. He prefers to watch people,
to understand them without words. I can always feel him on my
skin, his eyes studying me. He's always trying to remember it all
as if it wouldn't be there one day.*

*"It's my fault," he says, "I let my jealousy get the better of me, and
I hit him. That's not saying he didn't deserve it, it felt good to mess
pretty boys lip up." Sean winces even remembering that his lip is
busted. "I am sorry though, it was uncalled for."*

*"You boys need to learn that hitting each other isn't always
going to solve your problems. You also need to understand that I
understand you both feel something for Nora but if you continue
to treat her like an object that you feel the need to fight over—"
he stops, I know the tone in his voice, what he's going to say next.
"Then I encourage you to remember she has a mind of her own,*

74

*and one of these days she's going to stop forgiving you both. I think
you would rather see her happy, with one of you, than heartbroken
with neither."*

Both boys look over at each other, grim looks on their faces. "Nora
you can come down now," my dad says and it's clear to everyone
that he's known for a long time that I've been there.

"Sorry dad," I say, stepping outside with them in the sun.

"Nothing you haven't heard before, this is the third time we've
had this conversation this summer boys. I don't want to have it
again." My dad shakes his head, giving both their heads a rough
playful slap before wandering back inside.

"I'm going to kill Ben," Sean coughs as soon as dad disappears
back inside.

"If Ben wasn't there, you would have killed each other. You
certainly didn't stop for me," I pull my tank top up to show the large
bruise forming where Sean had thrown an accidental elbow to my
ribs. I walk down the street leaving them both standing there.

"Stay here golden boy," Bishop's voice is quiet but demanding,
it's not long before I hear the sound of his boots behind me on the
sidewalk. He walks behind me in silence for a while, following me
to the pier, then down to the beach and he sits beside me in the sand
as the sun drops in the sky.

"Does it hurt?" He asks, fingering the hem of my tank top.

"No more than any other bruise you idiots have accidentally
given me," I bat his hand away.

"Sean's been asking for it lately," Bishop lays back in the sand,
his fingers playing with mine absently.

"If you give into him like that then you're no better Bishop," I
look down at him, his blue eyes inviting me to join him. He tugs
on my fingers, silently asking me again.

I lay beside him in the sun-warmed sand and I tuck myself into his arm with a small whimper. *The bruised ribs are rubbing against his side.* "Are you sure you're okay," *he cups my head with his hand.*

"I'll be okay, it wasn't your fault." *I muse rubbing my hand along his bare chest, his dark shirt unbuttoned all the way to his shorts.* "I just wish you guys could get along, just for one day."

"I'll work harder, for you mostly, I guess if I ever want Sean to find his own girlfriend I have to stop messing up his face." *Bishop jokes but there's a pain in his voice I recognize.*

"You're enough Bishop," *I say quietly.*

"Am I?" *he asks, a whisper against the sound of crashing waves and seagulls.*

"You are to me," *I kiss him, over and over until he smiles up at me.*

"How did the appointment go?" Dad sits on the island, his dark hair graying and his glasses hanging off his nose.

"Good news for my hand, not so great for my head." I tap my temple with a finger. "Will you tell me what happened that summer?" My mom drops a plate in the sink, the noise ringing out throughout the house. "I keep remembering things, but I can't seem to remember that."

"Let's go for a walk," Dad extends his hand to me, helping me around the counter. The air outside smells wonderful, the smell of smoke is gone now and the wind is carrying the salt water smell around the air.

"Before I tell you this, I want you to remember that not everything was easy for you, and what happened broke you. If I'm going to tell you everything, I want you to use the memories but also I want you to build new ones with both of the men in your life." He says looking up to the deck, Sean and Bishop stand on opposite ends, leaving against the railing watching us.

76

"I promise," I say confidently.

"The summer everyone avoids talking about, I got sick. Really sick. I had a brain tumor and a lot changed around here. Everyone picked up extra chores, and you all took on jobs to help keep the house running. You all got very busy," dad explains. "Bishop took it the hardest, his father isn't a nice man Nora. We were going to lose the beach house because medical expenses were piling up."

"I don't understand," I say.

"Bishop went to work for his father, against his better judgment. To help us, to help you. You were ready to give up your entire college savings to save the beach house. Bishop knew the only way to make you happy was to make sure you had a home to come back to, even if it meant leaving you and hating him." My dad takes my hand and squeezes it. "I got better, and we got back on our feet."

"Why do you all walk on eggshells around him then, why is he the big bad wolf if he did this for us?" I ask, searching for answers.

"He did it all without talking to you. You and Bishop were different, he was a quiet kid, and didn't talk a lot. His dad and sister took advantage of him a lot until you started to notice the bruises and scars. You stood up for Bishop like no person had done for him before and he felt like he owed you. He did everything in his power to sabotage everything you were together." Dad's voice trailed off as we came to the water's edge.

"He brought girls over, he got in fights, you had to bail him out of jail more than once," he explains.

"Why tell me this?" I question.

"I'm telling you because I'm the only one who saw through

his bullshit. It was a self-defense mechanism for him. He started drinking around the time his dad came home from Romania. He did it so that he couldn't think, he knew if he was sober he would let you talk him out of leaving." A sigh leaves his lips.

"He asked you one day to go with him. He wanted you to live in Tokyo with him, I think he only asked to hear you tell him no. He wanted to make sure you truly hated him enough, he's truly a brilliant man even under the circumstances. He knew you could handle the anger better than the heartbreak."

"And did I handle it well?" I bite my lip.

"You didn't, but he put a fail-safe in place." My dad looks back up to the house, and both of them still stand on the deck. "He gave you Sean," he says. "They even got in a fist fight over it and for the first time in their entire lives, the fight was about something other than the possession of your heart my tiny, sweet girl. Sean refused to let him leave and tried to convince him to stay. For once they were fighting for a common goal."

"Where am I supposed to go from here?" I feel like all I do anymore is ask questions.

"Just go from here with an open mind, listen to what they both have to say, and decide what's best for you. You've spent your entire life living it for them. It's time you matter." My dad hugs me tightly and walks me back up to the beach house where both men stand a fair distance apart.

"I'm going to need both of your help to remember every-thing, which means I need you to be civil with each other. Can you do that?" I ask.

They both nod.

"Absolute honestly, from both of you—" I look at Bishop first and he tenses but nods in agreement. This would be difficult but if I'm going to make the best decision for myself, my memories, and the future I need to know everything.

11

"Hey," Bishop sits on the chair across from my bed. The sun is barely up and a warm glow casts over the room. "How are you?" He asks, there's a softness to his face this early in the morning. His lip curls up as he watches me sit up in bed.

I look to see if Nat is in the room but her bed is unmade, "guess it makes sense for them to sleep in Ben's room now." I sigh. It's weird having it so empty, without the incessant snoring coming from Natalie in the middle of the night.

"I can stay in here if you want, I'll sleep in her bed of course." He suggests, "you never liked sleeping alone."

"We shared a room my entire life," I say with a frown. "Did I live with someone in Atlanta?" I shake my head, this was a question for Sean. Not Bishop.

"Uh," he pauses. "I don't think so, you should ask Sean. He knows you better than I do now," he looks sad now.

"I didn't mean to upset you," I say before I can stop myself. *Focus on yourself*, that's what dad had said.

"You didn't, Darling," he muses and taps his fingers against the back of his neck. He leans back in the chair, his shirt rising up and exposing the tan skin of his stomach. He catches me staring and smiles.

"Will you come closer?" I ask and he tilts his head to the side.

"Are you sure that's a good idea?" He teases but his voice is soft and playful again. The voice I like.

"I have some questions for you, and I'd like to see your face properly when I ask them." He swallows hard, his throat bobbing. "Please?"

He stands, smoothing his shorts and fixing his hair with his fingers. I make room for him and he sits down at the end of my bed leaving space between us. I shake my head and hook my finger around his pinky to pull him closer. He scoots forward until his knees touch mine.

"Close enough?" He asks.

"Perfect."

He tenses, looking at me with a longing that should have made me uncomfortable but I just smile back at him. "Relax," I say, taking his hand in mine.

"First of all, why were you watching me sleep?" He chuckles, his tongue coming across his bottom lip. I want to lean in and taste it but I sit still and wait for his answer.

"You make these noises in your sleep, I missed hearing them," he pushes a loose hair back off my collarbone with the back of his hand.

"Is that the honest truth?" I question.

He sighs and removes his hand. "I've never been able to sleep, not properly. I used medication in the past to get a couple of hours here and there. The dark and I don't get along so well," he looks away from me but I turn his face back to mine with the palm of my hand. "God, this is going to sound creepy Nora, are you sure you want to hear this?"

"Honesty, remember? That's what I want."

"You are the only way I sleep anymore, I was asleep in that chair. I only woke up five minutes before you." He laughs softly, "the sound of you breathing beside me— it puts me to sleep."

"Yeah, you're right. That is creepy," I try to suppress my laugh but it comes out in a wave when his face drops into a scowl.

"Keep laughing," he says when I stop. "It's the most beautiful sound in the world." I smack him in the shoulder.

"Next question, why did you lie to me?" I raise my eyebrow at him. "Dad explained a lot about the summer he got sick. Why didn't you tell anyone you paid off the medical expenses and the beach house?"

"That man will be the death of me," he shifts uncomfortably. "I'm not that guy anymore, I won't lie to you again. Not even for your own good."

"You should have just told us," I say. "Maybe we could have figured it out. Helped somehow."

"You don't understand, it wasn't as simple as going to work for my dad. I had to make a deal with him. The deal meant leaving you behind." Bishop's eyes are dark now, something hollow had slipped in and I missed it.

"What was the deal, Bishop?" I wait, he's holding back a secret. I can see the pain flutter silently across all his hardened features.

"It was him or you, that's the only way he would pay the debt." His jaw twitches and his nose scrunches up to keep him from crying.

"How are you here now then, with me?" I ask.

"He's dead." The words are ice, I sit watching him process what he's said. "He died six months ago from a heart attack."

82

"I'm so sorry, Bishop," I say inching forward.

"Once you remember everything you won't be sorry, I can promise you that." He rubs a thumb against my jaw and I feel myself lean into his hand. "He doesn't deserve your sympathy baby," he coos "he never did."

"Bishop?" Glass crunches under my feet as I push the front door to their elegant beach house open. The walls are all painted various shades of white and gray. A stark contrast to the aquamarine tiles that floored the house throughout. "Baby?"

No one responds but I can hear the music pumping from one of the upstairs bedrooms. Bishop turned seventeen today. It was the first time in a long time any of us had seen his father. A brutal man with a pudgy face, dark eyes, and whiskery-like long dark hair that curled around his ears.

He didn't share any of Bishop's soft features, his kind ocean blue eyes, or his full gentle lips. No, this man was a marble statue.

The glass under my feet is from a vase, the black and gold one that usually sat in the entryway filled with flowers. It had been thrown across the room violently and lay in chunks around the floor. I climb the stairs to the bedroom with no signs of anyone else in the house.

I don't knock, it's Bishop's room that the music is blasting from. It's dark inside from his blackout curtains, all the sun trapped on the other side. "Bishop?" I say closing the door behind me.

He doesn't answer me but I can see the shape of him crumpled in the corner. His shoulders heaving in sobs as he cries everything out of his body. I get down on my knees and wrap myself around him. Letting him cry all the pain away. I try not to cry with him, it won't help him but I feel so bad. Every bit of agony rolling through him hits me too. Eventually, he stops.

I lean over and turn on the lamp. It lights the room enough for me to see how terrible he looks. I restrain a gasp, "baby—" a large gash runs the length of his cheekbone. It's clotted and still sticky with blood.

His eyes are so red the blue in them is the brightest I've ever seen. I just wanna take away all the pain. His jaw is badly bruised. The collar of his dress shirt is ripped open exposing the purple rings around his throat.

"You have to tell someone Bishop," I say like I've done time and time again. "He should be in jail."

But as always, he looks at me with sadness and defeat, "I'll be fine, just tell everyone I'm sick. The bruising will be gone before surf camp and no one will know."

I help him stand, leading him to the bathroom. I sit him in the tub and grab a face cloth. He's worse than I thought as he strips the torn dress shirt from his body he lets out a painful whimper. His ribs are purple all down the left side. I swallow my own fear and ignore them as I turn the faucet on. He sits in his jeans, the tub filling up to his stomach. I clean the dried blood from his face, careful not to hurt him further.

"Come here," he says. I tug off my shirt and jeans climbing into the tub in my black bra and underwear. I wrap my feet around behind him and rest my hips down into the space between his legs. I examine the bruising on his ribs and try not to wince as I run a finger over them. "I'm sorry it's always you who finds me," he says so quietly I almost miss it.

"I'm not," I say, raising my hand to his chin delicately.

"This cycle will never end, it'll never be enough for him to stop. To just leave me alone." The boy sitting in front of me is broken, defeated, and abused.

"You remember what mom always says when we're feeling down on ourselves?" I ask, staring across at him.

84

"Right now I don't think hearing that will help Nora," he admits.

"You are more than enough," I say it anyway because I know it's what he needs. "I love you."

He stares at me, his face shocked and bewildered. I had never said that to him until now. It's easy to forget how hard those words are to say to someone. I had been meaning to tell him for weeks but no time felt right. Someone was always around and watching us.

"I didn't want that word tarnished by a moment like this but I do, I love you." He shakes his head and grips both hands to my face.

"I've loved you since we were fifteen years old Nora, thank you for always being the brave one between us." He kisses me then. Slow and passionate like he had nowhere else to be in the entire world.

"I loved you a lot didn't I?" I stare at him now. His face is weathered with age but his eyes are still as bright as they were that day staring back at me.

"What did you remember?" His turn to ask a question.

"The day I told you I loved you for the first time," I expect him to grimace or scowl. Such a harsh memory could not bring such light to his eyes but he smiles at me. So big my heart skips a beat in my chest just seeing it.

"That was the best present I received for my birthday that year." He says. "I still love you that much, I will always love you that much no matter what you choose to do at the end of the summer."

The end is coming and he laid out a harsh reminder it was sooner than later that I would have to decide. I bit my lip and closed my eyes trying to sink back into memory so I didn't have to deal with real life but nothing came over me. Not this time.

"I have meetings today for work, but I would like to take

you all sailing tomorrow. Ben, Nat, and Sean." He pushes himself from the bed, a skip in his step.

"Even Sean?" I say teasing.

"Yeah, even pretty boy Roberts can come. I'll talk to you later," he goes to leave but darts back, placing a quick kiss on the top of my head. "Thank you for this, I think forgetting everything is helping everyone more than you know. We all have stuff we need to remember, we just need a push."

12

Ben stands against the railing of the deck in his wet suit, "we're going to go surfing, did you want us to set you up on the beach?"

"I'd like that," the wind is a bit chilly but Nat comes out with a blanket.

"Sean brought a chair down for you already," she says with a smile. "I got this for you," she holds out a plain black notepad and a pack of pencils.

"I can't draw worth shit," I laugh but take the book.

"You can. Trust me." She hooks her arm in mine and walks us down the stairs behind Ben. He carries a large yellow surfboard under his arm and a cooler in the other hand. She sets me up on the chair, nestled into the sand under an umbrella, and lays a blanket over my legs.

Sean is in the water, his blonde hair wet, it glistens under the afternoon sun. He stares back at us, there's a hesitation on his face that worries me. I can't read their minds, but he and Bishop alike must hate me right now. Everything I'm doing affects them, their minds and hearts.

I flip the hardcover of the book over, tucking it under the blank pages. I rip open the pack of pencils, and charcoal and raise an eyebrow at Nat. "Alright," she sets her book down and rolls her head to the side, looking at me above her sunglasses.

"You used it as a coping mechanism," she sighs, "you tried to hide it from me, both you and Ben but you're both terrible at secrets. It's deplorable."

She scans through the pages of her book until she comes to a small piece of folded paper that I had thought was a bookmark but as she unfolds it, she reveals a picture. It's messy, and sketchy and only hues of gray and black compose it but it's a drawing of us. Natalie, grips Ben tightly around the middle, with a giant messy smile on her face. Ben has his arm around Sean, an open-mouthed silent laugh coming from his figure. I smiled, running a finger against the paper, he stood taller than the rest of his, in his Harvard sweater a goofy grin on his face. I'm the next, shorter but my hand is tangled in the crook of his arm. Even still, my attention is to the right of me.

The page is empty there, with enough space for him but it's like I never got the chance to draw him. I scowled and handed the paper back to her, "you didn't draw him in there because you were hiding your therapy from me not because you didn't want to."

She extends the paper again, holding it out between us. "Finish the picture, Nora," she says gently, "he deserves a space there even after everything."

"Did you know?" I asked her finally, I had been avoiding dragging her into this. With everything going on with her there was no room for any more stress.

"I didn't," she wiggles her nose and looks out to the water. "I said a lot of awful things to him over the years. Dad never said a word, he just helped him keep up the facade that Bishop was a terrible person. I feel horrible." She rubs her tummy with a sad smile, "I would never want my child to be treated

88

how Bishop was growing up."

"Never," I lean over and rub her hand with mine. "I love you, Nat. Thanks for always being there for me."

"Finish that, it's time." I look down at the page, a sigh leaving my lips. I take the pencil to the paper slowly and carefully as I can. I'm not sure how but after some time, Bishop's face appears on the paper. His figure is slumped towards mine, he leans into my shoulder with a wide smile that scrunches at his nose.

The sun is high above us now, but the drawing is much more complete than before. I watch as Sean pulls a huge wave, riding it across the horizon as Ben hollers from a distance. His hands are in the air, and a wild laugh fills in the air as Sean fumbles and crashes into the waves.

"Am I still a terrible surfer?" I look at Natalie but she's fallen asleep. She looks peaceful, her usually concerned face is softened around the edges, her full lips half open.

I lift the blanket off myself and lay it over her. I wander closer to the shore, my toes digging in the warm, beige sand as I go. Sean saunters in from the water, dragging his board behind him. He unzips his wet suit and pulls it down over his chest until it hangs at his tanned waist loosely.

"Did you put sunscreen on?" He says, ripping the Velcro on his ankle. He slams his board into the sand.

"Good afternoon Sean, how are you? Oh good, I'm good too—" I tease his lack of conversation skills. "This isn't going to be awkward, I won't let it."

He kicks the sand under his wet feet and pushes his wet hair back off his face nervously, "I'm sorry. I just don't know how to act around you," he looks out at the ocean to where Ben still sits on his board letting the waves push him around.

"Walk?"

"Yeah, Nat fell asleep an hour ago. I could use some real company." I walk beside him, not close enough to touch him but close enough that if I want to reach out I can.

"How's your head?" He asks after a little while of silence.

"It's okay, I'll be grateful to be free of this cast. At times I wish it would all just come back, but the doctor said that could be dangerous too so I don't know anymore."

"When you get your cast off I'll take you out on the water. Remind me how good of a surfer you are," he smiles at me, and the blue in his eyes sparkles in the sun.

"I'd take a warm shower at this point," I laugh.

"I may have a solution for that if you're willing of course—" he stops and turns toward me. His chest is so sculpted that I can't help but trail my eyes over it. It's sandy and damp, water droplets stick to the ridges in his abs.

"I would be willing," I laugh nervously, "if it means I'm not greasy anymore."

Sean laughs back, taking my hand and leading me up past our beach house towards his. "Mom had this giant three-person claw tub installed last summer. It's massive. You can have a bath, it's not the same as a shower but it's clean water."

"Thank you, Sean," I smile at him. He unlocks the front door to their beach house and sets his keys in a small bowl at the main entrance. Their house was a little more extravagant than ours. Newer construction gave the entire main floor an open concept. It was painted in bright pastel colors and all the furniture was newer.

He points to the back, where his mother's room is, and leads me in the right direction. He's right, the tub is massive. It sits in the middle of a redone bathroom. The tiles are plain to compliment the beautiful sunny yellow shiplap that hung around the walls. The tub is white as well, with copper fixtures and it certainly could fit three people, if not four.

"I'll run it for you and then go get you some clean clothes. Let you have your privacy," he's so kind. His stance relaxes a touch when I nod in agreement. He moves to the tub running the water and checking it with his hand to make sure it's not too warm. "I'll leave all of this here, you should be able to reach it. You'll be okay to get in?"

"I think I can handle it," I say I can feel the color form on my cheeks, from his stare. He drags his mother's vanity stool towards the tub and sets shampoo, conditioner, and soap on top of it within my reach. He smiles warmly before he closes the door behind him and I start to remove my clothes. I would have taken help with my shirt but didn't want to impose any more than I already had. I push off my cotton shorts with my good hand, letting them fall in a pile along with my shirt and underwear.

The water is so nice, it stings my toes a little as I climb over the edge and sink down into the tub. It's a lot harder than it seems to sink into a tub one-handed. I fumble a little and decide my best course of action is to kneel first and then move my legs out from underneath me.

The water feels so good on my dirty skin. I use my fingers to clumsily pull the elastic from my thick, knotted hair and I chuck it away from me. I close my eyes and let the steam from the water brush along my jaw, and cheeks and clean the ash from my eyelashes that remains. I could feel my skin screaming with excitement to be soaking all the dirt, sand, and blood away. I had been cleaned at the hospital but this was a new sense of euphoria.

I take soap and run it over my body the best I can, I can't reach my back and it's near impossible to do it all well holding my arm above the water. A soft knock at the door interrupts my struggle, "Nora?" Sean's voice floats through the crack in the door. "I brought you clothes, do you need anything?"

He sounds so sweet like if I was to open the door behind it would stand my scrawny, fresh-faced quarterback Sean. That's not who was behind the door though, it was a different version of the boy I once knew. Now all I can think about is running my hands all over him, and feeling his hands all over me.

"Do you think you could wash my hair for me?" I ask, biting my lip. I know it's not the smartest idea but I'm not gonna leave this tub without clean hair. I have come too far for that.

"Are you sure?" He isn't even sure, I chuckle at his uncertainty.

"It's nothing you haven't seen before, Roberts, if you're too much of a gentleman I can get Natalie to wash it at home in the sink," I say and he sighs from the other side of the door. I turn, pressing my exposed chest against my knees, and wait for him to work up the nerve.

He's in a clean pair of jeans, but he's still not wearing a shirt. His face is flushed as he looks anywhere but the tub. "Sean, stop. Look at me," he turns slowly and stares at me. A huff of air leaves his beautiful pink lips and he wanders over to grab the shower head attachment from my hand.

He turns the water on and lets it run warm before taking it to my hair, I lean back into it as it sluices down my body back into the tub. He sets it down and lathers my hair, his strong fingers raking against my scalp firmly. "Is that too rough?"

I moan lightly and let him continue to massage my head,

he rinses it clean. I can feel his fingers trace the ridges of my hunched-over shoulder blades under the running water, slowly he runs them up and over my shoulders. He dips into the canals until he reaches my neck and returns back down just as painstaking slowly.

I dare to look back at him, all the boyish embarrassment had faded from his face and now he stares at me intently. He brings his hand to cup my cheek, a smirk on his lips. He removes it and slides over my collarbones until it finds the soft flesh of my breast, his thumb grazes my nipple. My body instinctively buckled, knowing how long it had been subconsciously since I had been touched like this.

Sean's tongue slides over his lips, his gaze sliding down my body.

"We shouldn't do this Nora, it will complicate everything." He pulls back but I grab his hand, sliding it lower over my nape, leaning back against the side of the tub until he can reach between my legs.

He presses his forehead against the side of my head, with a deep sigh. His fingers move fast, circling in a way I couldn't tell if I liked or not as my hips lift in time with his touch. I growl as he stops again, apprehensive to continue.

"It's just sex Sean," I say hoarsely, "Pleasure."

"Maybe to you," he pulls away and stands grabbing a towel from the bench and holding it out for me. "I can't be the person you use as a release Nora, not anymore. I'll tell you whatever you want to know, I'll talk to you for hours. Until you have a conversation with Bishop about what you want, this won't happen."

He leaves me standing here, leaving the bathroom. I hear the front door open and close. I dress and set out to find him, it doesn't take long when I spot him sulking in the sand close to the shore.

"I'm sorry," I say sitting next to him, he holds a hand out and helps me down beside him. "I shouldn't have expected you to do that, it was unfair."

"I wanted to, I really did." A raw and low groan comes from his lips beside me. "But I've always been caught between the two of you. That day at the diner, the day you met him—I had almost dared you to kiss me. I was so close, but I was so scared."

I draw circles in the sand with my finger as he talks, knowing he needs to get it out but waiting for the other shoe to drop. "I had to watch Ben struggle for so long with Natalie before he had the courage to say anything to her. How do you live up to that kind of love if you didn't feel the same I would have shattered our friendship. It would have turned the summers into endless days of awkward feelings." Sean sighs.

"And then he showed up and I had to watch you fall in love with him, summer after summer." He bites his lip and shakes his head a little. "I had this fantasy for a long time about what would have happened if I had just taken the chance that day. Bathtub sex is included in that fantasy, but I don't want it if it means you still have feelings for him. I won't be collateral damage in your journey back to yourself Nora."

"I'm sorry I don't remember the years we had together, not properly. I can't promise you that what I decide will make you happy but I know that this has made me a different person and I want you here with me while I figure it all out." I say taking his hand in mine. "I promise I won't do that again, I took advantage of your kindness, acting on feelings I don't even remember having. If I ever do it again, I'll be sure."

"That's all I ask," he smiles. "Your mom is making dinner, we should get back before they think you drowned in the tub or worse had sex with me in it."

13

"You know what Sean—" Bishop's voice floats up to the tree house, they're arguing again and there isn't a damn thing I can do about it. "I'm sorry that you constantly feel the need to undermine everything I do."

"You think that's what I'm doing? Undermining you?" Sean scoffs and steps forward into his face. "You do a damn fine job of screwing everything up on your Bishop. You don't need my help."

"You don't need to remind me every chance you get that I'm a fuck up, I know that already." He retorts stepping to come chest to chest with Sean. They're going to get physical. The air around them is charged and tense, "but leave Nora out of this. She doesn't need you whispering in her ear how terrible I am. News flash she knows it too."

"I don't think she does. She is so blinded by this grumpy puppy dog facade you have going for you that she doesn't see how awful you are for her. You are a brick, dead weight and she is a bird. You will tear her apart, she will never succeed with you tied to her ankles." Sean shoves him back, Bishop barely moves from the push. "Next time you have the chance, leave with your dad. It will do us all some good."

"Sean!" I've had enough, I won't listen to him berate him for no reason. It's clear they didn't know I was above them, sitting in

96

the tree house in tears because Bishop's sister Kate had said some nasty words the night before at a party. "Walk away," I snap and he grinds his teeth together but listens.

"This conversation isn't over," he looks back at Bishop.

"This wasn't a conversation, it was a trial," Bishop growls back but I nod to him, asking him to come up to the tree house. He obliges me, climbing the rungs slowly until he reaches the top and slides in silently.

"He's just on edge about school, the finals were hard enough without scouts breathing down his neck about football scholarship, and with dad getting diagnosed we're all on edge Bishop," I say as he slouches into the couch next to me. I rest my head on his shoulder.

"Making excuses for him doesn't make him wrong," he sighs and traces circles on my jawline with his hand. "I have to leave Nora," he says, but it doesn't register right away what he means.

"Sean isn't your keeper Bishop, he doesn't make the rules here. You don't have to leave because he says you do—" I stop and sit up trying to find the reasoning in his eyes.

"This isn't about Sean, I have to go. Dad offered me a position at the company, but I have to start right away." His jaw tenses, I know deep down he's hiding details from me, concealing the whole truth but I just don't have the capacity emotionally to question him further on it. To prod and find out why he would take a job with that monster.

"The man that did this?" I ask pulling his shirt up revealing the nasty gash on his collarbone that has barely healed over. "Or this?" I run my finger over the bruised skin of his under-eye. "Why are you running away?"

I stand up, moving away from him so he doesn't see my tears, the ones threatening to fall as he sits stoically on the couch like he *hasn't just dropped a bomb on our life together.*

"I'm not running away Nora," he shakes his head.

"That's the only thing that makes sense, this is too much for you and you're running away. I get it, I've been a lot lately. This has been hard, and exhausting. I'm sorry for not being myself, but that's not a free pass." I'm angry now, trying to control myself. I wanna shove him from the tree house, evict him from my safe haven.

"You heard what Sean said, he's right. I'm trash, it doesn't matter how hard I love you, Nora, I will always be the dead weight tied to you. How are you supposed to fly?" he finally speaks and it's like ice in my veins.

"I've never wanted to fly, all I ever wanted to do was sail away with you. You are not dead weight, you are my anchor Bishop. How do you not see that? The difference there?" I wanna scream at him.

"That's the thing Nora, we can't just sail away together. Not anymore, your dad is so sick. You can't leave him, can't leave this place but if I stay I will only make things worse. This is the only way I know how to help." His voice is silk, he's sitting on the edge of the couch with tears brimming his bright blue eyes. "I was never your anchor and you know it. I'm not that person, I'm not your person."

"Then get out," I turned away from him, so angry I couldn't speak anymore. I wanna throw things and cry but I won't give him the satisfaction of doing it in front of him.

"Hey, hey—" warm arms embrace me from behind, his legs come around my hips and he applies pressure to my entire body. "It's alright, you're safe." Bishop's husky voice floats over my body and everything relaxes.

"It was just a bad dream," he runs his hand over my head

and rocks us back down into the bed. He tugs the red plaid comforter over my shoulders and presses me against his bare chest. For a moment I think to pull away, I should. I remember what Sean had said about collateral damage, and them being caught in the center of it but it feels so nice to just breathe him in like this. Laying in the darkness, I can feel his chest rising and falling. I can smell the soap on his skin, the salt in his hair.

"It wasn't a dream," I can feel the anger, sadness, and frustration bubbling up and I know it's because I'm overwhelmed. I know all of the things he did were for me but it still hurt the same. Staring into his hollow eyes while he lies to my face. "It was bad," I sigh, pushing away from the comfort of his arms.

"Do you think I would have handled it differently if you had told me the truth from the beginning, Bishop?" I stare out the window, the moon hangs high in the sky and the ocean noises float through the open window.

He watches me carefully, shifting to create space between us. He sits up in the bed, his chest heaves with a heavy sigh so long and careful I can see it in the dim light. "I broke your heart regardless of the truth, Nora. Lying to you was the only way to keep you safe, and to keep you from trying to convince me otherwise."

"It was unfair to assume that of me," I say.

"You can't remember yourself then, you don't remember how fierce you were about everything. You would have never let me go, Nora. You barely let me go and you hated me." His tongue jutted out over his lips and he huffed a long sigh.

"Are you ever going to tell me what you did?" I don't mean to interrogate him but I need to know.

"I thought about it," he said, his voice husky from sleep. "If I tell you what happened from my perspective Nora you'll never truly remember everything that I did. I can't trust myself to leave out details that could sway you in my favor. As much as I never want to leave your side ever again, I want to be honest with you." He reaches out and cups the side of my face carefully rubbing my cheek with his thumb. "A fair honest shot, I won't undermine Sean. I'm not a teenager anymore."

He gets up from the bed and saunters back to his own. The old mattress creaks under his weight, and he lays his head on the pillow facing me. I can see the color in his as I lay back down facing him and pull the blankets up to my chin. "Are you cold?" He asks. "I can close the window."

What I want is for him to come climb back into the bed, I want to feel his bare chest against the exposed skin on my back. I want to fall back asleep with him as close as he can be. "No, I'm good. I have an extra blanket."

He nods and rolls to his back, his hands coming up to rest behind his head. He closes his eyes and within minutes light snoring comes from his side of the room. I sigh and try to fall asleep but nothing seems to work to put me back to bed. I quietly make my way down the stairs, hoping I don't wake Bishop as I close the squeaky door behind me.

The house is so quiet as I grab my coat from the hooks by the door and make my way outside to the main street. I can see the front lamp that illuminates the Bartley front porch and make my way down the street. The house is quiet, I know Kate and Curtis are inside. It's where they had chosen to stay. I press the front door open and step inside. The front entrance is almost exactly how I remembered it. There's no broken glass this time but there is a new vase sitting on the table.

Vibrant, fresh sunflowers fill the teal vase. I finger the pedals and continue up through the nearly empty house. I feel like a ghost wandering around but I wanted to know if his room was the same. If the walls were covered in posters, and the shelves with books. I take an educated guess that the door with the shabby door is his, it's in terrible shape like it had been slammed closed too many times.

Inside was exactly what I had seen in my memory. Two large bookshelves along the far western wall, are jammed with books so full that there are stacks beside the shelves and even beside the bed. It was massive, a king-size with huge posts reaching to the ceiling. They are draped with soft black linen that blows in the wind from the open window. He had been in here recently, the sheets on the bed are messy and thrown about. In the opposite corner was a plush-looking armchair that had a book overturned on the arm of it. It was a book on memory loss and recovery.

He loves you more than you could ever remember, I shake my head and wander over to the bookshelf. It's covered in everything from fiction to non-fiction, the most curious is his collection of high fantasy novels that are roughly crammed into every space possible. I run my fingers over the leather bindings and pull out the Hobbit.

I tiptoe back over to the chair, dragging a blanket from the bed as I go and rest on it, careful not to disturb the open book on the armchair. The chair is so cushioned, it's worn in and shapes to the curve of my body when I sink into it.

I curl my legs up under me, pull the blanket over my body, and open the book. I don't know when I'd fallen asleep but the sun creeps into the room and the book is sitting on my lap half read. I can hear people arguing outside the house, I slide out of the chair clumsy. My feet are both asleep and it's like walking on pins and needles as I cross to the open window.

"I knew you sleeping in her room was a bad idea Bishop," Sean throws a pointed finger in Bishop's face. He's wearing a cream-knitted sweater and blue jeans. Bishop barely moves away from the finger, standing in his dark gray shirt and shorts. "It's hard enough keeping track of what's going on with her without her wandering off. How did you not hear her leave?"

Bishop looks at him with intent to harm, I can see it on his face. Any trace of the soft Bishop I had been receiving was gone but as if he silently counts to ten in his own head. The harshness leaves and he smiles slightly, "I did hear her," he shakes his head. "I also watched her come down here from the living room window, she wasn't in danger Sean. Unless you have a reason to believe she should be."

"I do," he snaps back at him. He steps forward getting in Bishop's face. "I don't trust you, not for a fucking second."

"Language Roberts," Bishop smirks. "She came down here because she couldn't sleep, she couldn't sleep because she can't remember anything. I was just giving her the space to explore what she can't. It's not our job to watch her every move, Sean."

"That's been my job for three years Bishop," Sean all but yells, a few seagulls close by fly off the beach startled by him so early in the morning. "All I have done is watch her every move. I've made sure she didn't drink herself to death, or worse actually try to kill herself. All well you were fucking every girl in arms reach in Japan. So it's really rich coming from you thinking it's not *our* job. It certainly isn't. It's *my* job."

"We've been having this fight our entire friendship Sean, a lot of the time it got rough. Broken noses, bruises all over us

and almost always she was the one to get hurt breaking us up."
Bishop ran a hand through his hair, "She's not our possession,
she's not property. She's a living and breathing human being
that's struggling right now to remember her life. She's the
toughest person we know, she's fallen out of trees, broken
almost every bone she has, and still stood up ready to go on
the next adventure."

"This is different Bishop, how do you not see that?" Sean
breathes out heavily, his chest heaving. "It's not a broken bone,
it's her mind Bishop! It's her intelligent, caring, and beautiful
mind that's broken."

"When I left, Sean, she needed you. Needed someone to
protect her from herself. I watched you get closer from a
distance and it hurt but it's what she needed. She doesn't need
you anymore, all of her memories the ones she needs back.
She has to get them from me, not you." Bishop sighs, his whole
body tenses as if he's waiting for a punch.

Sean just stares at him, his fist is balled at his side but the
punch never comes. "You're wrong," is what he says instead,
"just like you always are."

He walks away with that, ramming his shoulder into Bishop
before he stomps down the stairs that lead to the beach.
Bishop looks at his shoes for a long time, his shoulders move
with each deep breath he takes. He doesn't say a word as he
turns his deep blue eyes up to me, a silent moment passes
between us because he knew I was there all along.

14

"Nu este vorba de bani," Bishop says into his phone, he's standing in the foray when I emerge from his room. "Nu-mi pasă ce vrea el," he's speaking a language I don't understand. He sighs and rubs his neck, "Listen to me Scott, get it done, and don't call me until you have the information I want."

He hangs up and throws his phone back into his pocket. "Hey, are you ready to go sailing today?" He asks, his tone changes so easily back to being soft and welcoming.

"Who were you talking to?" I question, I meet him on the first floor still carrying the Hobbit under my arm.

"That's a good book, I've read it three times." He deflects, "A colleague, he's taking care of things for me while I'm here."

"How many languages do you speak now?" I smile, he opens the front door for me, and the warm weather floods into the house.

"Six," he answers, closing the door behind us. "English, French, Romanian, German, Japanese, Spanish, and Portuguese."

"That's impressive," I smile as we walk down the street. "You'll have to teach me your favorite," I tease, "swear words obviously being the most important thing. I want to be able to insult you in all your languages."

"Do you now?" He shakes his head, "Orice pentru tine dragostea mea," the words flow off his tongue in a husky tone, he stares at me for a moment and then winks before opening the door to the beach house for me.

"What does that mean?" I know better than to ask because he won't tell me regardless.

"Wouldn't you like to know?"

"You!" My mother shakes her finger at me, "don't do that. What if you had wandered off farther and couldn't find your way home?"

"Less work for everyone else I suppose," I shrug my shoulders. "I won't do it again," I say when she narrows her eyes at me. "I promise," I scrunch my nose at her and wander away. I can hear her and Bishop speaking in the kitchen as I collect my notebook to retreat upstairs.

"I'm doing my best not to let Sean under my skin, but it's so hard Marianne. I put them in this position, I can't just expect him to not be fiercely protective of her."

"Don't get discouraged. I know my daughter and she'll make a decision with her heart, and her head Bishop. Just give her time, and don't give her a reason to favor Sean in the meantime." My mother hushes him and goes back to preparing a salad, her knife hitting the cutting board as she slices through the raw carrots.

"I'm glad you could join us for dinner, Nora. Bishop here says you're so busy, I keep inviting you but you always have better things to do." Bishop's pudgy-faced father circles the table and sets down a bottle of wine in the center.

I fidget with the fork on the table, running my finger along the cool metal methodically to keep my emotions at bay. I wasn't busy,

I'm sixteen in the middle of summer without a part-time job and I spend all my time with Bishop. It was his choice not to bring me over. I know why he doesn't want to, why he keeps his family at arm's length.

"It's my pleasure sir," I say as Kate loads her plate with lettuce and vegetables. "It's nice to finally meet you, I've heard so much." I smile but I want to throw my fork at his face, Bishop's hand squeezes my knee under the table and I let it go.

I've seen the bruises you give him, I want to say.

All the scars that paint his body like the most brutal form of artwork.

I've protected his secret this summer from everyone we know. I've helped him protect you.

You are a monster in a man's body.

"All good things I hope," there is a venomous tone to his statement and I nod my head.

"All good things," I smile. Bishop hands me serving bowls and plates, full of food and I take my share. Kate waves off anything that has a calorie and eats in silence. "It's nice that you're able to join Jason's birthday."

Before we had left the house Bishop had given me the rundown of everything I could, and shouldn't say. His middle name is one of the trigger words. Bishop was what his mom called him before she died. His father hates that name and refuses to acknowledge it, "use Jason or nothing." He had said before placing a long, slow kiss on my lips.

I'm being careful, I watch every word I say and I cannot imagine what It was like to grow up like this. Constantly watching every word, every movement, and action I make so that the man that's supposed to be my father doesn't ruthlessly beat me for a mistake.

My heart ached for him. I dare turn my head to catch his eyes, so blue like the ocean after a thunderstorm, and they are filled with fear. I told him, "I'll be fine Bishop, I can handle this and if it means he never asks to meet me again then it worked." He smiled at me then, but it was tense and forced.

"It will be fine," I said to him. But whatever this is, doesn't feel fine. The table is charged with tense energy, all of us walking on glass to appease him long enough to survive dinner without a scratch. My parents didn't know his father, not really. He's very good at showing face when everyone is around, waving and smiling at whoever needs one.

In the privacy of his home, I can see how dark of a man he is.

After dinner, I help Kate clear the table, and the house cleaner deals with the dishes and shoos us from her sight. Bishop doesn't leave my sight, and the moment he does his dad swoops in and leads me towards a closed-off room that looks like an office.

It has high bookshelves, and dark walls, and the lights are dim inside. There's no window to see the beach or to let in the sunlight. It's a cave. "I can see on your face that you care deeply for my son," he says, shutting the door behind him.

"I can tell you right now you're making a mistake falling in love with him." His words cut through the silence, I look over and all I am met with are dark, an endless iris' that stare back. "He has a way of letting down people that love him, every single time. He's been this way since he could talk."

"He hasn't let me down," I say, trying not to lose my cool.

"You all but said 'yet' dear, Nora. He's not someone you can love, he's not capable of that. When his mother died she took all the love with her. Now he's just a useless waste of space. He's not going anywhere in life. Did he tell you why we moved here?" He pauses, his face is dark.

I shake my head, "He hit someone with his car, Nora. He killed

107

someone. He's a murderer."

I don't say anything, my stomach rolling with nausea. I take a long deep breath to steady my feelings. "I'm rich, we have lawyers. I made it all go away and moved him across the country so he could feel normal on the condition that he stayed out of trouble. As usual, Bishop cannot do a single thing right, and now he's brought you and your little family into it. I want you to grab your jacket Nora, and I want you to leave my house. If you call him, see him if you even say goodbye to him after I let you out of this room." He stops, clicking the lock but before he turns the knob he looks at me. "He'll pay for your mistakes as well as his own."

He lets me out without another word, I am shaking and I can see Bishop standing by the staircase. Shock rattles through me, he killed someone. Why wouldn't he tell me this? I take another deep breath and begin to walk, I wanna ask him a million questions. I want to hear his side of the story but I don't want his father to punish him for it. So I continue by him, even as his fingers reach out and graze the skin on my arm, I keep walking.

I wouldn't be responsible for any of his bruises, I couldn't do that. He can handle me walking away, at least for now. I could find a way to speak to him, I had to. But until then this is all I can do to keep him safe.

I don't even know how I ended up in my room, but I collapsed on the bed. My legs are weak and my head spins, I can't get my thoughts organized. My breathing picks up and it feels like my lungs are strangling in my chest.

"Nora?" Sean slides down on the ground, he sits on his knees between my legs and wraps his hands around my face. "You're having a panic attack, you need to breathe."

I want to breathe, I tell my body to do just that but nothing happens. He locks his blue eyes on mine and smiles sadly,

"You get them all the time, you need to close your eyes. On the count of three, I want you to breathe the biggest breath you can handle."

I close my eyes and let the feeling of his hand on my face ground me, "One," he says and I let his voice roll over me. "Two," he says, rubbing his thumb against my cheek. "Three," I breathe in, filling my legs with as much air as I can. We do this three more times before my breathing is back to normal.

"All better?" He asks, I nod. "Are you going to be okay today?"

"You aren't coming," I manage to choke out.

"It's probably better if I don't," he slides back from his kneeling position and stands.

"It'll be fun, no talk of my head all day. Please?" I ask him and he smiles at his shoes. "You'll be so bored all by yourself here."

"Fine, twist my arm why don't you." He shook his head in disbelief.

15

"Take this," Ben slings a cooler to Sean over the edge of the boat. "This vessel is beautiful, Bishop."

Bishop is organizing ropes, wrapping them about his palm and elbow to form a tight circle. "I haven't had a chance to take her out yet so this is her maiden voyage."

"Really?" Nat throws her beach bag onto one of the bench seats that are recessed into the back deck.

"I wouldn't take her out without Nora, it is her boat after all." I can hear Sean's inner monologue simmering as he turns to eye Bishop.

Today would be long. I had to have hope that I could bring them back to whatever they were. They had to be friends at some point. Right? I would have never dated Bishop if Sean had a problem with him. At least in the beginning before I knew what Sean was thinking. His misplaced protection was overbearing but I can understand what he's gone through to get me to this place. It just took him ten years to fess up to his feelings. Ten years too long.

He wears dark blue board shorts and a gray tank top that curves to the shape of his tucked waistline. His muscles strain as he pushes the boat from the dock and then uses them to hoist himself onto the deck over the side.

Ben helps Natalie unpack the lunch mom made us. She was kind enough to make more than what any one of us could eat in the couple hours we would be on the water. Salads, sandwiches, fruit, and more. Ben had filled the cooler with alcohol which seemed intriguing until Sean reminded me I couldn't mix it with my pain medication.

Bishop steered the boat across the water pushing her out until we could no longer see the shore. Ben step up his fishing rod and Sean had fallen asleep with the bottom hem of his tank top pulled over his face to block out the sun.

"How are you doing?" I ask Nat, who frankly looks like she's going to be sick.

"I'm going to be sick, " I laugh and shake my head.

"Nora, " Bishop calls me over, "take the wheel. I'll take Nat downstairs so she can lay down." I do as he says, wrapping my hands around the solid wood wheel. He walks over to where she sits, taking her hand and leading her downstairs.

He returns after a while, holding two bottles of water, and leans against the railing to watch me. "You're a natural," his blue eyes are so fierce under the sun.

"There's nothing for me to hit out here, " I tease. *He's a murderer*, rings through me. He had hit someone with his car just after getting his license. A sick sensation rolls through me and he wrinkles his forehead in worry.

"What did you remember Nora, " he doesn't move. I don't speak. "If you don't tell me when you remember something I can't help you make sense of it."

I let my stomach settle and turn to look at him again, but I still don't speak. I don't want to ask him. I don't want to know. Not really.

"How old were we?" he asks and I tilt my head in question.

He sighs lightly, pushing his tongue against his cheek in frustration. "I guess what transpired if you tell me how old we were. Do you remember?"

"It was your sixteenth birthday, " I whisper.

"Mm, " he looks out to the water. "Come here, " he motions for me to leave the wheel and sit. "The boat is going anywhere."

I wander over and stand next to him, "the first time I stood up to my father was that following day. After you left I destroyed all the wine in the cellar, drank a lot of it but smashed it all to the floor in rage. What he told you was true, what he didn't tell you is that he was in the car with me."

He stops, his Adam's apple bobs in his throat, "he was teaching me how to drive that night, he forced whiskey down my throat. I was barely alive when I hit that girl, I tried to swerve the car but he held the steering wheel. He forced me to hit her."

"How did he get away with it?" I ask, shock sinking in. I wanna comfort him any way I can but he's got his hands curled up and his body is leaning away from me.

"Lawyers, and what could I do? When the cops showed up I was blowing over the legal limit of alcohol. He set me up to fail so he could have something over me." he sighed. "He found me later the next day I went to his office. I didn't have a plan. I wanted to burn it down but there was a little voice in my head. My songbird, you, telling me he wasn't worth it."

"What did you do?" I want more information.

"I sat there. Drank an entire bottle of wine and waited for him to show up to work. I wanted to know what he said to you but I already knew deep down it was that. That could have been the only thing that would scare you away. I thought I had lost you so I didn't care what he did. He didn't lay a hand on me. Not in public at least. You found me a week later in bed, dad had returned to Japan and Kate called you." Bishop pushes the loose hair back. "You hadn't given up. You just needed a way around my dad so he couldn't hurt me because of you."

"Did you tell me that day what happened?" I lean forward to make eye contact with him.

"No, I didn't want to seem weak. You already pitied me enough, I couldn't stand having you look at me like that anymore." He stands correcting the wheel and then comes to stand in front of me. "You saved me more times than you understand, Nora."

He must see the concern on my face because he doesn't move, "I write letters to the girl's sister every Christmas. I sent a card, money, and a donation receipt. It took her a couple of years to write back. The first letter was awful, she was so angry at me. I learned that forgiving myself meant apologizing even if it hurt me to do it."

I touch his scruffy face and rub my fingers into it gently, "I wish you would have told me then if I was brave enough to come to find you. I was brave enough to know the whole truth. Thank you for telling me now."

"Of course," he smiles and presses his hand to mine. He closes his eyes and leans into the affection just for a second before moving back to the wheel.

"I'm going to go check on Nat," he nods at me and I disappear under the deck. I gently tap on the bedroom door, she groans and I push it open to find her rolled over into a bowl. Bishop had left her a towel, a bowl, water, and gravol. Such a sweet boy.

"God I hate boats," she moans and rolls back over.

YOU LEFT US IN GEORGIA

"The baby must be making it worse," I say with a laugh and
sit next to her. "Can I do anything?"

"For me? No. For Sean and Bishop, pick one already.
They're driving Ben and me insane."

"How am I supposed to just pick?" I ask and she laughs.

"You only get one date for the wedding. I'm making it easy
for you. Your dress is emerald green, Willa's is maroon." She
is interrupted by more vomit before she continues. "Sean and
Bishop will each get a bow tie. You decide who gets what
color. End of story, you hear me. I will not be responsible for
this choice."

"Seems a little extreme Nat," I roll my eyes.

"They both want to make you happy but you aren't going to
get away having sex with both of them for very long without
it exploding. Do me a favor and sort your brain out." She
waves me off and I let her go back to sleep.

Ben stands outside the bedroom having heard our conversation. I'm grateful it's him and not one of the other men. "She's
so cranky lately," he groans. "But she's not wrong. It's not
healthy for you either to be bouncing between them."

"Sean said you studied therapy in school, do you like it?" I
deflect the conversation.

"I enjoy the challenge." He smiles, "you're still an awful
patient."

"Isn't that a conflict of interest? Being a shrink to your
future sister-in-law?" I ask.

"It was. I'm not your therapist anymore. You see one of my
colleagues. That doesn't mean I don't recommend courses of
treatment for you." He explains.

"Like the notebook, " I say.

"Notebooks, plural. There were at least six I knew of, "

114

he leans against the counter in his floral tank top and board shorts. "It worked well, after the attempt on your life you needed an outlet that wasn't going to harm you. You also burned all the books you brought here in the tree house, so those are gone."

"Attempt?" Ben's face tells me he's said too much. He fixes his glasses and stands up straight.

"Last winter, " he grimaces, "it was a wake-up call though."

The air is colder than usual. Winter in Georgia isn't awful, but today of all days it snows. I don't remember in the last twenty-two years on the planet it ever snowed. I wonder if it's snowing in Tokyo? The news outlets were all over him, it was new year's after all. Infamous rich kid lawyer Bishop Bartley, out in the town, a girl on each arm.

Each one is more beautiful than the last, but none that ever looks like me. They are always opposites of me, blonde and taller than him. Models. My shoes were on the roof, I had kicked them off before climbing up on the ledge.

The ground doesn't seem so far away. It's quieter than the voices in my head. Everyone nagging me. Get help, stop drinking, and think of mom and dad. It's always something and someone telling me I'm loved. I am also a burden, constantly in distress and filled with suffering. I am misery and spite.

I would make a much more beautiful snow angel than a person I think. I creep closer to the edge, wrapping my toes around the cold metal. It's harsh against my skin, biting at the soft flesh under my feet.

"Nora!" someone screams my name but it's too late I am already falling.

The darkness is colder than I had imagined. It wraps me in ice and feels like needles all over my skin. My lungs are pleading for air but I can't seem to open my eyes. A set of arms find me, wrapping around my waist and pulling me rapidly to the surface. My lungs take in a raw breath as we break and I finally open my eyes.

Sean grips me tightly, his face in shock and his muscles so tense I don't understand how he's swimming. Bishop reaches for me as we reach the side of the boat.

"What the hell was that?" Sean asks sliding out of the water still fully clothed.

"I— it was a memory but then I was in the water, " I still talking.

"You walked to the edge of the boat and stood there like you were going to jump but you just toppled over the edge without a word." Sean is baffled.

"This is my fault, " Ben speaks up. "I told her about last winter."

"Why the hell would you do that?" Sean stands up, he's in Ben's face before anyone can do anything about it.

"What happened last winter?" Bishop's voice breaks them apart like a clever. He didn't know.

16

Bishop stands rigid, hands both curl into closed fists. He stares at Ben and Sean in shock, "tell me, now."

Both men shift uncomfortably at the command but Ben opens his mouth to speak first. "New year's eve, we were out. All of us. Celebrating. It was the first time she had touched alcohol in a long time but she was feeling good and we were still tiptoeing around every move she made. No offensive Nora, but you weren't the most stable even in your stable moments."

"We were at some dive bar downtown, live music, and drinks." Sean finally finds his voice. Bishop looks at me and there's a pain behind his eyes I can't explain. I sit still soaking wet but don't dare move to get out of the clothes. I want to hear the story as much as Bishop does.

"When the band ended they turned on the TV to catch the ball drop but it was only eleven-thirty and they were just showing coverage of events. You were on the TV for less than five minutes but it was enough. You had your tongue down some Ukrainian model's throat and the other model had her hand down your pants. The news was having a field day." Sean shakes his head. His emotions flaring again, Bishop says nothing.

"We lost track of her when I turned around and she was gone," Sean confesses. "She was so drunk and it was so cold out."

"Apparently and fortunately for us, Willa had lost her before. She had turned on find my phone on Nora's cell and they found her on the rooftop of her apartment. She was huddled in a corner freezing but there were two distant footprints pressed into the snow on the ledge of the building. When Willa called me she was in tears because it was obvious Nora had meant to jump. I don't know what stopped you, " Ben looks at me finally, a huff leaving his lips. "But you didn't jump. We've spoken about it once since it happened. When Natalie told you that you needed help. You listened to her and got it."

"Why didn't you call me?" Bishop's question is pointed at Sean now.

"You didn't need to know Bishop, you couldn't change the outcome even if I had." Sean's words bite through the tension, he steps forward but Ben puts himself between the two of them hastily.

"I would have come home, talked to her," Bishop's reply is cautious.

"You didn't deserve to talk to her. You're the reason she was on that ledge. She would have rather ended her life than see you ever again, " Sean's words are a direct shot at him. No remorse in them.

"Sean, " Ben's tone was a warning to stop.

"No, I'm right and you know it. Stop coddling him, " Sean all but growled at Ben. He was willing to go through him to get to Bishop.

"He's right, Ben." I look at Bishop, a defeated look fills his features. "I didn't deserve to talk to her but had I known how bad it had gotten? I would have come home sooner." I know full well that if his father was alive last new year's, he would have had a hard time accomplishing that.

"You always were a shit liar, Bartley." Sean spits.

"God Sean, drop your superiority complex for five minutes and use your brain. You and I had a deal, I leave, I break her heart—" my heart picks up and my chest gets tight. Sean knew, and now he won't even look at me. "You pick up the pieces."

Sean doesn't say a word and Ben's reaction time isn't fast enough as he pushes out of the hold and lays a heavy fist on Bishop's jaw.

Bishop retaliates with a hard punch to Sean's midsection causing the six-foot man to double over. He recovers quickly and charges toward Bishop wrapping his arms around his hips and slamming them both into the side of the boat.

Natalie appears from below deck with a look of shock and confusion. "What the fuck are you idiots doing?" she yells.

They don't immediately break apart, Sean lands another good punch before Bishop shoves him off with a kick to the thigh. They stand panting across from one another, Bishop's jaw is already starting to bruise and a matching one forms around his eye. Sean has no noticeable face injuries but he grips his rib cage uncomfortably.

"You're both going to sit down and tell me, in length, about this deal you made." I stare at both of them. Bishop's tongue runs along his bottom lip roughly but he nods. Sean hesitates but turns to me.

"His jaw needs ice, and then we can talk." He points to the cabin "Ben can you steer us home? I want to get off this boat." He starts to move to the stairs without another word. Bishop follows when Ben takes the wheel confidently.

Natalie sighs as I walk by her, "I didn't start this fight." I assert.

"You always start the fights, Nora. That's the problem, " Natalie wanders over to stand with Ben and I shake my head at her. I had nothing to do with this argument, that I am sure of.

Bishop leans up against the counter holding ice to his jaw when I make my way downstairs. Sean yanks his shirt over his torso but I catch sight of a nasty bruise forming over his abdomen.

"Natalie is ready to rip my head off so this better is good enough to explain why you just tried to kill each other on the deck, " I snapped. I'm done being soft and careful with their feelings. I'm sick of avoiding hard conversations because they're too scared to talk about them.

"You knew?" I direct my question to Sean who rolls his eyes at me. "Without the attitude please, you're an adult. Act like it."

"You sound like your dad, " Sean laughs under his breath. "Yeah, I knew what Bishop was doing. He and I had a conversation before he spiraled."

I turn an eyebrow to Bishop, "I never wanted to leave you, but knowing I had to. I made a decision. I made Sean promise to be there no matter the situation. He was to be your safety net after I left. And it worked for a long time until he took it upon himself to get too comfortable with you." The last words come out in a snarl, but Sean just laughs at him.

"Bishop wanted the best for you until his jealousy got the best of him." Sean growls, "he's not innocent here. You're all acting like he did everything for a reason but was it really worth it? She didn't care about the beach house, she hasn't been back here since you left because she can't stand it anymore. So yeah, Bishop you saved the house, you kept the Quinns out of debt but you almost killed Nora. Good job."

Sean, having had enough, stands up and moves towards me standing at the door. "He won't tell you about that summer because he's ashamed of who he is, it's selfish and cruel. When you remember," he looks back to Bishop standing with his head down. Staring at his feet, "It's going to break you all over again especially if you let him back in, Nora. Just be careful please." Sean presses a light kiss to my head and disappears back to the upper deck.

"I'm sorry," a choking sob comes from his throat, when he looks up at me water floods his eyes. "I'm so sorry," he repeats himself and the sound of his voice is more painful than the first time. He moves so quickly I don't have time to react but he wraps himself around me, not caring about getting wet as the water still drips off of me. His body heaves as he cries into the crook of my neck, I wrap my arms around his back and pull him in closer.

He stays like that for a long time. A mess of a man huddled into my arms like a small child. He pulls back and runs his hands all over my face, "I'm sorry I did this," tears still stream down his face. "You're here now, like this because I was a stubborn, selfish idiot. Nora," he says so quietly I almost don't hear my name come from his lips. "Sean is right," he stops and pulls away from me finally.

I feel cold without him standing so close, he feels a million miles away. "When your memory comes back it's going to be overwhelming. I didn't think anything could hurt me ever, not after my father. I was wrong. Knowing you tried to kill yourself because of me, makes me just as bad as him. The one person I didn't want to become and here I am, exactly who he wanted me to be. A murder."

"I'm alive, Bishop. You didn't kill me." I say confidently.

"Not for a lack of trying," he growls but the agitation isn't directed at me. It's frustration boiling under his skin, frustration because of his own choices. "Ever since that day in the diner, you've been in danger without even knowing it. From me, my actions, the people I've wronged, and from yourself. Your sweet, caring, and agonizingly beautiful heart. I've put you so close to death for so long."

"That's not true and you know it," I respond calmly, he's spiraling and I don't know what to say to him that will bring him back. Unfortunately, as much as I want to remember him, I don't, not really. "Everything that I've learned over the last week has proven to me that my choices were my own. I could have come home, I could have gotten my life together but I didn't. I let myself get out of control. I put myself on that ledge. Not you."

He stares at me, his jaw ticks under the layer of scruff and his eyes are red from crying, "I wasn't strong enough to protect you, Nora. I never have been."

"Maybe it was never me who needed the protection Bishop," he lets out a huff of air, a breath of realization that he has never had control of anything. He's just been hanging from a rope, waiting for the chair to be kicked out from underneath him. Teetering on the edge of the chair, struggling to keep his balance on his tiptoes as the only thing keeping him alive tips back and forth uncontrollably.

He doesn't say anything, not a single word as he takes in what I have said to him. A dark moment of knowing that I'm too right about too many things without all the facts to be so confident in my answers. "I've been selfishly hiding from you. I came here ready to beg you for forgiveness without planning on telling you the real truth. Then you hurt yourself," he stops, a breath catching in his throat.

"There was so much blood, you were so still I thought maybe this had been the time I finally subconsciously killed you. You were so angry with me, and nothing I said was worthy of your forgiveness. I was just trying to make myself feel better. This isn't about me, it's about you and how you've felt all these years thinking I didn't love you anymore. I went up into that tree house with fake words and empty apologies." He scrunches his nose to keep from crying again, I recognize that facial tic in my soul, even without memory of him ever doing it before. I feel it like a tidal wave crashing into me.

"You had covered the entire tree house in these, dark and haunting charcoal drawings of me. My sad, broken eyes bore into me like a mirror while I tried to justify my actions while omitting the truth. I don't know if it was an accident or not that you lit the tree house on fire but it was still my fault, Nora. I owed you the truth and I couldn't even do that properly. I carried you all the way back up to the house, not knowing if you could even survive after the amount of blood that was covering me. They wouldn't let me ride in the ambulance with you and I started to panic so Sean sent me down the tree house to be helpful. Keep my hands busy, even when I'm messing everything up he still has it in him to help me slow down and hold myself together." He runs his hands through his hair. I know nothing I say can help him, so I just let him work through the information on his own.

"I've never been the right choice, Nora. I've held on for so long because you make me feel alive. No one has ever looked at me the way you do and I was greedy with you because of how you made me feel. I didn't care, not really about how I made you feel and I'm so sorry." He swallows hard, before I can say anything he moves past me, stopping as he brushes past my shoulder and studies the side of my face momentarily. "I love you, Nora."

I stand watching the light pour into the empty cabin of the boat. Ben brings the ship back to dock, I don't even see Bishop leave but by the time we get back to the cars he's gone. I wish I knew what to say to him, and how to handle the information he presented. Sean helps me into his truck, but he stops short of closing the door. "I shouldn't have said those things today, but it doesn't mean I take back all of them. Bishop needs to tell you, and you had a right to know he passed you off to me like that. I shouldn't have let him, but at the time I was being selfish too. I was too young to realize that maybe that's not what you wanted and too stupid to ask you how you felt about it. I just took advantage of the situation."

"I have a lot to think about," I say with a pitiful smile

17

No one saw Bishop for five days, Mom asks every time she sees me but I have no clue where he could have gone. I can't even remember where I put my own shoes half the time. Sean had taken me back to the hospital, the cast I had been wearing wasn't protecting anything so the nurse put the brace on early and sent me home.

On the sixth day, a shiny black land rover pulls up the street and parks outside our home. A handsome man stands opposite of me in the living room, his eyes scanning and studying the room around him. "I'm Scott Wilson, a colleague of Bishop."

"You were on the phone with him last week," I say with a polite smile.

"The one and only," he responds. Ben stands by the backdoor watching the interaction from a distance. Sean had taken Natalie into the town to collect her wedding dress leaving Ben and me alone for a change. The house was so quiet and still without everyone inside of it. "Bishop sent me to collect some paperwork and his computer from the house but Kate doesn't seem to be home and the door is locked."

"There's a spare key in the kitchen drawer," Ben unfolds his crossed arms and walks over to it. Sliding it open and tossing me the key.

"I can take you, just let me grab my coat." Scott backs up from me, as I reach for the coat hook. He takes the coat from me and holds it open so I can slip into it and I grab the umbrella from the bucket. The rain outside isn't coming down hard but it hasn't stopped raining for four days. A steady downpour and heavy gray clouds covered the entire beach in darkness.

"Thank you," I say as he holds the door open for me, "where is Bishop?" I ask, wasting no time.

"I don't mean to sound rude ma'am," his voice is velvet, and his eyes are soft and watchful. "Bishop asked me to come to get his things and try to keep to myself. If Kate was home you wouldn't have known I was here."

"Well she wasn't, and I do. So if you want in that house, I would like to know where Bishop is?" I stop, the rain pattering gently against the shell of the umbrella is the only noise between us.

Unexpectedly, Scott smiles. A wide and brilliant smile that makes me forget it's raining just for a moment. "Bishop warned me about you," he admits. "He told me to avoid you if I could because you're very convincing and you're very good at getting what you want from people."

"That makes me sound like a brat," I laugh under my breath.

"No," Scott chuckles, "he speaks highly of you, he always had. For the last three years, all I've had to listen to is how much he admires you. Nora, this. Nora, that. He's a man without direction and you are the north star."

"Oh, you are smooth with words aren't you Mr. Wilson?" I smirk at him as we reach the front door of the Bartley house. "You talk quite a bit but you never once answered my question.

126

Where is he?" I demand this time, not rudely but with a stern look that cracks his tough exterior shell enough for me to see that he in fact knows exactly where Bishop is.

"Nora," Scott says, "if I tell you where he is, he'll probably kill me."

"Scott," I mock him back and he shakes his head. "I'll get to you first if you don't tell me. He left so suddenly and I'm kind of tired of him doing that."

"He likes to do that, he has this complex that he thinks he knows what's best for everyone around him but he's so blind to his own well-being. He's so bad for concealing himself behind a wall." Scott's face tells me he's more than just a colleague.

"I worked for Douglas Bartley for a long time, too long before I met Bishop. I was assigned to him to watch over him, but it was more like I was policing him for years. His father didn't trust him or love him. He saw Bishop as a threat," the use of his middle name makes me smile but Scott continues. "He did a number on him. The wall was and still is very necessary. It's to protect him but also to protect you, Nora."

"You're making him sound dangerous," my smile drops and so does Scott's.

"I'm going to collect his things, but maybe you should talk to your friend Ben some more. He's had more contact with Bishop than anyone over the years." Scott slides the key from my palm and unlocks the front door. He hands it back to me with a smile. "It was a pleasure to meet you, Nora."

I walk back to the beach house, my hand squeezing so tightly around the key I can feel the intents of the groves dig into the soft skin of my palm. Ben leans back on the couch with a book in his head, his eyes perk up when he hears the screen door shut behind him.

"All done?" He asks with a smile.

"I have a question," I say and he nods for me to sit down across from him. He shifts slightly, the gray long sleeve shirt he wears tugs at his arms as he crosses them. "Scott mentioned just now that you kept in contact with Bishop, is that true?"

Ben sighs but nods again. "It is, yeah. Uh," he stands up and moves to the kitchen. "Do you want some tea?" he asks and I accept. "Bishop needed therapy, like a lot of therapy."

"You're his therapist?" I sat in shock, all this time I thought he had ghosted all of us.

"I am," He hands me a warm cup of tea, I let the fragrant steam rise to my nose before I take a small sip.

"That's why Sean thinks you're coddling Bishop," I nod. "Because you are."

"Bishop shows patterns of extreme psychological and physical abuse," He stops, he looks up from his tea. "I'm telling you this because I trust you not to use this against him, Nora, and because I think you know a lot of his story that I don't even know."

"I promise. I won't break your trust, Ben." I say reaching across the island to touch his hand.

"He suffers from prolonged abuse, it's a form of post-traumatic stress disorder. It affects his ability to regulate his emotions, he's dealing with crippling anxiety and depression." Ben sets the cup down on the table. "He has a history of lashing out negatively. He's mimicking his father's behavior without even knowing it. At first, therapy started as a way for him to talk about you and that was it. But eventually, it turned into weekly calls to keep him from hurting people." Ben shrugs his shoulders. "Violent tendencies are hard to curb and harder to deal with but he's been doing better."

"Do you think with everything that happened on the boat," I pause, "that he went..."

"To act upon these tendencies?" Ben shakes his head, "It's possible. I know where he is, Nora. We had a deal that I would help him work through his problems if he was always honest with me about his whereabouts and actions." He wanders over to the coat rack and pulls on a jacket before grabbing his keys. "Are you coming or not?"

I collect myself and follow him to the car, he drives for what seems like over an hour, at least. "Where are we going?" I ask more than once but he just keeps his eyes on the road. "This is cryptic and frankly I'm a little nervous. Can you at least give me a hint?"

He nods his head out the front window as he turns the car onto a heavily forested gravel road, it winds for a while until a small cottage comes into view. Covered in vibrant green vines, the bushes out front have beautiful yellow roses and the windows are all closed. It backs out onto the water and there in the driveway, sits a lone motorcycle.

"Are you coming?" I ask him as I reach for the door of the car.

"No, this isn't my place to interfere. I brought you out here because he doesn't need a therapist right now." Ben gives me a sad smile. I hesitate nervously and Ben leans over to touch my shoulder. "He won't hurt you. I've spent hundreds of hours talking to him, Nora. He always starts and finishes the phone call by reminding himself that he loves you more than the world. You have never been the source of his sadness or his anger. Just take it slow."

"Sean and Natalie will be home soon, what will you tell

them?" I ask.

"The truth," he smiles, "Sean pretends to be the big guy, the level-headed one but Bishop is his best friend whether or not he wants to admit it. Natalie, well let me deal with the hormonal pregnant woman."

"Thank you, Ben, for doing this for me," I say.

"I'm doing this for him." He gives me a shove and I open the door fully. The ground is soggy from all the rain and my feet sink into it as I walk. The door is painted a pale yellow color, I stand and stare at it for a long time as I listen to Ben pull away from the house.

I can't hear any noise from inside, so I put my hand on the knob. It turns open with ease, the door creaks open so slowly that I feel like my heart is going to pound out of my chest. The inside is quaint, a small navy blue couch sits in front of a small fireplace that isn't lit along with a plush-looking rug and a sitting chair that mimics the one in his room. Again there are shelves of books that line the back wall of the small sitting area.

To my right is a small kitchen with dark wood cabinets, on the counter is a vase full of the same yellow roses from the bushes out front. There is a door open off to the left and I can see a comfortable-looking bed with a few dark quilts piled at the foot of it. Bishop doesn't seem to be in the house, but the screen door leading out the back hallway is open.

Off the back of the house, is a small beach that opens up on the lake. Out on the horizon, he sits, floating aimlessly on his surfboard staring at the sky as it rains down around him. Just as I turn to go back inside and wait for him, his head turns towards the house finally.

"I'm waiting," I whisper, and as if he can hear me all the way across the water, he nods.

18

Bishop walks up the sandy path back towards the house, his surfboard is tucked neatly under his left arm. The weight of the board causes the muscles to pull against the wet suit. The scruff on his face is trimmed down, and his hair is wet, falling out of its normal pushed-back style. He sets the board against the back of the cottage. He strips the wet suit down, the sound of the zipper filling the tense silence between the two of us. I stand at the end of the narrow hallway watching through the screen door as he peels the suit completely off.

I watch as the water rolls down over every muscle on his body, the swell of his biceps, the ridges along his abdomen. Trickling down the soft skin of his pelvic muscles until I wrenched my eyes away from what hung below. I hear a soft chuckle from his lips as I turn away, catching my breath. I wait until I hear the click of the bathroom door to turn back. I can feel the red flush on my cheek. When he returns he has a towel wrapped around his waist and he silently makes his way into the bedroom. I stare out the small window that hangs lonely, between two large bookshelves. Outside the rain still patters against the glass pane, cleaning all the dirt away from the world one drop at a time.

"Where's Ben?" is the first question he asks, he returns from the bedroom in a simple black t-shirt, and a pair of jeans, and his hair is pushed messily off his face.

"He didn't stay, and said this wasn't this place to interfere." I play with the Velcro on my wrist brace nervously, trying to avoid making full eye contact.

"That's a first," he walks around the island to the heart of the kitchen and pulls two cups from the cupboard above him. His shirt pulls up and exposes the soft skin of his back, along with multiple scars. He pulls a bottle of whiskey from the shelf beside the fridge and turns back to me. "Do you want some?"

"Given what I know about myself and liquor, I shouldn't." I honestly say, staring at the cups now.

"There are no rules here," Bishop's voice is low, I can feel his eyes on me as he unscrews the top of the whiskey bottle. "That being said, I won't let you get drunk or do something foolish. Just one shot to help calm you down. You're shaking."

I hadn't noticed but he was right, my hands shook against each other. I hadn't expected to be so nervous. I'm not afraid of him, I'm afraid of all the things unsaid between us. The things I don't know, and the things I'm told to forget. He slides the cup across the counter to me, his knuckles are red and sore. Old scabs mix with fresh wounds. I swallow hard before I grab the cup from him and down it one shot. The taste is horrible, warm, and lingering as it sits on my tongue even after I swallow it.

"Better?" he asks, and I shake my head. He laughs softly and pours another before moving to the living room. He sets the cup on the brick framing that lines the small fireplace and begins stacking logs inside. "Grab a blanket from the bed," he points to the room as he continues to start the fire. I kick off my dirty shoes at the door and backtrack to the bedroom.

The room is smaller than it looks from the hallway, it barely fits the bed that's inside. I go to grab the top blanket, a thick quilt made of dark red fabric that is soft to the touch and something catches my eye. Across from the bed, hidden by the door unless you are all the way inside, is a wall of photos.

"Smile," he says to me, standing across the pier. His hair is so long now he has it pulled back into a bun near the nape of his strong neck. "Nora," he whispers the awful nickname, to catch my attention again. I can feel it under my skin when I hear him whisper to me. The sun is setting and there is a flock of sailboats varying in size floating around the pier.

The oranges, reds, and pinks cast off their sails so beautifully, that it looks like a painting and I am mesmerized by them. "Bishop," I reach out my hand without taking my eyes off the horizon, he comes to me wordlessly and wraps his arms around me. "They're so free."

"One day my love, that will be us." He nuzzles his face into the crook of my neck and breathes in slowly. It tickles the skin there, but I don't dare move. There is nowhere I would rather be than standing here with him, so warm and protected from everything that threatens us. He kisses the exposed skin around my tank top strap, slowly and carefully making sure his lips press down fully before pulling away. There is nothing fevered about them, they are patient and purposeful.

When he pulls away it's sudden and I almost gasp from the lack of touch but he raises his camera again, the sound of the shutter telling me he's taking more photos. He's always taking photos, never with his phone, always with this shitty little camera, Sean had gifted him last Christmas. He took it everywhere.

134

I understand why, for such a ratty-looking thing. With the dirty knobs and broken plastic pieces, the camera took the most spectacular photos. The light leaked through the lens in a strangely beautiful way that never seemed to ruin the photos but frames them. I climb up, using the rickety running boards to reach the flat base of the boardwalk railing. I hear Bishop sigh, but he doesn't move closer.

He's so used to the fearless attitude that flowed through me like wildfire. The wind whips through my long auburn hair creating tangles I'll have to brush out later but for now, I felt as free as the sailboats. "You're always so nervous, Bishop." I laugh and tip off balance on purpose to gain a reaction from him behind me.

The drop from where we are is at least twelve feet into freezing cold water, I would only break a few bones if I fell. My mother always says it was like she was gifted a boy in girls' clothing. I had no fear, no shame, no guilt. I was a force, a hurricane that gave little reason to my direction or destruction in life. "Can you come down now, if you break anything else your dad will kill me?" Bishop asks, he never begged or pleaded he knew that would only make me more likely to jump.

"I know you enjoy the rush Nora," Bishop says, his hand trailing up the bare skin of my calf until it found the round swell of my thigh. "There are other ways to feel that rush," he kisses the back of my leg with his warm and welcoming lips. "Let me show you," I can hear the smirk on his lips loud as can be. I giggle a bit and let myself tip backward, as always I fall carefully and gracefully into his waiting arms. His camera tucked back into his bag in preparation for the trust fall.

"Do you remember the first time you did that?" Bishop laughs, setting me down onto the boardwalk, and an old couple that had been walking back shakes their heads at me in disapproval.

"I yelled a warning that time, and we were standing on solid ground. I had to know what your reaction time was like. I'm lucky you caught me then," I smile, and rub a fleck of dirt off his stern cheekbones. "You've always been ready to catch me, I've never had a chance to doubt that you wouldn't."

The smile disappears from his face for a moment, a fleeting show of sadness in his eyes but he quickly recovers with a quick kiss. When he pulls back the sadness is gone and he's smiling again, "I'll always catch you, Nora."

"I know," I muse back at him, returning the generous kiss. "If you weren't so dense I would catch you too but I'm afraid the impact alone if you jumped would kill us both."

His mouth gapes open at my mockery but I don't give him time to give a response, I turn on my heel and run as fast as I can down the boardwalk, hollering with laughter as I go. I make a sharp turn, taking the stairs down to the beach two at a time. I kick off my shoes as I reach the sand and keep running, my feet sinking into the ruts. He crashes into me, arms tangled around me, and lands on top of me in the sand.

His hair has fallen from the bun and it hangs loosely on his face, his eyes trace the features of my face slowly. The blue reflects off the dimming sunlight making them sparkle. "You're a brat," he pushes a loose strand away from my face, hovering just above my lips. His legs straddle me and I can feel the breath on my face as he studies me. "But you're wrong. Every day I wake up falling, and somehow you are always there to slow me, to make sure I don't ever hit the bottom. So you're wrong Nora, you do catch me."

"I remember that day," his voice brings me back, it's older, deeper, and sadder than the boy in the memory. "You loved those boats, every Sunday they sat in the harbor like that. Floating along. We would sit there for hours. I would read and you would just," he pauses, staring at the photo. "Exist. It was peaceful."

"I liked your long hair," I looked at him in response. He drags a hand through the shorter, messy version of the same brown locks.

"I know, you were upset the day my father cut it," he comes to a step closer, looking at all the photos on the wall. "This one," he points to one of me sitting at the end of a pier, my hair wild and my face turned towards the camera. There's no smile on my face though, I look sad and so far away. "That's the day it happened. I surprised you and that was the face you made. You tried so hard to hide the disappointment, mere seconds after I took that you plastered a smile on your face and showered me with compliments. But you knew what happened, you could feel the gashes he left from the clippers. It was so short, cropped so tightly to the sides it was hard to hide the nicks and cuts he left."

I step towards him, I'm so close I rub against his chest. He stands so still I might think he's frozen but his eyes move to the side to avoid looking at me. I reach my hand up, pushing hair out of the way, and without thinking I can find the one large nick that left a scar. "I remember that now," his eyes flash to mine, and hold them there.

We're so close that I can feel his breath on my face, I could lean in and finally figure out why I loved him so fiercely. His lips were right there, begging to be explored but my head was screaming at me to pay attention, and a sharp pain shot through me making my eyes water. The pain registers on my face and Bishop steps back a touch.

"That was after your eighteenth birthday. He only ever came to Georgia for that week. We were sitting in the living room when we heard the car pull up and you shoved me out the back door so he wouldn't see me. I couldn't leave you there so I watched from the back window as he yanked on your hair. The sound you made, I can't believe I ever forgot that noise. He dragged you by your hair out of sight and the next time I saw you it was all gone." He stares at me, the distance between us feels like a canyon. "He never hurt Kate," I pause looking back at the photos.

"He wasn't grooming Kate, she couldn't offer him anything. She couldn't run the business after he died so it didn't matter, not in his eyes at least." Bishop sighed, "come it's cold in here. The fire will warm you up."

I sat on the couch and he wrapped the quilt around me, making sure I was warm, and retrieved the bottle of whiskey from the counter before sitting on the couch next to me. I study his face, the tired look in his eyes. The bruise from Sean is fading but even in the dim light of the cottage, you can see the bruise. "Ben told me about your therapy."

I know I shouldn't say anything but I can't lie to him, "Of course he did," Bishop downs a cup of whiskey, setting it aside and not bothering with the cup anymore. He takes a long swig from the bottle and smiles, a painful smile at me.

"I needed to," I say, trying to comfort him.

"You needed it because of me," he retorts, "I needed it to stop," he pauses, catching himself before he says too much.

"Bishop," I look at him, "no more lies. I don't know this version of you, even with my memory I know that in my soul. You're so far away from me and I just want the chance to get to know you again. The real you. Not the role you played to save face in front of everyone all those years, not even the version of you that you used to protect me. I want the truth,

138

all of it. Let me catch you."

19

"What did Ben tell you about my therapy? I'm assuming he didn't follow protocol," Bishop set the bottle by his feet.

"He said you were working through your *PTSD*," I look back to the fire.

"So he told you about my violent past, no wonder you were shaking. You're terrified to be here alone." He swallows, his jaw gets tight and he shakes his head.

"I'm not scared of you," I say confidently, "I was scared of what you were going to say. Scared that you were gonna kick me out or worse ignore me."

"How is ignoring you worse?" He looks over at me.

"Walking home in the rain isn't so bad, standing here staring at you in silence is a lot worse." I smile softly at him and he returns it. "Will you tell me why you disappeared after our talk the other day?"

His tongue runs against the harsh scabbing cut that split his bottom lip, "The truth?" I nod for him to continue and he shifts uncomfortably against the back of the couch. "Sean was right, I'm a coward. It had never crossed my mind that you would harm yourself because of me. I thought the worst thing you could ever do is fall in love with someone else. Love someone else other than me."

He stops, reaching for the whiskey bottle, and downs another shot of it. "It was a selfish thought, but I didn't think about how I would feel if you had followed through. When they told me the story that day, I would have let Sean beat the life out of me. I deserved it and more, but seeing how sad you were in the gally. Seeing how disappointed you were in me, and how I handled my feelings about you and about us. It snapped something else, this need to hit something, hit anything."

"Bishop," I say but he stops me.

"Not you, never you. My father never laid a hand on my mother, it was the only kindness he showed me as a child that was not harming her. I think he hated me so much because I look so much like her. I realized that if I didn't leave and cool off I would do something that my father would do. I would take it out on someone you loved. I can't control my anger as well as I would like. It's gotten worse since I left you, but in turn, it's gotten better since working with Ben."

"I never once thought you would hurt me, even when Ben told me about your tendencies. The thought didn't cross my mind, I just wanted to make sure you hadn't hurt yourself." I say sadly.

"That's my fatal flaw, Nora. I'm built too much like my father, I'm too selfish to hurt myself. It doesn't offer a release from the emotions. I came out here because I needed time to think, this has been that safe space away from every tempting moment in the last three years. Close to home, but not close enough to hurt you or anyone else." Bishop takes another swig and finally returns the cap to the bottle.

"I remembered a moment two days into your disappearing

act," I lean back on the couch resting my throbbing head against the backrest. "You talked about the day you went to see your father, after dinner. After he told me that story. I don't know if you were too drunk to remember or just chose not to tell me the day on the boat. But," I swallow my thoughts and center myself, "I was there Bishop, I had gone to talk to your father. When I showed up he was all over you, saying these awful things to you. That's the moment I knew I didn't need more information from him. I needed to talk to you."

A piece of him realizes where I'm going with the story. "I knew at that moment that you would have risked your life to stand up to that violent man, just to make sure I knew the truth about what happened. And maybe you didn't tell me the full truth that day, and if I could remember everything I would be pissed about that. You had your reason Bishop, you were trying to protect me."

I shift so I'm turned towards him on the couch now, "You keep calling yourself selfish, but I think it's a front because it's the only armor you have left to keep us all at arms reach. We're just asking for you to let us get closer."

"We?" he smiles and every part of my body reacts to the sight. It's beautiful and warm, it feels like the sun has filled the space around us. He tugs on the end of the quilt, pulling the edge that is tucked into the back of the couch around my body, free of its confines. He tugs at my socked foot and it's enough for me to move from my safe, warm spot on the couch.

"You?" he asks again and shifts.

He leaves a space between himself and the couch, perfectly sized for me to slide into. He tenses as I come close but I ignore the reaction and settle in beside him. "Are you okay? I can move back," I shift to leave his side but rough fingers dig into my waist and hold me against him.

"Give me a moment, it's been a long time since I held you like this," he sounds strained but his fingers loosen and he slides back against the couch. He relaxes a bit and presses his cheek against the top of my head. "What else have you remembered this week?" He asked to fill the silence.

"Some of the stuff was inappropriate for a lady to repeat back," I laugh, the redness flooding back to my cheeks.

"I hate to break this to you Nora, but you have never been a lady." I love the feeling of his wild laugh against my back, "anything appropriate to share then? I don't want to hear about you and Sean's downtime, no offense."

"I only slept with Sean once," I answer honestly and move positions in his arms until I can see his face.

"You can't remember half your life, Nora." He grimaces, I know he doesn't believe me or my brain at the moment but I knew I was telling the truth. Sean had told me as much. It was only once.

"It was only once Bishop," I say again, staring at him sternly until I know he's registered the serious tone of my voice. "And it was the beginning of this year after I saw you at my event with that woman that you introduced me to as your girlfriend."

"May, that's right. Her name was," Bishop pauses to think but can't come up with it. "Why are you here, trying so damn hard if you remember how much of an asshole I was the last time I saw you?"

"It doesn't matter anymore, who we've been the last three years don't matter. Not really. We both did very dumb things when we weren't together." I say, flicking his chin gently, I rub the scruff on his jaw.

"I did dumb things when we were together too," he reminds

me. "My list outweighs yours by a lot."

"Are you keeping a list? I didn't know we were writing things down," I sigh. Frustration laces my voice, I just want him to be serious for a minute, not crack self-deprecating jokes. "I don't know how long Ben can keep Sean at bay before he comes looking for me. You have a limited amount of time to tell me everything."

"Nora," he says my name so softly it sends goosebumps running the length of my arms. "You're asking to relive a very painful time."

"I'm going to remember everything eventually, with or without your help. So why not tell your side of the story before I remember how much I hate you?" *Before I stop wanting to listen to you talk, the soothing tone of your husky voice is in my ear.* I think and he bites his lip.

He stares at the fire for a while before clearing his throat. "When we found out your dad was sick, at first you held yourself together really well." He moves his arm to pull something out of his jean pocket. I feel his hand digging around and when he holds his palm up in my face there is a small oval-shaped, silver pendant in it.

"It's an archangel, the patron saint of healing. Raphael. Natalie bought it for your dad, and he wore it the whole summer around his neck through all the chemo and radiation. Even after every foolish thing I did that summer, he gave it to me." He drops it in my hand, "I snuck out while you were asleep thinking that would be the easiest thing to do. I had tried so hard to make you hate me that summer and you still let me crawl into your bed to sleep that night. It broke everything in me to slide out from under you. You're perfect face sleeping so soundlessly you looked like an angel yourself."

144

I run my thumb over the cold, shiny necklace and look up at him. He's staring down at me, his fingers wrapping gently around a loose strand of hair. "Nothing has ever gotten past your dad, not once. He stopped me before I could leave. I always admired your dad's ability to love his family so quietly. He never raised his voice, he loved you all with such a fierce silence. He didn't need words to show you. But he looked at me that day and he said something to me I'll never forget, *"Don't chase bad dreams, feel everything even when it hurts and remember where home is.* And then he dropped that in my hand, gave me the longest hug I've ever experienced from a father figure in my entire life, and told me to keep it because it was my turn to heal."

"And did you?" I ask, I pull away from him slightly, sitting up and resting my legs underneath me. He studies me for a long moment. "Did you heal?"

"I did not," he swallowed hard. "Not for a lack of trying, but there was always something missing. I carried this necklace every day for the last three years wondering why he would plague me with such a responsibility." He rubs the back of his neck and groans, "It was worse than taking on my father's business, harder than paying off all the debt. Living a life of fear not knowing when he would strike out like a rattlesnake and end my life. That necklace came from a man I truly admired, who loved me like his own son and with it held this expectation to be the man he knew I could be. I've never lived up to that expectation and that haunts me more than the memory of any beating I took from my own father."

"I believe you have become that man," I say, touching his face with the palm of my hand. "My dad never believes in anything he isn't absolutely sure of. If he gave you this and told you to heal all he wanted for you was to be happy. It wasn't an expectation to be a superhero, Bishop."

"It felt like it. It wasn't until my dad," he pauses and takes a long moment to catch his breath. "Died. That I was able to realize I had forgotten the three rules your dad taught me. I was chasing nightmares, I couldn't sleep. I was exhausted and overworked. I wasn't allowing myself to feel anything, I kept myself so dumb with drugs and alcohol that I didn't even know what it felt like to smile for real anymore. Worst of all, I forgot where home was. I was living in Japan, treating it like a home but it never was. It wasn't until I was back here, the air in Georgia clearing my senses that I knew I was home, and then seeing you. You're my home, Nora and I am ashamed to say I forgot you were."

"I wish I could forget you," I whisper into the phone, he calls every night and never says a word to me. I know it's because he doesn't sleep, he can't be without me. Some things never change. "Everyone said it would get easier, get a job, Nora, get an apartment, Nora, make some new friends. It doesn't matter what I do, how much money I make, or how many friends I have. Not with you calling me every night to remind me that you're still there."

A sharp intake of air lets me know the words are still wounding him. It's been two years since that day, I'm not the only one in pain. It offers such a small comfort between us. Together in misery, but separated by the world. By his actions.

I stare out the window, the rain falls against it in heavy, hail-like drops. It had been raining for days with no signs of stopping any time soon. I love the smell of rain, the clean smell that resides after it stops like everything awful has been washed away with it in a matter of hours. A fresh start.

That awful, painfully sad Lord Huron song plays over the speaker connected to my Spotify. I want to chuck the phone, the methodical blink of the time ticking away. Three hours were spent laying in the dark listening to him breathe. Neither of us would get any sleep ever again. I can't chuck my phone though, this would be the fourth one I've bought in two months from throwing it at a wall. Logically, if it doesn't work, he can't call.

"Why do you do this to us?" I ask into the silence. "Is it to remind us how much we suffer every day because you are stupid, selfish, and stubborn? If you don't want to talk, or come home then stop doing this to me. I can't take it anymore."

He says nothing, as per usual. I don't hang up, as usual. I need the silence just as much as he does. I can hear the busy state of his office in the background, and the people talking around him but he just sits and listens to me. I don't know how but I know he can hear me even in the noise of his surroundings.

"Mr. Bartley you have a call on line four, it's Stockley." His secretary even sounds beautiful. It pains me to hear her sweet, lulling Japanese accent. He hangs up with a click and without another word. Leaving me alone just like he always does.

"Do you need something for your head?" Bishop is kneeling in front of me now. Concern floods his stark blue eyes and he rubs a hand over my head. "You're remembering more and more every day."

A tear streaks down my face, "Hey," he muses and wipes it away with the back of his hand carefully.

"I needed the phone calls just as much as you," I say but a choked, forced sound leaves my lips. "I acted as if I hated them but I needed them too."

He lifts my chin with the crook of his finger, "I know." He presses his lips to mine, slowly. They are so warm, and he is so gentle as he brings us together. I lean into it, my fingers digging into the edge of the couch to hold my balance. My chest feels so hot and short of breath when he pulls away that I almost force him to come back.

He sits on his heels and smiles at me. "Let's see how much conversation we can get through before Sean breaks in my door," he laughs, his smile grows tenfold and he scrunches his nose at me. "I might need more whiskey though," he looks at the half-empty bottle on the floor.

20

His pace quickens, his hand down moving inside his jeans. My center throbs despite myself and the warmth beneath my legs ache. "Bishop," I whisper, begging him. "Slower. I like watching you. I like it slow."

He turns his blue eyes on me, his lips brushing against mine, "Nora—"

"Take your pants off," I lick my lips. The night sky above is so dark, the large trees that hang above us provide cover from the chilly wind that whips off the shore.

He obeys, bending his knees up and pushing his pants down. He pulls his cock out, thick and hard. I watch him rub his thumb over the wet tip and continue stroking it. He's only got eyes for me, watching intently.

I slowly start to unbutton his shirt. I push it open with my hands, his bare skin from neck to groin all waiting for me. I want to touch him but I resist.

"Slower baby," I tell him. He'll finish when I let him.

"Open your shirt," he meets my eyes and there's fiery frustration behind them. "No one can hear us, please open your shirt for me."

I pause, my pulse throbbing. I want to but we didn't venture far and I can hear the laughter of my sister and Sean rising over the waves through the night air. They're too close.

149

"They're not looking for us," Bishop says, he follows my gaze through the tree line. At any second they could do just that, come looking for us.

"Open your shirt, Nora." It's more of order this time, a growl in his voice.

I listen, holding his gaze as he rubs himself. I unbutton the light shirt I'm wearing. Underneath is the bright yellow swimsuit I wore earlier in the day. He licks his lips, yanking it up over my breasts.

He dips his head and licks across the hardened nipple. Still jerking himself, his eyes trailing up from my breasts to my eyes. He fists himself hard, cum dripping from the tip. He lifts his hands to touch me but I shake my head.

"Not tonight. Just you."

"This is torture," Bishop groans, I smile a little. "Just one more taste."

I shake my head, my skin tingling at the idea. To have him all over me, take me here in the middle of the woods with everyone mere feet away. He dangles on my words and tries to kiss me.

"Faster now," I push my chest out. He breathes through his teeth restraining himself from touching the breasts I push in his face. I slip my hand down my jean shorts and into my underwear. He growls watching me finger myself.

"Take your pants off Nora, I want to watch."

"No," I say simply knowing it will drive Bishop nuts.

I see his breathing turn rabid as his eyes fall down my body and I smile back at him as he loses all control from the sight of me touching myself. "I want you," he breathes like he's in pain.

He takes the chance cupping my chin roughly with his free hand. His mouth on mine, gently kissing my lips. He runs his tongue over my bottom lip, his teeth grabbing hold of it and sending a warm pulse through my body to my toes. His lips leave me just as

150

suddenly as he completely comes undone.

"I'm the boss next time," he growls. He uses his discarded shirt to clean himself.

"You do owe me now," I lean over and kiss his nose causing him to scrunch it up.

I wake short of breath, but he sleeps soundlessly beside me. I roll onto my back and stare at the ceiling. I am hot and I ache from the memory that startled me awake. I am tempted to push my hands between my legs and settle the throb that comes over me like waves.

Bishop stirs beside me, the thoughts of his hands around himself make it worse. I need a cold shower. I slide from the bed as quietly as I can manage. Last night he was so kind, so sweet, and honest with me. I feel guilty because as much as I know I love Sean, there is a draw to my dark, handsome Bishop. I stare at him from the bedroom door. His hair is messy, pushed around his face in his sleep.

I refused to let him sleep on the couch, but he had curled onto the bed at a distance with a blanket of his own pulled around his hips. The hard ridges of his abs, the subtle dip in his hips where the blanket met skin all moved in slow deep breaths. He looked so innocent, so untouched by all the harm he's suffered. When he sleeps it's the one time he looks at peace.

I don't know where this is going, but I know at this moment staring at him from a distance that I would fight a thousand fights for him. I would fight to remember him for the rest of my life.

I turn away from him, walking silently to the bathroom and running the water in the shower. It's cold at first against my skin but it turns warm and soothing. It smells like cabin water, the stuff that comes straight from the ocean unfiltered and it reminds me of all the summers we spent in the water.

I hear the bathroom door creak open and for a second my heart flutters in my chest. I know he's seen me naked before but there's something about this. Without my memory, I can't remember the first time he had. What was his reaction, did it make me feel beautiful?

"Towels," his voice is deep and husky from sleep. "I didn't hear you get up."

"You were sleeping so sounding I didn't want to wake you," I say, pushing my wet hair back off my face and letting the water run over my closed eyes and down the front of my body. He's so close, when I open my eyes I can see the outline of his broad shoulders beyond the thin shower curtain.

I hide the sound of my breathing, nervous and shallow as he stands so still. I wish he would take the chance, pull the curtain back and get in. He just stands there, I want so badly to know what's going on in his head. I hope that after yesterday he doesn't revert to silence, that things aren't awkward because I know about his therapy.

My heart cracks as I see him back away to the door after another moment, "I'll leave you to shower in peace," he says quietly and closes the door behind him with a soft click.

"Bishop," I whisper but it comes out as a plea, a begging noise that is strained with pain.

"Do you love him?" Bishop asks, I am pressed against the bathroom wall. My red hair is messy and falls around my shoulders. It's covered in sand, salt, and other gross things from spending the whole day surfing. I had gone with Sean, alone.

Bishop had been acting weird for weeks, avoiding spending time with any of us. His nineteenth birthday is coming fast and I

152

know he's so on edge about his father returning. Every year is like clockwork, he shows up to remind Bishop that he's a failure. But this was different. We had all felt the pressures of my dad being sick, we had all become so busy.

I picked up a new part-time job that doubled my time away from the beach house, lucky Sean had also gotten hired at the gold club. I was at least able to enjoy some of the summers with people I knew. We had been let off early and spent the afternoon surfing the cove. The waves were so nice, easy surfing and relaxing. I got home and stripped out of my wet suit, the dark blue bikini I'm wearing covered in sand.

Bishop had cornered me in the bathroom, where we stand now. He stares at me so furious, his hand pinning my arm to the wall and he leans into me like he wants to kiss me but doesn't. I'm not scared of him, I'm concerned.

"Do you love him?" He asks again. I know what he saw, I know why he's so angry but there's no way to explain it away. "I saw you, and Sean," the way he says his name has changed so much over the last few weeks.

Even in their long weeks of arguments in the past they always came around. They were best friends. This though, the anger he feels is warranted. "I saw him kiss you," he growls. "Did you like it? Do you enjoy it when he puts his hands on you? Do you get wet when he kisses you? Do you want him to fuck you?"

"Bishop James Bartley," I growl back, furious with him for even asking me such a question. Disgusted with his lack of kindness. "Watch your tone with me and don't you ever accuse me. Ever."

He looks to the ground and his jaw tenses against his will. A tell that he's sorry but doesn't know how to apologize. His anger gets the best of him and he says stupid things. Not able to take them back. Past the point of self-control, he slams his hand against the *wall beside my head.*

"Do you love him, Nora?" This time the question is heartbreaking. He says it so slowly as he looks up from his feet. His eyes are piercing, blue like the purest wave first thing in the morning before the tourists have time to dirty the ocean.

"I love you," I say without pause, "I'll always love you," I press a hand to his face. "What is going on with you?"

Instead of an answer, he kisses me. It's feverish and heavy against my lips. He drags his tongue on my bottom lip and presses in tightly. My back pressed to the bathroom wall, still trapped by his hold I gave into the moment. "Bishop," I push him back finally, he won't stop unless I make him. "Until you tell me what's going on. You don't get to do this, you're cut off."

"Fine, not like I can't find a piece of ass to fuck somewhere else. It's tourist season, Nora." He snarls, leaving the bathroom. I slam the door closed behind him and press my head to the cold wood.

I don't know how long I sit under the water, it turns cold but I don't care. A soft knock comes from the door but I don't answer. It creaks open slowly and Sean's figure stands on the other side of the curtain. "Nora?"

I try to answer him but a sob leaves my lips, he kneels by the tub, pulling the curtain back. I still sit in my bathing suit, the freezing water pelting my skin so hard it's red and irritating. He says nothing, for which I'm grateful. He climbs into the tub in his jeans and shirt, wrapping himself around me, and sits in the cold water in silence.

These are hard memories, to remember a time when Bishop lost control and to try to focus on the future. That he's not that man anymore, but all I can feel is the warmth of Sean. The protection he brought when Bishop lost control. I'm so angry as I climb from the shower, all thoughts of Bishop's smooth stomach, and bare arms touching me leave my body.

I take two long deep breaths and pull on the clean shirt Bishop had set on the counter for me. I tug on my dirty pants and set out to find him. He's making eggs in the kitchen, still shirtless. I stop in my tracks. I seem to always forget just how many scars riddle his back. His father was meticulous with his placements. He would create scars over scars. Leaving ugly ridges cut into Bishop's back. He was just a boy trying to do what he thought was right for everyone.

"I never realized how much you protected me until you were gone," I say from the hallway and he turns, a confused look on his face. "The day you saw Sean kiss me and accused me of loving him," I pause and he takes a long breath.

"Please stop, I remember everything I said to you." His voice cracks and he drops the spoon to the counter.

"It's not about what you said, you knew you were leaving then?" I ask him and he nods carefully, "you were trying to push me away. Sean did the best he could to pick up the pieces that night, but he never touched me romantically, ever. Not until I wanted it. He did exactly what you asked of him. He protected me like you had been doing our entire childhood."

He runs his tongue along his lips and tilts his head, closing his eyes for a moment. "I think you and Sean need to sit down with Ben. You need to talk just as much as I need it."

"That won't end the way you want it, Nori." He grimaces, and I'm sure he's right.

"It doesn't matter, things need to be said. On both sides. You'll do it for me, I know he will too." I raise an eyebrow at him.

"Fine, call Ben. They can come here, that way I can kick them out after." At least he's being honest. I dig my cell from my back pocket and call Ben.

21

Bishop looks nervous.

He fidgets with the sleeves of his white shirt, carefully cuffing them over his biceps. I can see him breathing, counting his breaths in his head as he focuses on the shirt. I walk over to him and take his hand away from the fabric and into mine.

"Stop," I laugh softly, "this is a good thing. You're the two people I love the most in my life. I can speak for everyone when I say we're sick of you fighting." He looks up from our hands, the depths of his blue eyes filled with uncertainty. "You'll be okay, I promise."

"I'm not worried about me being okay after this, Nora. I don't think you should be here for this conversation." His jaw tics and he shakes his head. "There are things you shouldn't hear."

"All or nothing, from here on out. I didn't leave after this morning. I remembered all those horrible things you said to me, didn't I? I'm still here."

"I said horrible crap to you that day, but—" he pauses, "it's not the *worst*."

I shake my head, knowing full well that what happened that day was the tip of a very large, dark, and ominous iceberg that crashed into us that summer. He looks so unsure of everything to come. I wish I could convince him that I had no intention of leaving. I didn't. I can't promise my emotions won't get the best of me, or that I'll be angry with him for a while. All I know is that I have spent my entire life running back to him, regardless of our issues. We need each other to survive.

"I know Bishop," I smile at him, a careful smile that is hiding my own fear. "You can't control the outcome of today. You've spent the better part of your life trying to protect me from the bad things in life. It's time you let me take care of myself, just this once. Let go."

"Easier said than done, my love." He lifts our tangled hands to his mouth and kisses the ridges of my knuckles.

My love.

I lay in bed, I can feel his arms around me. Even after all this time, how horrible he's been this summer I cannot stand to sleep without him. It's his birthday tomorrow, his father's car was in the driveway this morning. I all but begged him to stay with me. Just tonight.

Now his head presses into the space between my shoulder blades, I can feel the crinkles of his furrowed forehead on my bare back. Tears fill my eyes. I just want everything to be okay. I want my dad to be healthy, he looks so brittle, so thin, and sick. He's been a force my entire life, a guiding light. So strong and capable of anything the world threw at him. As though he was made of marble. Now he was showing those cracks. He and his mom switched rooms so he didn't have to climb the stairs, he barely ate or smiled. He couldn't even get down to the beach.

I want to roll over, to press his face into my chest. To remind him what beats under the skin, and why it does so rapidly. I want

*to say to him, 'you're here, in my arms but it's like we're oceans
apart.' I want him to fight for this, I want to know why he hides it,
the pain he carries. He's hiding it from me in the form of fucking
other girls and getting so drunk he can't stand straight.*

Oceans apart.

*I can feel his hands squeeze around my waist, holding me so
tightly as if I may slip through his fingers if he doesn't grasp it. I'm
not the one pulling away. I should be the one gripping him, I'm
falling so fast, scared to hit the bottom but he's barely there to catch
me anymore. 'I'll always catch you, Nora,' the words play over and
over in my mind.*

*I close my eyes, but sleep never comes. The moonlight cracks
through the room, the rings on his hands reflect the light and when
he finally slips out from underneath me I almost cry out for him to
come back. He kneels in front of me, I can hear him even with my
eyes closed. The breath on my face from him being so close.*

*"Hey baby," he whispers so quietly I almost burst into tears but I
continue to pretend that I am asleep. "My love. My world. I know
in the coming weeks you're going to be very upset with me. I tried
so hard to prepare you for tomorrow but I wasn't strong enough to
do what needed to be done. Not really. I shouldn't have come here
tonight, laying with you was a mistake because now I don't know if
I can do this. My heart is breaking, you are so beautiful. I'm doing
this all for you. I will not be the anchor tied to you, my sweet bird.
You were meant to fly and you cannot do that with me. Your dad
will be okay, he'll survive this and he'll be here for everything going
forward. He'll be there to hold you when you wake up tomorrow,
to comfort you when you're sad. He will be there to meet the next
man you love, to bless your engagement, and walk you down the
aisle." He pauses and it sounds like he's finished.*

He takes a long deep breath to steady himself and that's when

I can hear the tears, the soft sound of sobbing coming from him. I want so badly to open my eyes and tell him it's him that will be there on my wedding day, to grow old sitting on the back porch with me and my dad. It's us, it's always been us. My soul.

"He's going to be the best grandfather ever because he's the best father in the world. To you and me. He will live and eventually grow out but he will do it all right here. The beach house is ours, and I will not let anyone take that from us ever. You pulled me from hell Nora, you showed me how beautiful the world can be when you just open your eyes. Please never stop dreaming, watch the sailboats, and dream to be that free forever. For you and me." His voice cracks, "but you have to let me go, you are better without me. I need to do this, I need to redeem myself. I don't deserve your love, not even close but I thank you, for giving it to me unconditionally always. My sweet Nora, you are stronger than you know. Use that. My love."

Bishop rubs a thumb over the tear that streams down my face, "I didn't mean to make you cry. It's a habit of calling you that, I'm sorry."

"It wasn't that, I was awake that night, the night you left," I say staring at the floor. I feel like I was intruding on the memory like I didn't belong there. It was a moment I was never supposed to hear.

"I knew you were awake," he raises my chin so I look at him. "It made it excruciatingly hard to leave you. I took my bike down the docks and sat there alone for hours before I returned to my house and told my dad my decision."

"I'm sorry you felt that was your only choice, my *soul*." He smiles softly, and he leans in like he may kiss me but a car door slams outside and he drops his grip on my hand. "Deep breaths," I say and walk to the front door.

160

I hear him slump into a chair behind me with a mumble of words. "Hey boys," Ben hugs me tightly, his sweater is itchy, and rubs against my face. "He's okay."

Ben nods, he's just as worried about him as I am. I can see it on his face as he pulls back from me. Sean comes into view, wearing a dark zip-up hoodie. His beard is out of control and he looks like he hasn't slept all night. "He is not," Ben mumbles under his breath leaving me. He wanders into the house and Sean comes to stand in front of me.

He's inspecting my face, neck, and hands, "Are you actually looking for bruises right now?" I scoff at him and it snaps him from his trance.

"I'm sorry, I just know how he gets when he's upset," Sean grumbles, his hands shoved into his pockets like a child.

"This is a good thing, he's scared too," I say looking back at the cottage. "You need to have this conversation, and if not for yourself Sean, do it for me."

"That's a low blow, Nora." He sniffles, fidgeting and shifting his weight uncomfortable.

"Is it? You two claim to have done this all in my protection, to take care of me. Me, me, me. What's one more thing? If you two can spend years fighting over me, you can spend one evening having a grown-up conversation *for me*." I say with my eyes narrowed at him, I tilt my head and wait for his answer.

"You're manipulative," Sean says with a smirk on his face. "Are you truly ready to hear everything?"

"I've been ready for a long time, I may not remember a lot but I know in my soul I've been waiting for an explanation for years. So go in there and try your best." I hold out my hand to him, he stares at it. And then up to me, my heart clenches.

I know how he feels about me now, and it makes everything so much harder to work out. I extend my hand in friendship, but it is more than that to him, to both of us.

"Nora," he sighs, "do you love me?" He asks and I should have expected it. I knew I couldn't get out of this without explaining my own feelings. He doesn't take my hand and I retract it back to my pocket, shoving the embarrassed feeling into my jeans with my hand.

"Hey Nora," the message on my answering machine vibrates through my hungover head. Sean's voice is so loud this early in the morning but he's called twice already. I should really be out of bed, I have to be at work in twenty minutes.

"I," he pauses, this is why he's called twice. He can't seem to get his words out. Sean can talk himself in circles but when it matters the words get caught. He invented the phrase, cat got your tongue? I'm sure of it. "We haven't talked since the other night and I'm feeling kind of weird about it all because you seem to be ignoring me completely."

I sigh, I've been avoiding him because I don't know how to explain myself. It felt so good, and it was Sean, I've known him for my entire life. There was no hidden side to him, no darkness or unforgivable past. He was just my golden boy, my Pony boy Curtis. Pure and kind, he was a dream. So why did I feel so conflicted about what we did? At first, I thought it was because I didn't care because it was a mistake and I was drunk.

"I know you're drinking that night, and I'm giving you a free pass here if you want to say you can't remember it or you don't feel anything now but, I just need an answer, Nora. I'm going crazy." His voice cuts into my thoughts, I could remember everything. Every single touch, the way his fingers felt against my skin. How I felt when he pushed inside of me, the feeling of us moving together

as the water ran over us in the shower.

It wasn't that I didn't feel anything, it was that I felt guilty for feeling everything.

"I haven't," I stop, unsure how to explain myself to him. His blue eyes trail across my face, waiting and watching with bated breath for my answer. "I haven't remembered anything from our time together except that night Sean," I swallow hard. "I don't remember my feelings for you."

"Yet," Sean says so confidently I hear the world halt, it stops spinning just for a moment to revel in his confidence. "If you don't hate me after this, I would like to take you surfing tomorrow."

"Deal, as long as you promise not to hit Bishop today. He hates himself enough right now, he doesn't need to be in physical pain too." I say, and he nods. This time it's him who extends his hand to me and I smile while taking it. I pull him in for a hug. I forget how warm and safe he feels when he wraps his arms around my small frame. A blanket that covers my entire body, it's weighted and pushes all my fears down just for a moment.

Bishop still sits on the chair in the corner, his face stern and tense. I know he saw the hug but it was nothing but that. A hug. He sits up on guard when Sean comes in behind me. He stands up against my back, so close I can feel the curve of his body against mine. Using me as a shield.

"Time to figure this out," I speak first, Ben nods.

"Bishop, SHARK!" Sean calls from the pier, the shout travels across the water loud enough to cause Bishop to lose his balance and slip off his board.

"He's going to kill you for that," I laughed while taking a bite of my hot dog.

"He's doing an amazing job for a kid who's never surfed before. He refuses to give up." Sean turns and leans against the pier with his arms crossed.

"I think he just wants to fit in with you guys," I say, cleaning my hands and throwing out my garbage in the bin next to me. Sean's body is slowly starting to fill out, over the last summer he's looked less scrawny, and malnutrition. We start Sophomore year in two weeks. "With school starting soon he's going to need all the friends he can get. He doesn't exactly fit in."

"You mean with his endless closet of dark clothing, his unnerving silent stare, and his all-around shining personality people won't like him?" Sean laughs, his shirt is tucked into the pocket of his obnoxiously loud board shorts. Polar opposites.

"You like him," I say, "that's enough for me. Thank you for giving him a chance," I say, leaning my head against his shoulder.

"I'm struggling here, Nora. I do like him, he's a good guy but there's something he's hiding from us." I give a sad smile and turn *back to watch him appear from the water. Ben slaps his shoulder and they laugh about something. Bishop shakes the water from his hair in Natalie's face causing her to howl and run from him.*

"He's not hiding it from me, I know what goes on inside of his house, and if we're able to give him just some sense of a normal childhood? The kind with friends, laughter, and surfing. The kind of childhood we grew up having, don't you wanna try?" I can see the glimmer of jealousy in his eyes but I keep the comment to myself. I'm not here to tell Sean he can't have feelings, I could only control how mine felt.

"Sometimes Nora Quinn, you sound exactly like your dad and it's terrifying." Sean laughs, the concession kid yells for him to pick up his order and we take the rest of the food back to the beach.

"How'd I do?" Bishop asks, throwing his arm over my shoulders and kissing my cheek. I lean into it, craving more from him.

"Not bad," Sean interjects, "you need to learn to shuffle your feet and you tend to bend at the back and not your knees. Eat your hot dog and I'll show you some tricks."

I smile softly at Sean, a silent thank you between the two of us. He nods, shoving a hot dog into his mouth with a goofy grin on his face.

I'm focusing so hard on the crumbling brick below the fireplace that when Ben coughs loudly to break me from my trance I barely look up. They've been sitting staring at one another for the last hour, in silence. Not a word has been spoken that hasn't been prompted by either Ben or myself.

"Alright, I'm done with this shit," Ben swears and I flinch at the use of the word, he's mad now. "You two get to run around making a mess of everyone else's lives and take zero responsibility ever."

"Is that your professional opinion?" Sean rolls his eyes, I

shoot him a dirty look. He lets out a huff of air and sits forward on his knees, covering his face with his hands.

"Can I ask a question," I say, both of them looking up, absolutely terrified of what I'm about to say, "what happened?"

Neither answers me.

"What happened that turned you against each other?" I ask, Bishop licks his lower lip in silence and Sean just shakes his head. "Well? An answer would be nice," I snap.

"You," Bishop speaks first, always incapable of staying silent when I beg him for sound. "You happened."

I inhaled sharply, I had expected this answer. "You can't blame everything on me, I want to know the exact moment. The snap."

"It wasn't Sean's fault," Bishop sighs, he slides forward on his chair and sits up properly. "Your dad threw an eighteenth birthday party for me, this was before—" he stops and Ben nods for him to continue. "This was before anyone but you and your father knew what happened behind closed doors, Nora."

I look at Sean, he won't look back at me. All this time he's known what Bishop has been through and never said a word to make himself look better. "My dad was late that year, we thought maybe he wouldn't show up at all and your dad was so kind to me I couldn't say no to dinner. You guys decorated the whole house, the deck, and even the tree house. It was amazing."

"His dad showed up," Sean finally speaks up. "He tried to get Bishop to leave but your dad stepped in the way. He knew what was going on in that house and asked his father to leave him just for the night. That Bishop would be home the next day, no harm, no foul."

166

Bishop grimaces, "You know my dad, Nora. Whether or not you remember the worst of him, you know deep down how he would have taken that."

"What happened?" Ben shifts beside me on the couch, there if I need him.

Sean looks to Bishop, encouraging him to speak up but Bishop can't seem to find his voice. The muscles in his neck strain and he rubs his face with his hands. "His dad pulled a gun out, he put it in your face, Nora. Your face," Bishop sighs when Sean speaks, fear and anger dripping from his lips.

"Neither of them said a word, Bishop just stood and left the house. He left you standing there with a gun in your face." Sean sits back against his chair again. "That's when it changed. You see, not a single person was concerned about your safety when he showed back up a week later. It was all about Bishop, if he was alright, where his father went, and what they needed to do for him. But not one person saw you standing in the room, not even him. Scared to death, reverting to yourself. All I could see was you, standing in the middle of all these bodies, pale and terrified."

"All I ever did was care about her safety," Bishop's face changes from grief to anger in a second. "Why do you think I walked away that day? He would have killed her to make a point, so yes Sean, I walked away from her."

"That's all you've ever done, you think walking away makes you some kind of hero," Sean growls.

"I can't be what you want me to be, I can't be what you don't want to see Sean," Bishop goes to stand but Ben shakes his head and he stays sitting. "It doesn't matter what you think of me. You've never understood that. I don't need your approval to love Nora."

167

"But you do need me to pick up the pieces, you need me to be there when you leave. You need me to watch her, to keep her safe, to do your job when you decide it's too dangerous or hard to do it yourself. Right, Bishop? Or am I missing something?" Sean's body is tense, even in his sweater his muscles bulge and his jaw grinds together.

"You're missing something," Bishop sneers, their tempers flaring. "You forget that you begged me to break her heart. You asked me to be cruel, to treat her so badly that she couldn't look at me. To want her so heartbroken that she'd have no choice but to turn to you finally. How did that work out for you Sean?"

My heart sinks, they were both right. I didn't want to hear this. But what I wanted, and what I needed are two very different things right now.

"I told you that I had to leave, I told you what I was doing. All these years you've played the knight in shining armor to protect her, to be there and hold her when she's upset. I'm not going to sit here and let you throw me under the bus any longer. She knows the truth about why I left and it's time you own up to your part in why she is the way she is." Bishop pointed a finger at me in anger and then back to his own heart, slamming it against his chest. "I didn't want her to turn into this, I just wanted to leave. You convinced me that the only way she would let me go was to destroy her. I did what you asked because I believed in you, you were my best friend and I thought you were doing what was right for her! But it was what was right for you, Sean."

Sean said nothing, he just took the onslaught of accusations. "For the last three years, I have been meeting with Sean to check in with you. Every year it gets worse, he didn't even tell me about the suicide attempt because it would have been the end of our deal. I would have come home right there, risked everything to come home and make it better. But he hid that from me because he enjoyed crawling into your bed so much, he enjoyed the fact that you needed him so much," he snarls now, his eyes brimming with tears and his face red with anger. "That he didn't care what happened to you anymore."

He stares at me, his eyes so blue they are gateways to his soul. I can feel everything that's going on inside of him right now. His jaw tics and Sean shifts uncomfortably in the chair beside us. Bishop makes a move and the whole room finches.

"Alright Bishop," Ben interjected, "take a breath."

"I'm not going to hurt anyone," the strain in his voice is painful to hear because he wants Ben to have faith in him. A young boy was just desperate for the friends he never knew he needed. "He's still my best friend, regardless of what he did over the years. The stupid, cruel, and unfair things he's whispered in Nora's ear while she drunkenly slept in his arms. They mean nothing because at least she was safe."

"Sean," I look at him but he refuses to look back at me. "Sean," I say it again, louder this time and he turns his saddened gaze to me. "Is he telling the truth?"

"Yeah," is all he says, tears rolling down his face. "You gotta understand that when I asked him to do those things, I was eighteen. I was stupid. I had been in love with you since we were ten and you never noticed. It wasn't until the dark horse arrived in town that you had any interest in boys. I felt," he rubs his hands on his knees, "betrayed. I know that you didn't mean to make me feel that way, it wasn't your fault I never acted on my feelings."

"When Bishop came to me and told me he had a solution.

A way for your family to keep the beach house, to get out of debt I didn't question him. I just went along with his plan. I knew you'd never stop loving him, it didn't matter if he broke up with you normally, or disappeared in the night. You would have followed him and demanded a reason. I knew that with him gone, maybe I could love you, I could be that person for you. So I convinced him to sleep with other girls, to get so drunk, and to treat you like garbage. I told you, I was selfish too but I should have explained why a long time ago." He explains.

"That's why you called that week, after the night we spent together," a violent hiss leaves Bishop's lips from the confession. "You felt just as guilty as I did. You felt guilty because you didn't know if I was just too drunk to remember Bishop or if I was actually falling for you. You felt guilty because your five-year plan worked."

Sean stood and before Ben could stop him he left, the screen door slamming behind him.

"That went well."

"I'm going to go talk to him," I say more to Bishop than anyone, who looks over at me with a worried look on his face. "This isn't me choosing Bishop." Relief sweeps over his features and he nods.

"Talk to Ben for a bit, cool off," I say standing and following Sean out the door. I find him walking towards the driveway. "What are you going to do to walk back to the pier? That's a solid four-hour walk, easily."

"Maybe, it's better than sitting here hating myself under watchful eyes." He throws his hands in the air and I almost laugh because he looks like a teenager again. Ranting about his dad's expectations, and his school grades, or girls. He looks young again.

"Don't do that," I say walking up behind him. He looks over at me and shoves his hands in his pockets, "Don't beat yourself up for things that happened a long time ago."

"It feels long to you, Nora. But the last conversation Bishop and I had about you was only a month ago. Right before you decided to come down for the summer, I met with him. He knew you were coming long before Kate called him. Ben let it slip that you were thinking about it," He sighs, "It wasn't a nice conversation. I told him to stay away against my better judgment and because I knew if he came home he'd tell you everything and then I would have to deal with my actions."

"And here we are anyway, so let's deal with them," I say, grabbing his wrist I pull his hand from his pocket and link it with mine. "We were kids, Sean. You were in love."

"Yeah, I was in love. I am in love," he squeezes my hands. "But I had my chance, and I screwed it up pretty badly. The only thing Bishop is guilty of is being an idiot, I manipulated him and you to get what I want inside of just fighting for you the good old fashion way." He leans in and kisses my cheek. "I can't promise I'll be his best friend anytime soon, but I promise not to start any more fights."

"How about you trust me?" I say squeezing his hand back, he pulls me in for a long hug. The smell of banana surf wax and salt-washed over me just like it always does. "I love you, Sean. I'm sorry none of this turned out in your favor."

"Wrong, I didn't lose you even after you heard all that. You still love me, and that is all I need." He lets go of me and flicks my nose. "Let's go make sure Bishop hasn't killed Ben."

"Sean," I scoff, shaking my head.

"Sorry," he smiles and holds the door open for me.

23

My head is pressed against Bishop's back, the smell of fresh rain and open highway rushing around my face. The bike rumbles between my thighs and a rush of feeling alive rolls through me as he takes a sharp turn away from town. I pull his leather jacket tighter into my fingers and close my eyes, letting the feeling of flying wash over me.

The sounds and lights of Atlanta are bright against the night sky, office buildings lights flickering off as bar signs flicker to life. We're going to a movie but I was just grateful for a night off. Sean turns the truck down the main street towards the theater.

"Natalie is going to go with you to the movie," he says, but there's an annoyance to his tone and he pulls the truck up in front of the theater. "I have to go deal with something."

"Alright," I smile, "meet us after for food?" I ask and he nods but won't look at me.

"Just call me, and I'll come to get you. Don't wander around downtown." His jaw tenses. I get out and lean against the side of the truck, peering into the window.

"Sean," I muse, begging him to look at me just for a moment. "What's wrong?" He had been on edge for weeks, the stress of graduating mixed with working was getting to us all but there was

something else eating away at him.

"Nothing, just have somewhere to be and you're going to be late for your movie. Shoo!" He waves me off with a forced smile. "I promise, I'm okay Nora." He says when I don't pull away from the truck.

"Be careful," I say, it comes out barely a whisper but he nods with a grim expression. He's going to see Bishop.

"Hey!" Natalie yells from the ticket booth, she's standing with a couple of girls from school and their boyfriends. I fix my worried facial features and make my way to them. "I thought Sean was coming too?"

"Yeah, me too. He had some stuff to do I guess," I trail off looking down the street at his ugly pickup truck as it rattles to a stop and makes a left turn. "He'll catch up later."

The movie was terrible, a romantic comedy about a girl in her late thirties. The other girls chatted about it while we stood out in front of the theater. I had texted Sean to check in on him a couple of times during the film but got no response from him.

"Hey, there's a party a couple of blocks over, do you guys wanna go? Lang just texted and said things were getting rowdy. Sounds fun to me." Kate looks at me with a pathetically fake smile and winks. "Or are you going to be a boring little girl tonight and do what Roberts tells you to do?"

I all but hiss at her, an insult on my lips. Lately, Kate and I have come to head about life. I don't blame her, I can't because she has to deal with her father more than anyone. I see the way he treats her like she doesn't exist. So she demands attention from everyone else around her.

She crosses her bare arms over her chest, the soft pink tank top barely containing her as she settles her arms against the fabric. "Well, what's the verdict, Nora?"

Natalie gives me a soft smile, tilting her head causing her soft red hair to spill over her shoulder. Her green eyes glittered under the warm glow of the theater lights, "It can't hurt," she shrugs her shoulders.

"Mm, not so boring after all." Kate laughs, linking her arm through the arm of Joshua. His tall, six-foot frame compliments Kate's tall thin one. His dark eyes follow the curves of her body, a smile curving on his lips as he reaches the plump shape of her ass. Josh would follow her all night if it meant a chance to get into the tight jeans she wore.

She's not lying, the sounds of the party float down the alley after only walking a few blocks. A large gate swings open and an equally large man in a heavy leather jacket stands beyond it. His face is scruffy and covered in scars, and his eyes are darker than the alley itself but I can feel him looking us over. He lets us in after some sweet talking on Kate's part. Natalie tugs me along until the red light is visible.

The alley is shoved full of people, a small stage tucked up against the back of a restaurant has a DJ settled up top pumping loud music out into the narrow space. Couches and chairs are set up around the alley, in circles, and in gathering spaces. People have draped over the furniture and each other, tipping beer into their mouths. People slip tiny capsules into their tongues, while others prefer to suck them up their noses.

"Sean is going to kill us," I whisper to Nat and she shakes her head, pointing towards a set of couches that are shoved into the darkest corner of the alley. A single red lamp hangs over them, barely illuminating their face but there's no confusion that it's Sean and Bishop. "Check that, I'm going to kill him."

Natalie grabs my arm, twirling me back to face her. "Sean probably has his reasons. Why don't we just go find some sucker willing to buy us a beer?" She smiles at me, but I can feel the anger festering.

Not two days before I caught Bishop with his hands down another girl's pants. I could still see the look in his eyes while he stared at me, her moaning his name in his ear but his eyes locked on mine. He had shaved his head again, leaving him looking like a hardened, ruthless version of the boy I knew. His facial hair had started to grow thick along his face, making him look older. I took a fleeting glance back at them, they still hadn't seen us. Bishop runs his tongue along a cigarette wrapper and his eyes glance up, catching mine.

He says something without breaking eye contact and I see Sean stir out of the corner of my eye. "Not this time Natalie," I pull out of her grasp and make my way to them. Bishop leans back on the couch, his eyes downcast as he smokes the freshly rolled nicotine.

Sean steps in front of me before I get too close, he's wearing a dark black coat and his hair is pushed under a backward hat. "How was your movie? I see you didn't listen to me and have wandered around downtown."

"I'm not a little kid Sean," I bite back. "Hey Bishop," I say with venom, it drips from my lips as a snarl form. "And you don't answer your phone so," I shake my head. Over his shoulder I can see the tense posture of Bishop, his eyes carefully watching the interaction but never looking at me.

"You shouldn't be here," he says under his breath and puts his hand on my wrist, his fingers wrapping around my skin gently but firm and commanding.

"What's wrong with him?" I ask, completely ignoring his comment. I stood by what I said, I wasn't a child. I was the same age as them, we were all eighteen and fully capable of taking care of ourselves. They had made that clear when they started fucking *other girls in my tree house. Our tree house.*

"His dad is home," *Sean swallows hard. That's wrong, it's not his birthday and his father never visited any other time during the summer. "I know, he won't tell me why," Sean says as if he can read my thoughts.*

"You're just not going to talk to me? Tell me this yourself," I *push Sean away, his shoulder turning enough that I can make eye contact with Bishop. "You're a coward."*

"Hey," *Sean growls as I shove his grip off my arm and walk away. He calls after me, I turn and give them both the middle finger.* "Nora!"

The worst part of the memory returning is the pain that comes with them. Bishop carries me to the bed, his arms cradled underneath me as my head lulls against his chest. I run my fingers through his hair as he settles next to me, his face turns towards me, and a smile forms on his face.

"Anything we need to discuss?" He asks, knowing the sadness that flickers across my face is probably something to do with him. He runs his thumb along my jaw and leans in to place a gentle kiss on the skin.

"Don't cut your hair anymore," I whisper, "I don't like it short. It makes you look too hard, worn out, and old."

"Oh, now I'm old hey?" He teases pushing a stray hand back off my neck. "You never did like it short and you always voiced it."

"Good, don't. I like it long." It's grown more since he's been home, the first time I saw him standing on the deck it was cropped shorter, with most of the length on top. Now more and more strands started to fall behind his ears.

"When I knew you were coming home after Sean met with me," he pauses, still uncomfortable talking about everything so openly. "I started growing it. I knew you would be upset with how short it was cut and I wanted to make you happy. I knew better, I knew that a haircut wasn't going to make you any less upset with me. The love-sick teenager in me thought it might work though," he smiles at me.

"Lovesick hey?" I continue to play with his hair.

"No cure." His tongue runs across his bottom lip as he watches me carefully. "All these years and I never get sick of staring at you."

"You are exceptional at staring," I laugh but a sinking feeling creeps through my insides as I remember the dark look on his face that night.

How different, savage and unhinged he looked staring at me with the red light casting down on all his sharp features. I realize there was a moment in time when I was scared of him, maybe I hadn't admitted it then but I could now.

"Sometimes I feel so empty, so void of everything but rage. Then I look at you, and realize that something, somewhere deemed me worthy of you." He swallows hard, a devastating look fills his eyes turning the blue so vivid I can see myself in the reflection of the pools.

"Nothing about you is empty," I whisper. "I can feel every part of you."

I press his hand to the skin above my breast. I close my eyes, letting him feel the thumping in my chest, "I fear no matter what you do in life, you'll always be the reason my heart beats so fast Bishop," I sigh. "Just don't break it again, I don't think I'll live through it a second time."

24

S inking into his mouth, I knit my fingers through the long strands of dark hair down the nape of his neck, feeling him melt in my arms. I glide them down his back before sliding them around his waist, hugging him to me.

My injuries are a million miles away, the pain in my pelvis has subsided and only a soft throb remains in my leg. The cast had finally been removed and I felt so free after being trapped in the hospital for months after the accident.

I kiss him everywhere, along his sharp jaw, down his neck, behind his ear coming back for his lips between each one. He doesn't rush to move inside me, closing his eyes instead. I hold his head and graze my lips over his eyelids pressing my mouth softly. Taking a long painful moment to savor him.

His forehead falls against mine. I stare down between us, as he enters me, his mouth hovering an inch from mine. I know he's watching me, he's still scared. Terrified that any wrong move will break me. I should be angry with him, furious for everything that's happened but when he holds me like this. When we fuck slow and quiet in the dark hours of the night I forget everything he's ever done, all the wrong things he's said. More importantly, the things he hasn't had the courage to say.

Only the sound of heavy breathing fills the air as he finishes, *falling weighted against my chest. "Bishop you have to stop this," I say but he doesn't respond. "Not talking to me, it's immature and unhealthy."*

His blue eyes are stark against the darkness. He bites his lip and pulls back from me, his naked chest still moving rapidly. He grabs his dark shirt and pulls it over his head, fixing his long hair behind his ears with his hands. He doesn't say a word.

"Fine," I scoff, shaking my hair loose from the ponytail that restrained it. "If you want to walk around silent and like a ghost. Not talking to anyone, at least talk to me. I deserve to hear your voice Bishop, this is cruel."

He stops short of leaving the room, he's been walking away more than ever. The usual arguments have turned sour and lengthy, as I fight to get him to talk to me. Scream, throw things, get mad. Anything. I am instead met with more silence.

I climb from bed, stumbling on my sore and weak leg. He catches me before I fall and his jaw is so tightly wired shut I can hear the teeth grinding together. "You can't even walk," he mumbles. His voice after weeks of silence is a breath of fresh air; it doesn't even matter how angry he sounds. "I feel like a ghost, Nora. I can't walk around with your pity weighing over me. You should be furious but instead, you're... sad for me? I don't understand it."

"I am mad at you, I'm furious and frustrated that you won't talk to me about the accident. I'm sitting alone here, on the deck, on the beach. All alone trying to make sense of what happened without your help. So I am mad," I say, pushing away from his grip. The dizzy feeling passes quickly and I am able to support myself properly.

"Will you tell me what happened the night of the accident?" I ask him, his bare chest stands over the counter, his back turned to me. All the muscles in his shoulders and arms contract when I ask, his body going rigid. "I just," I stop and sigh. "I keep having memories of things that happened after but I can't remember that day."

"Can we leave it like that?" Bishop asks without turning around. His voice is strained and hung between us in the air. "It's not an easy day to talk about."

"None of this is easy Bishop," I scoff and he turns around to face me.

"I don't want to talk about that." The tone of his voice changes, it's no longer soft and understanding. It's demanding, it's the voice he used on the phone when he was talking to Scott.

I don't respond, I just pick at the fruit he cut for me. I push it around my plate, my eyes downcast because if I look at him, I may just lose it. The plate shifts away from me and his fingers grip my chin, he tilts my head up so I'll look at him.

"Take the good days, Nora. They weren't all like that." He searches my eyes. "Eventually you'll remember everything that happened that night and remember those feelings, so forgive me if I'm reveling in what little time I'm being given to make it up to you."

"I've forgiven a lot Bishop," I say with his fiery grip still holding true.

"I'm not talking about that day, anything else but I won't make you relive that." He snaps, his grip tightening. "That day was the worst day of my life."

I don't say anything about his grip, I settle into it instead. "I'm going to find out regardless, so you either tell me yourself. Or live with me resenting you for not having the courage to tell me yourself. It doesn't matter what happened that day, I forgave you for it once. What matters right now is you

180

hiding behind this opportunity, what did you say? Revel in what little time you have. Stop making the same mistakes you made when we were younger, stop pretending you have this open door policy and will tell me everything. Just talk to me."

"Sean is coming to get you," he says pulling his hand away, I tilt my head in question. The skin on my chin burns from his touch, aching for him, not in spite of him. "You have a dress fitting in town for the wedding."

"Why aren't you taking me?" I question him. I know better than to push his ignorance of the story, he'll have to tell me eventually. I was starting to think something worse happened that night, something nobody wanted to admit to me.

"Despite being here the company will not run itself, I have meetings this afternoon I need to take care of or I'll be forced to return to Japan sooner than I would like." He answers as honestly as he can.

"Why do you still run the company if you hate it, Bishop?" I ask. Genuine curiosity fills me, I want to know everything about him.

"Because we're adults now," he laughs. "Adults do crap they don't want to do all the time."

"That's not true," I say sadly, "Ben told me I plan major musical events, I wish I could remember that. It sounds like a dream come true."

"You were very good at it, every event you've ever planned was amazing." Bishop smiles and sets a fresh cup of coffee in front of me.

"How many did you attend?" I take a sip of the warm caffeine and smile into the cup.

"All of them." Bishop sets the coffee carafe back on its warmer.

A soft knock on the door drags my eyes from his and to the screen where Sean stood. His hair is flipped back, he was wearing a thin gray shirt and a red over shirt. His smile is bright when he looks at me, I smile back and slide off the stool.

"Good morning," I say, opening the door to him. He leans against it, his arms crossed over his chest. I turn back to see if Bishop is going to say hello, but he's disappeared from the kitchen. "One step at a time I guess."

"I brought you some clean clothes," he hands me a bag. I look down at the oversize shirt I'm wearing bare-legged. "Are you ready to rejoin society?"

"I am," I say quietly, "not sure about him though."

"He'll be okay, let him pull away for a week and he'll be following you like a puppy dog soon enough. He just adjusts differently than you or me to confrontation." Sean assures me. I take the bag back to the room where Bishop is pulling on clean clothes. A pressed black button-down that he leaves unbuttoned around his collar.

He runs a small amount of gel through his hair pushing the growing lengths back against his scalp until they all sit nicely in place. He turns when I enter, his sharp aquamarine eyes staring back at me. "I'll come back to the beach house tomorrow when I'm done with all my work."

I roll my eyes throwing the bag on the bed, "Bishop," I turn to him as he begins to tuck his dress shirt into a pair of clean pressed black slacks. "Don't come back until you're ready, to be honest with me."

"I thought I was being honest with you?" He leans back against the dresser with a heavy sigh.

"It's half-assed and you know it. You're being honest when it

182

suits you," I say, pulling my shirt over my head, but the collar gets stuck on my jaw. His fingers find the hem and pull it gently away from my skin until the shirt is free. "Thank you."

He nods and steps back again, he licks his lips and runs a heavy hand over the back of his neck. "I could be mad about this but it's nice to see you getting back to yourself," he grimaces.

"What's that supposed to mean?" I snap, pulling a clean shirt on by myself this time. I slink into a pair of tight jeans and pull clean socks over my feet.

"I just miss bossy, Nora. She knows what she wants, it's sexy." I glare up at him through my lashes and he chuckles.

"I'm serious," I threw his dirty shirt back at him and left the bedroom.

"Ready?" I brush my fingers through my hair and toss it into a ponytail. Brushing past Sean as I exit the house, Bishop says something to him but I'm too far away to catch it. Sean shakes his head as he opens the truck door for me.

"Up you get," Sean's hand presses into my lower back. "You're lucky Willa called me. How were you going to get home?"

The lights of the pier flicker in the wind, a storm is coming. I knew full well I shouldn't be out here but there was a force that pulled me back to the beach during storms like this. I could have let the hurricane take me away without another thought, the wind and rain would wash away all the awful feelings.

"God damnit Nora!" Sean yells as he slams his own door. He never yells it's not in his nature but his eyes burn into me. A wave of nausea comes over me and I'm forced to open the door again as quickly as I can to puke onto the road below me. "What were you thinking?" He says, holding out a napkin when I finally pull myself back into the car.

"I missed the smell of the beach," I say without remorse.

"There are plenty of times you could have visited, during a category two hurricane is not one of those!" He slams his hand against the steering wheel. "The road off the island is closed, you're going to have to stay in the house. It's boarded up well enough, we can stay there tonight and ride out the storm."

"No," I say turning on him finally, his eyes are furious as they bore into me. "No Sean, I can't stay there. Can't you take me home?" I beg, the words that come out of my mouth are pleading. Groveling.

"It's too late Nora," he shakes his head. "You should have thought about that before you came up here alone and got too plastered to drive home yourself."

"Sean, I would rather drown in the ocean a thousand times than sit in that suffocating house for even five minutes. You can't make me." I cry, tears streaming down my face.

"We don't have an option Nora, it's the only house boarded up. You're just going to have to deal with your feelings for the night." He starts the truck, pulling away from the pier and driving back towards the house.

It looms, I can feel the emotions crawling up and out of me. Ripping apart my insides, my heart is in shreds, ribbons of what it used to be. He opens the door, soaking wet it had started to pour on the drive back. His blonde hair had been cropped short for the academy, it made him look so old. He pulled the wood off the front door, pulling out his keys and letting me inside first.

"There should be clothes upstairs in your room," He says, handing me a flashlight. "Get out of those wet ones." He carefully re-boards the front door and throws his keys in the bowl by the front door.

The stairs creak under my weight as I make my way up in the dark, and my phone buzzes in my back pockets.

Excuse me?
Did you drive to the beach house in a fucking hurricane?
Are you mental?

I shake my head at Natalie's text and shove the phone back into my pocket, it was none of her business. She didn't want to deal with me anymore anyways. She had her lover, Ben, and they were happy and getting married.

The door to my room creaked open as if it hadn't been touched in years. I shudder at the thought of trying to control my breathing. If I didn't I may just puke everywhere. The walls were lined with photos, concert stubs, movie tickets, and fairy lights that didn't work anymore. I sighed, touching the quilt on my bed, the fabric still soft and inviting.

I hate it here.

Every single photo, the tickets, and fabrics. Even the smell of the room, musty and dark, his smell and presence lingered inside. "I hate that you are still here." I curl onto the bed, not bothering to change the damp clothes. I bring my knees up to my stomach and sob softly into the pillow I lay my head on. After a while the bed dips and silently Sean wraps himself behind me, pushing the wet hair away from my red cheeks.

"You'll be okay," he whispers in my ear. "Just sleep it off."

"You can't sleep off this kind of pain, Sean. It doesn't work like that." I mumble between sniffles.

"Just this once, let it." He nuzzles his forehead against my back. "Just this once."

25

"Bishop was different after the accident. He—." Sean pauses and turns onto the main highway. "It was a turning point for him. He wasn't that kid we met in the diner anymore. He was this empty shell of what we grew up with."

"But I forgave him?" I say flipping the hem of my shirt through my fingers over and over again. I missed my violin, playing music to drown out how I felt.

"Instantly, you were in a coma for a week and the first thing you said when you woke up is, 'where's Bishop?'" Sean shakes his head. "Because you forgave him, we forgave him just the same but I don't think he ever believed you. No matter how many times you tried to convince him something had snapped that day in him. Seeing you so close to death because of him, changed who he was."

"I wish he would talk to me about it," I say as Sean pulls into town.

"I hope he never does." He sighs and I turn my head to look at him. "And not to protect you. To protect him. I saw him that day, I was behind you on the road. I can't talk about it, and he was—" he stops and turns off the engine in front of the small dress shop. "He had picked you up, hobbling on a twisted ankle. His shoulder was ripped to shreds but he was walking. He was going to carry you to the hospital. I had to force him to put you down so the paramedics could help you."

"I'm sorry. I don't mean to put you through that again. I'll stop asking about that." I say with a small sigh.

"Let him come to you," Sean smiles, and I can see the pain flicker across his stern, handsome features. "He always goes home when he's ready. Sometimes it just takes him a little longer to get there."

"Wise words for a man who failed English more than he passed it." I joke.

"I don't think you're remembering that correctly." He laughs and climbs from the truck. He opens the door for me and I hop out onto the pavement below me softly.

"I have a surprise for you!" He says, extending his hand to me, a boyish smile on his face. "There are some people that missed you, and I know you may not remember them well but they wanted to come to see you. Hopefully, it stirs something in there," he taps the side of my hand with his free hand.

A beautiful-looking woman sits in the window of the coffee shop, her fingers tangled around a teacup and a bright smile on her pale face. Her auburn hair is tucked into a messy ponytail and she talks to the man sitting across from her. He catches my gaze, his dark brown eyes lighting up when he sees me. He gives a small wave as we move to the door.

"Willa, and Nick. You lived with them for a long time in Atlanta. Went to school with Willa, she's your best friend... you know besides me." Sean winks, opening the door for me. The coffee shop smells like roasted beans and cinnamon, and baked goods line the glass display cases around the counter. Workers wearing black aprons work like bees behind the black counter as people order off the large wall-spanning, a chalkboard that hangs above them.

"I'll get you a coffee, go say hi." Sean nudges me towards them, Nick stands instantly wrapping his arms around me so tightly I almost stop breathing.

"Man we missed you," he whispers in my ear as he pulls away to pull the chair out for me, "Sean told us you don't really remember us. It's okay, we're not completely offended."

"Nick," Willa shakes her head and gives me a pitiful smile. "He's always an idiot, you'll get used to it, or remember soon I guess. I'm sorry, this is hard. I'm being awkward aren't I?" She takes a sip of her tea to stop herself from saying more.

"We heard Bishop is back," Nick says, taking a bite of what looks like a strawberry danish.

"Nicholas!" Willa spits hot tea all over the table, furiously wiping it up with her napkin. "I'm sorry, oh god."

"Willa!" He scoffs back, "so details? What the hell happened?" He sits back in his chair, as Willa continues to clean the table nervously.

"I fell out of a tree?" I look at him awkwardly, "and now I can't remember half my life." He laughs at me, it's warm and chaotic as he throws his head back.

"At least you didn't lose your personality on the ride down?" He jokes. "Where does the dark horse come into all of this?"

"Dark horse?" I laugh nervously, and Willa rolls her eyes.

"He calls Bishop, the dark horse. He's trying to be funny," she sneers. "But seriously, did you know he would be here?"

"I had no idea from what I could tell, I guess I started the fire in the tree house. I did this to myself and now I'm stuck trying to remember everything. Half the time I can't control when I remember something and I come to completely unaware that

I've just been staring into the distance like an idiot for twenty minutes." Sean sets a large mug of warm coffee in front of me, the smell of freshly steamed milk and caramel wafting up into my face.

"It's pretty adorable, to be honest, she goes all deer in headlights." Sean widens his eyes and pretends to look shocked. I roll my eyes and slap his chest with the back of my hand. "How are things in Atlanta?"

"Her plants aren't dead yet, so that's a plus," Willa says quietly, even though I couldn't remember who they were, they had been taking care of all my things while I was away.

"Josh has been a handful since she's been indisposed."

"Is Josh my cat?" I ask and they all break into laughter.

"Josh is your boss." Nick says, "you're the thing that holds that company together. It's been difficult to organize everything without your help but we're managing. Oddly enough a week after the accident, your laptop was couriered to the office, with the password and all the files and contact information for the party was on it. All we had to do was make sure everything was paid for basically."

"My laptop just showed up at the office and neither of you questioned it?" I chuckle nervously.

"It was weird but we figured maybe you or Ben had sent it along." Nick shrugs.

"Yeah maybe," I say, either way, I'm glad that it had been taken care of. I sip on my coffee and let them tell me stories. I had lived a whole life with them, away from the beach house and away from my family. It was hard to understand because my brain was stuck at being fifteen and never wanting to leave the beach for anything. But I had been happy in Atlanta, I had friends and a job. I had a home and I was happy.

"What about this one?" Willa steps out of my closet with a slinky sheer black dress hanging over her body. I shake my head wrinkling my nose at her. "Do you know how hard it's been to get his attention? It's like he doesn't even have human, male emotions. It's like talking to a computer most days."

"Jarvis likes you, I don't think you need to show him that much skin to get a response. Just be yourself, Willa." I laugh as she disappears back into the closet.

"Have you talked to Sean?" She asks her voice a muffled holler. "He called me yesterday, he sounded pretty upset."

"Great, now he's calling you too." I lay my head back against the couch and close my eyes. "I was so drunk and I wasn't thinking straight but it's Sean..." I groan.

"And?" she reappears wearing a tight red dress that comes to her knees. I clap my hands in approval and she curtsies like the dork she is. "Do you want it to happen again?" She asks while sitting next to me on the couch, she pulls my head into her lap and brushes her fingers through my hair.

"Every time I close my eyes I see his face," I sigh, "how he looked at me when I opened the door that night. A flicker of sadness, just a momentary glance at me that screamed defeat. Like he had lost the game he was playing but I don't know the rules, I've never known the rules..." I almost cry but she shushes me.

"Oh Nora, he doesn't even know the rules." She stares down at me, sweet, caring, and protective Willa. "I have to tell you something," she smiles softly, "it wasn't just the last event. He's been at every single one since you started with Josh. He's never missed an event, he's always on the list."

"That's impossible, I would have seen him sooner," I say sitting up and staring at her in shock.

"It's not, up until now he hasn't wanted you to see him so you *don't. I think he wanted you to see him this time, Nora, it's the first time he's ever brought a woman to one of these things." Willa plays with the necklace around her neck.*

"Why didn't you ever tell me?" I say, trying not to overreact.

"Because being unaware wasn't hurting you but him being there was torturing him. It seemed like fitting justice to the man who broke your heart. Nora, you haven't slept with another man until Sean, ever. Not even in college, and he shows up the night you go home with Sean? You go home with him once a week, you never sleep together but from the outside eye you would assume you were." She sighs and shakes her head. "I just think there's more to the story than just him breaking your heart. There's more going on. Did I think maybe eventually he would talk to you? But what happened last week was not how I imagined that going."

'There was more going on.'

Willa had already been figuring things out before I could have. She had seen the connection between Sean and Bishop before I could wrap my head around their deal.

"I need to speak with you," I say, snapping from my trance. He swallows hard but nods his head. "We'll be right back, order me another coffee. I want to hear about Jarvis…" Willa smiles widely, her cheeks turning a bright red but she nods and stands up to go to the counter as we make our way outside.

"You called him that day," I say, "was it before or after we had sex?"

He looks like I've slapped him across the face. "Answer me," I snap when he doesn't say a single word for far too long.

"Before." He groans, "I called him after Nick called me to come to get you from the pub."

"What did you say to him?" I demand.

"Nora," he growls under his breath like a warning but I tilt my head and wait. "Don't make me repeat this, it's..." he stops.

"It's about me, and I deserve to hear what you said to him because whatever it was he came running like he never has before." I step forward into his space. "What did you say to him, I won't ask you again Sean."

"I called him to ask what he was doing showing up like that with another woman, he couldn't answer me straight and I got upset. I told him you were drinking yourself into another coma because of him and he wouldn't respond." Sean grumbles.

"All the things you've said to him before and he never responds never comes home. So what else happened?" I demand.

"I got angry and started telling him all the ways you like to be fucked, Nora. That's the only way I ever got a response out of him. Was to remind him that it wasn't his job to do those things to him anymore. It was mine. Are you happy now? I feel like an asshole enough already." He clears his throat.

"Willa will drive me home," he stares at me when I say it, but I'm serious and don't say anything else before walking back into the coffee shop.

He stands outside the window as I sit back in the chair, his blue eyes burning into me glossed over and red. Willa stares at me uncomfortable but I just keep looking out the window at him until he gets the hint and leaves. Nick stands to go after him and I let him.

"What the hell was that?" She asks me.

"You were right," I sigh. "They've always been a team, there was always more to the story."

She looks from me to where Nick talks to Sean on the sidewalk, "Sean?" She looks back at me. "Oh my god. The night Bishop showed up, he called him, didn't he?"

"Yeah he did," I swallow hard.

26

"You looked amazing tonight," he says to me, spinning me around. The fabric of the thin white sundress I wore lifted and danced in the breeze around my thighs. He pulls the bobby pins keeping my long hair back out and lets it free around my shoulders. "You are the moon and the stars Nora Quinn, don't ever forget that."

I kiss him, dragging my hands along the sharp curves of his jaw line until he tugs back and away from me. "You've had quite a bit to drink tonight." He muses playing with a loose strand of hair, he takes the half-empty wine glass from me and sets it on the table beside his bed.

He pulls me into his arms, pressing his hands firmly against my ass, and pulls my legs up around his hips until I am firmly in place and he makes his way towards his balcony doors. Outside he's laid blankets on the ground, pillows, and a small glowing lamp.

He sets me down, his blue eyes watchful and slow as he rolls them down my body. I push the straps of the dress off and let it fall to the ground. The stars above us are the only witness to my bare skin and the wild smile on his face.

A low growl leaves his lips as he closes the gap and plants two simple but painfully slow kisses against either side of my collarbone. He kneels, falling back onto the nest of blankets, and removes the *dark dress shirt he had worn that night. His eyes sparkle as I take in the site of his hardened chest and tanned skin, and his arms flexing as he rests them behind his head on a pillow.*

"Come here before the neighbors see a naked girl standing on the balcony." He beckons with a laugh and takes my hand. Pulling me down into the covered half of the fenced-in deck. I straddle across him, already feeling him growing hard between my legs as I lean in for another taste of his mouth.

He moans as I push my hips back and down against the fabric that restrains him. He pulls me in for a feverish, hungry kiss that pulls against my bottom lip. His eyes came to meet mine alight with fire and passion. "You know I love you, right?" he whispers against my neck, leaving small, delicate kisses in his wake.

"You'll have to show me how much," I tease, pulling back, grinding against him again, causing him to growl and grab me. He flips us over, laying me on my back. My hair sprays out across the pillows and he stares down at me like he's never seen anything more beautiful.

He kisses me again, hovering so close to my lips I'm sure I can taste them from proximity alone. I angle up for another but he dodges, placing one on my collarbone and then another against the soft skin of my breast. Taking the nipple in his mouth he sucks until my hips rise from the blanket in protest, a moan leaving my lips. He trails down, cupping the sore nipple, rubbing the pad of his thumb against it to soothe the tender skin as he leaves more kisses against my bare stomach.

"I owe you, I believe." He says his tongue flickering over his thick bottom lip, a wicked smile forms on his lips. Spreading my legs apart, he puts one over his shoulder and presses his face down against my thigh. He bites the inside delicately, biting and kissing until he's so close to me I can barely handle the teasing. I wiggle

against him but he presses his palm against my stomach holding me still as he tortures me.

He smiles against me, his lips curling up against my skin as he runs two fingers along the soft skin of my core. He moans as he slides within, "Nora," he growls, it's so wet his fingers pump in and out without resistance. Bishop leans down, licking long, torturous stripes along my center while he continues to move in and out with his fingers.

Just as my stomach fills with warmth and screams for more he pulls his face away, looking up at me the moon catches his eyes and ignites them. I run my fingers roughly through his hair, tugging at the ends, forcing him to look at me as he moves his tongue back to my clit. My back arches against the blankets, rising without control as the feeling overwhelms me.

Coming undone he pumps his fingers harder as I moan out, "Oh god, Bishop don't stop." I push against his hands hoping for him to get deeper somehow as the sparks take control of my insides. When my body finally relaxes, he sits back admiring my exhaustion, and places both fingers in his mouth. Licking them clean while watching the rise and fall of my breasts.

He stands and strips the pants he was still wearing over his hips. His dick springs free, long, thick, and deliciously ready for what would come next. "Is this how you like me? Exposed?" He growls looking around at the surrounding beach houses. All their lights are off but the thrill of someone seeing us rushes through me.

He towers over me on his knees now, lazily stroking himself. I prop myself up on my elbow and run a hand along the thick muscles of his thighs, up and around his ass, and along the rail of hair that leads to the base of his hardened cock.

I replace his hand, stroking him with purpose until his hands are gripping the sides of the balcony railings so tightly they shake under his hold. He stops me, "I'm too close," he growls leaning down. "I want to be inside of you."

He hovers over me again, lining himself up with my entrance, and finally, he pushes into me while holding myself against the railing above me. The feeling of him inside of me forces me to shut my eyes. I let go of the metal railing and ran my nails down his back, crying out in pleasure as he stretched me around him.

"You like that?" he says with a hard shove inside, causing me to cry out his name again as he forces himself roughly inside over and over. "You feel amazing."

He slips an arm under my back lifting me to his chest and rocks into me again. Each pulse a little farther and faster until he has set a fast pace of deep thrusts in and out of my soaking wet center. His hair falls, wet and sweaty from the pony that had kept it neatly swept back most of the night. It hangs in his face, his eyes closed, and he moans, and growls above me.

"I want it all Bishop," I moan as he sits back on his knees, pulling me up into his lap. He grabs hold of my hips in a vice grip and slams himself as far as he can inside of me.

His cock throbbing in heavy pulses. His free hand rubs the soft upper skin of my clit as he groans against me. "Keep going, I want you to cum with me again."

A second orgasm crashes over me, my pussy spasming around him as he comes undone fully in waves of growls and moans. He grabs hold of me again, thrusting harder until I could feel the hot sticky liquid of his cum running around me, down his shaft, and onto his thighs.

"Bishop," I whisper between ragged breaths.

"Shh, I pulled out in time." He pressed a quick kiss to my lips, but I'm still nervous that he hadn't done it in time. His eyes held mine, sure of what he said and he kissed me again. "Are you alright?"

"I'm perfect," I say, leaning my forehead against his.

"Hey," Bishop stands in the doorway of my room, his bare arms crossed against his chest. It's the middle of August now, we only have a few weeks left before the wedding. It took him a while to return to the house but I couldn't have been happier to see him.

"You're up early," I give him a soft smile and lift the covers enough for him to get the hint that I want him to join me. The smell of fresh rain, musk, and wood wash over me as he wraps his arms around me just under my chest. He nuzzles his face into the crook of my neck and takes a deep breath.

"I've been working on something," he whispers. I lean back into his chest and let him cuddle a little more. "If you get dressed I'll show you," he kisses the back of my neck gently and my stomach warms up from the soft touch.

"And what if I don't want to get dressed?" I say with a smile. Thinking of the dream I had, how it felt to have him touch me that way. Everything inside of me lit up with desire. We hadn't spoken much since our argument, I was still upset that he wouldn't talk about the night of the accident but a small part of me missed him too much to care.

It's always the same problem I had figured out, missing him always won over his shortcomings and flaws. It didn't matter how much I hated him, I always missed him more.

"As much as I want to stay right here, with you, like this and show you how badly I don't want you dressed. You're going to love this even more," he mumbles and the heat from his breath on my neck makes me swallow hard. He pulls away and opens the dresser beside me as I roll over. He hands me a clean shirt, pants, and warm socks. "It's cold out today."

He carefully lifts the pajama shirt from my body and helps

me shimmy into a bra, clasping it at the back. Each delicate swipe of his fingers against my skin tingles like miniature electric shocks. He pulls the clean shirt over my head and before he buttons my jeans he places a soft kiss on the edge of my underwear line. "You're a tease," I say pulling away from him.

"I haven't had you naked in my bed in a very long time Nora, and the first time I do it again it will not be under your parent's roof with everyone listening." He says it so seriously I get nervous.

"Embarrassed?" I tease, and he shakes his head the dark strands of long hair falling from the top where he has them slicked back.

"No one needs to hear how many times you scream my name, that's for us only." He leans in closely, his eyes drifting to my pouting lips but he doesn't kiss me he just takes my hips and presses me back to the bed. "Feet," he says, putting the thick socks on me one by one.

I know my face is red because I am so hot I'm tempted to take a cold shower before we go anywhere. "Come on," he says, placing a quick kiss on my cheek and taking my hand. He leads me down through the house where mom sits on the island talking to Nat about plans. Dad watches football on the T.V. pretending that Ben is listening to what he's saying. Ben is not watching football, he has his nose in a book and only looks up when he sees us appear from the stairs.

Sean has made himself scarce since the day at the coffee shop, Willa took the guest room and Nick chose to stay with Sean. They were surfing, only their silhouette visible against the rising sun in the water. They bobbed up and down against the waves and I wonder what they were talking about. I know what he said was cruel, it was disrespectful. Not only was my pride and dignity hurt by his actions, but he had also chosen to use me as a pawn to hurt Bishop.

Kate was laying on the beach in a shawl and long pants with a coffee in her hand watching Curtis run the length of the beach. His arms had new tattoos since the last time I saw him, but he was still in decent shape for his age. As much as I hated Kate I was happy for them, they were a good fit, a balance to each other that both of them had gone through a lot to find.

I slip on my shoes at the top of the deck and follow Bishop down through the winding path towards the beach, but he turns off and goes towards where the tree house had sat high in the trees.

"Surprise!" He says pointing up, just off the original placement of the tree house, high in a set of new trees sits a tree house. A new rope ladder leads up the trunk to the middle where a trap door was on the floor.

"Bishop," I gasp, "Did you do this yourself?"

"It's been a hard two weeks but I wanted to make sure that you didn't lose your tree house too, because of me." He says it so nonchalantly, but my heart cracks when he says it's because *of me*.

"I have gained a lot because of you too Bishop, it wasn't all loss," I say squeezing his hand. "This is incredible."

"Up you go," he says, letting go of my hand so I can climb up and into the house. It smells like fresh lumber and paint. The two windows he put on the front, have cute little teal window shutters and flower boxes hanging from them.

The inside is almost exactly how I remember it, "is that a *new*, old couch?" I laugh looking at the pilled blue fabric and deflated cushions.

"It had to be authentic trash, nothing but the finest for my baby doll," He coos from behind me, wrapping his arms around my middle and resting his chin in the crook of my neck. "It's still weird, being this close to you without being afraid of what's behind me." He swallows tightly and I close my eyes letting the sadness pass through me.

"The pictures," I say, finally noticing that the wall facing the couch is plastered with them. As if they are a part of the wood. "I thought they all burned with the original tree house?"

"I had copies made a long time ago before I left." He smiles at them.

"You brought us with you?" I chuckle lightly.

"I did yeah, and now I've brought you all back cause this is where these belong." He touches one of me while I sleep with a sad smile on his face.

"Have you shown the others what you did?" I ask and he shakes his head no into my neck. "You should. They would absolutely love this."

"Alright, I'll go get them then." He says making towards the hole in the floor. "I forgot how much I loved your smile, Nora. Don't lose it again."

27

"Y ou look beautiful," I say, touching the hem of her white dress. It wraps around her chest firmly, holding itself up. The bodice is covered in lace and leads to a flowing white tulle skirt that drags along the floor.

"I feel like a whale," Natalie says, rolling her hand over her swollen tummy. She had grown so big since the beginning of the summer. "She's sucking the life out of me and now I'm going to look fat on my wedding day."

"She's perfect," I whisper to her tummy, "and you look like a goddess."

Her red hair is curly and is half up in a messy bun the rest falls around her face in soft bounces and twists. Her makeup is subtle and highlights the gentle green in her eyes. "I know this isn't fancy or expensive but I have something for you."

I had her a small box, she lifted the lid and inside is an exact replica of the ugly blue friendship bracelets we wove each other when we were younger. She gave me a soft smile, pulling the thin aquamarine thread from the box. She holds out her wrist, allowing me to wrap it around and tie it at the back.

"Thank you, Nora," she kisses my cheek and plays with the bracelet, rolling it around her wrist slowly and methodically.

"Will you be alright today? I know this is going to be overwhelming for you."

"I'll be fine, I should go get into my dress before mom freaks out again about being late. I'll meet you downstairs." I smile, pressing my fingers to hers in passing. Trying to reassure her that everything will be perfect, just like she's always wanted.

My green dress hangs in the window, staring at me ominous like a dark cloud over the day. The two bow tie boxes sit on the dresser, I knew they would come for them eventually but I was given time to think about it for now. I slip on the green, velvet dress, the straps coming up over my shoulders and settling into the skin comfortably. I fit like a glove.

The fabric hugged around my waist, fit snugly under my breasts, and pushed them up to provide more cleavage than is actually there. "You look hot," Willa appears from the bathroom, her identical dress fitting her similarly but in a deep maroon color that compliments the copper colors in her hair. It hangs loosely around her face, subtly done with makeup and paired with a pair of gorgeous diamond earrings. "Presents from the man himself," she hands me a box, the tag reads *for my little sister, love Ben.*

She helps me zip up the side of my dress and holds my hair back as I slide the beautiful square earrings into my lobes. A knock at the door startles us from our routine and she floats over to open it.

Sean stands in a crisp dark blue suit, tailored perfectly to his broad shoulders and fitted waist. His shoes are brown leather and his cuffs are linked with fancy diamonds much like our earrings. Another gift from Ben. Willa looks back at me, "you want me to stay?"

"No it's okay," I say quietly, my eyes not wandering from the icy blue ones that glare back at me. His jaw is as tense as his shoulders but he relaxes a touch when Willa nods, she kisses him softly on the cheek as she slides from the room leaving us alone.

"You look beautiful," he says as she leaves, he walks into the bedroom and stops by the dresser. "Your mom sent me up for the ties."

"Thank you and yeah they're right here." I stare at the boxes, two ties, two colors, and one massive decision to make.

Sean reaches for the maroon one before I even have a chance to really think about it, making the choice clear and easy for me. He touches the fabric of the bow and pulls it out of the box. "Will you help me?" he asks politely and I nod.

I move in close to him, my fingers carefully flip up the brim of his white dress shirt and loop the bow around the back clasping it at the base of his neck. I move closer, onto my tip toes so I can make sure the back is neatly pressed back into place.

"I'm sorry for what I did," he apologized. His hand comes along the small of my back holding me close to him, the smell of his hair gel tingles my nose and makes me want to sneeze. "I shouldn't have ever sunk to his level."

"Sean," I do all but scoff, his name leaving my lips as an annoyance. "When you are ready to apologize and mean it, come find me." I step back forcibly from his grip and push my hand against his chest to move him back as well.

"He's got you wrapped around his finger, Nora but when you realize that he's hiding all these dark little secrets from you," he paused, his jaw ticking in frustration. "You'll need me again, just like you always do. The difference this time is I won't answer the call."

204

"I was never the one calling you Sean, it was always someone else, you were just always the one that came running." My anger is boiling over with him, he's mad at me but I do not deserve his wraith. Not today. Not ever. "Stop acting as if I owe you something," I growl.

"You're lying to yourself," he shakes his head, and the blonde hairs bounce around as he paces. "You may not remember the worst of it, but you will and it will destroy you." He snarls at me, his face so close to mine that our noses touch. "I refuse to watch that again."

"Do not ruin my sister's wedding today, act like an adult." I snap and point to the door. He takes the hint and leaves.

The room feels so large when he leaves, as though he was the only thing taking up any space. Stealing all the air from my lungs, I feel so dizzy and light-headed.

"Hey, hey!" Bishop rushes into the room, his hands all over me, and eases me into the chair behind me. "Breathe, ready?" he says and his voice is muffled in my head. "One," his voice is sturdy, I take a deep breath in and out. "Two," he continued and I took another one, the feeling coming back to my toes. Darkness surges at my eyesight, fading out and giving me a clear picture of Bishop kneeling in front of me.

"Three," he rubs his thumb on my jaw and waits for me to steady before standing back up and giving me space. "You alright?"

"It was just a panic attack, nervous is all. You look so handsome," I say taking him in finally, his suit fits much the same as Sean's. Perfectly tailored to his shape and navy blue. His hair is pushed back, slick over the top of his head in a small bun at the back of his crown.

"This for me?" he asks, sliding the emerald bow tie from

YOU LEFT US IN GEORGIA

the box, I nod slowly and watch him put it on in the mirror. He holds his hand out to me, waiting patiently for me to take it and when I do he lifts me back to my feet. "You are pure radiance in this color," he stands me in front of the mirror. Admiring me from behind. "We should get going, your mother is a very impatient woman."

"Nora," Bishop pauses before we leave the room. "Are you sure you're okay, you're shaking?"

"I'll be alright, just nervous," I lied to his face. Inside I am panicking, the conversation with Sean has left me rattled and unnerved. Bishop's blue eyes meet with mine and my breath slows a touch, my heart beating at a normal pace again.

"Just hang on tight, I won't let you fall." He winks, putting his arm out for me to link into.

"Alright Bartley, let's do this."

The beach is lined with white chairs and filled to the brim with bodies. Willa waits in the kitchen with Sean and Ben, both fidgeting with their hair and suits. I pause in the stairwell and Bishop turns back to check on me, "Something happened," he implied. "Are you going to tell me or make me guess?"

"It was just a stupid fight with Sean, it's done now," I answer honestly and he narrows his eyes at me in question, *is that really everything?* They ask silently, his jaw clenched and his hand blocking my path gripped tightly to the banister. "It's done. It's time to celebrate."

Bishop holds my hand as the music starts, ushering Ben to his place at the front of the crowd. A huge arch, made of wood and flowers is draped with luscious rich fabrics that stand out so stark against the soft sandy beach and baby blue sky.

We stand and watch Natalie come down with my father, a smile plastered on her face and the wind in her hair. Everyone turns to watch her, in awe of her beauty and the grace she uses to float down the aisle towards us. My father hands her over to Ben with a quick kiss and takes his place. Bishop winks at me from across the gap standing behind Sean who glares at me, through me, like I'm the ghost haunting him.

The commissioner talks for what seems like forever, reminding the crowd that love is work, love is respect, and a lifelong challenge that you had to be committed to for it to work. Ben pulls a ratty-looking folded paper from his breast pocket, his shaky hands taking care to open it.

"I didn't always have the words to tell you how much I cared for you when we were younger. They usually got stuck in my throat like sand anytime I tried to express how beautiful you were when the sun catches the strawberry color of my hair. Or how brilliant you are when you figure out all the small details of a movie before it's even really started." He stops and looks up from the paper at her. "I wish I could say that I outgrew being a nervous teenager around you, but standing here in front of you now and how astonishing you look today. I'm just as tongue-tied as the first time you spoke to me."

I can tell Nat is crying by the way her shoulders heave gently. Dad shuffles forward and hands her his handkerchief before finding his place beside mom again. She doesn't have paper, or anything written down. Her shoulders rise and fall in a long well-timed breath to steady herself before she begins.

"I was an idiot," the crowd laughs and she turns to them, "no really, I was. I," she pauses, and a soft chuckle leaves her lips. "I spent so long wandering around this beach trying to get people to pay attention to me. I cared too much about how I looked, how I dressed, and who was staring at me. Ben always saw me. He knew who I was before I even realized it and he guarded that secret until I was ready to be that person. I have no doubts that in this life and the next, he'll be the man to take care of me because he was put here to save me. I love you," she whispers.

I look over from her expression and see Bishop staring at me, his eyes a bright blue under the beaming sun. He doesn't move his lip, they stay pressed into a warm smile, but I can feel him reach across the distance and wrap his words around me like a blanket. *I love you in this life and the next.*

"I believe that makes you husband and wife," the man says, breaking my eye contact. Ben and Natalie tangle together as they kiss for the first time as a pair. They break apart and lead the rest of us back up to the house where fairy lights cover every inch of the deck and awning. The tables are dressed with white linens and dark plates, just how Nat wanted them.

Everyone danced, sang, and partied late into the night. Most of the old family friends poked at me, asking me questions that would be rude for me not to answer. So I did. Over and over, how are you? How's your head? Do you remember me? Can you imagine losing all your memories? Must be hard, and oh you poor thing. My head hurt from the prodding, they didn't actually care. They just wanted the town gossip.

It made it worse having Sean's eyes follow me around the deck, I slipped away from the noise and found myself on the beach. "Hey gorgeous," Nick comes up behind me with a drink, I shake my head no but he extends it anyways. "It's just water."

"Thank you," I took it from him, coating my throat. I hadn't realized how thirsty I was until I downed the entire glass. "Thanks for not asking how I am, I'm so sick of that question."

"I don't need to ask, you have that *'Nora needs a minute'* scowl on. Are you cold?" He asks and I shake my head, my skin feels like it's on fire even with the cool summer breeze blowing across the sand. "Sean is pretty rattled about what happened."

"Did he send you down here to play advocate?" I ask not to turn my head to look at Nick, I focus on the soft lapping of water over the shore as the sun dips beyond the horizon.

"No he did not, he just won't shut the fuck up about it, or you." Nick laughs and looks up behind us to the deck where Sean stands pretending to be busy in conversation when really he has one eye on his back. "He made some mistakes Nora, we all do. Bishop has made more than anyone. I think all he expects is that same allowance for fuck-ups."

"Bishop may have done questionable things, but he never spoke about me like a possession, not the way Sean did. He didn't use me to hurt Sean and get under his skin. What he said to Bishop that night was disrespectful and instead of apologizing earlier he jumped down my throat." I shake my head, playing with the soft velvet fabric at my waist.

"I think he's scared Nora," his fingers are cool against my bare shoulder, "you're his best friend and he's running all these worst-case scenarios through his little jock brain that you don't want to be like that anymore. Bottom line, he doesn't care that you chose Bishop. He cares that it's put him on the outside again after so long is the only thing you had."

"I thought you were supposed to be the goofy one between you and Willa. No one warned me you were some kind of Yoda." I roll my eyes and lean into his side as he wraps his arm around my shoulders fully. "You're right though. I think one more night of guilt will do him some good. I'll talk with him tomorrow."

"Atta girl," Nick chuckles. "Josh has been asking once a

day minimum when you'll be returning, so you call me when you're ready and the job is still yours." He bumps his head softly against mine before disappearing back up the stairs to where Sean stands rigid with anxiety and waiting for the worst news possible.

Nick pats his shoulder after some time and leaves him to be alone again. Staring down at me, our eyes meet and for the first time in a week, he gives me a soft, hopeful smile.

28

"Hey you," he whispers, his breath tangling in my loose hair. He presses against my back, a shiver runs up my back, the blood rushing to my cheeks. I let him hold me together, hip to hip I lean back and relax just for a moment.

"Hey," I smile, the smell of his cologne washing over me.

He dares wrap his arms around my waist, pulling me closer. The pleasure is intoxicating, I can feel my skin tingling. I can see Sean watching us. His eyes thread through the crowd of participants dancing like a needle. I let my eyes fall shut, for a moment I just want to forget I'm angry with him. I want to forget his guilt-casting blue eyes and his tight chest every time I walk by him.

"How are you doing? There are a lot of people here who think you owe it to them to remember their faces and names. It must be overwhelming," he sighs into the crook of my neck.

"I told Mr. Abottsford, to take a hike after he tried to grab my ass," I tilt my head back. Laughter shakes his body, rich and indulgent.

"They're all watching me as I might explode," I sigh, "maybe I will eventually but I definitely will with them all staring at me like I'm a ticking time bomb."

He touches me lightly, his thumb rubbing against the stomach of my soft velvet dress. "They're not watching you, not tonight." He touches my cheek and takes a sharp breath. "I've gotten too comfortable and they're worried I'm going to cause trouble."

I turn to him, and his sad eyes tell a thousand stories. I look away quickly, I don't want to feel this. Not tonight. He sees my avoidance, notices plain as fat what it does to me and his fingers graze the side of my jaw. Lightly and quickly so no one sees him do it.

"You say the word and we can leave. No one will mind," he brings his lips so close to mine I can feel the warmth kiss mine. But it's not the same as a real kiss, my body subconsciously leans forward but he stops me. A hand on my hip, I look to find his eyes squeezed shut. His face is tangled in expressions that resemble pain and confusion, but suddenly his hand is tangled in my hand and his lips are a touch closer.

"Is this a smart idea? Acting on feelings I don't remember?" I ask, and he pulls back from me. His eyes still shut tightly he sighs, the sound is strained and agonizing.

"Ever since we were younger you had this wild personality, uncontrollable. You just did, you never stopped to think but after everything you've grown so cautious with your feelings and I understand why," he grinds his jaw together before saying anything further. "I have no control here, if you want to go we can but I won't do anything until you are absolutely sure it's what you want."

He opens his eyes finally and everything around me stops. The center is so dark, sturdy, and deep like the ocean but the ice around the edges that frames all the pain. Trapping it inside like a cage with no key. I remember to breathe, my

212

lungs catching up to me. "It's what I want."

"Are you sure?" He searches my green eyes for any flicker of doubt, for a reason to say no to me. Fear twists on his features, and he touches my face, his hand raising to my chin so slowly from his sides I almost flinch when he finally makes contact.

"I'm just going to say goodnight to Natalie and Ben." He nods and removes his hand from my chin, stuffing it back into the pocket of his dress pants.

I move through the crowd towards where Nat and Ben sway delicately together. Ben looks up from her face to see me coming. "Hey bug," he says, Nat turns and smiles so brightly the room becomes the surface of the sun. I smile back at her, my heart so full and warm. Their happiness fills the space so effortlessly, tucking into everyone's moods and lifting the emotions in the room.

"I'm going to go, I think I've had enough of prying eyes and stupid questions tonight. Do you need me to do anything before I leave?" I ask. Natalie removes one hand from Ben's shoulder and takes my hand in hers, "I love you," I mouth to her and she returns it.

"Be careful okay," she grimaces looking over my shoulder. "He loves you so much but sometimes he can't help but hurt you. It's just his nature, so go slowly back into this, for me?"

"I promise," I say and Ben nods.

"Call us if you need anything, and don't stay out too late young lady." He laughs, spinning his new wife in a wide circle suddenly. Her laughter explodes around them and everyone claps as he dips her into a low arch over his arm.

Sean sits at his table, arms crossed over his chest. He's stripped his suit jacket and he's downing glasses of whiskey. "Looks like I'm not the only one who likes to drink my problems away," I move the glass away from him.

"It's better than feeling sad, Nora." He mocks, his hand wrapping around the glass but I press it back to the table away from his lips. "I'm not a child."

"Then stop acting like one, you're worried about ruining our friendship but you aren't doing a very good job protecting it right now. Let's get you to bed," I say and without protest he stands, taking my hand and leaning into me. He's drunker than I imagined, his feet shuffling clumsily as we weave through the crowd of people pressed into the deck. "Bishop," I say and he turns. "We have to get him home, he needs some sleep."

Bishop doesn't say a word, hooking his arm under Sean who eclipses his size by a whole foot and takes the weight off of me. Nick follows us out of the house and down the street, fumbling with the keys to the house in his hands. "God, you weigh a ton," Bishop groans, pushing him up the stairs. "What the hell, are you a moose?"

I can't help but giggle at the sight of them fighting with him until the very last step. He falls into bed like a tree and is out cold before Bishop even removes his shoes. "How much did he drink?"

"He started early and hasn't stopped all day." Nick comes into the room with a bucket and some water. "He'll be okay, he's just going to have a wicked headache come morning. You kids, go have fun, I'll stay here with this idiot." He laughs and shoos us from the room.

Bishop links his fingers in mine, and the warmth of his palm pressing against mine spreads across my body like wildfire. I look over at him, the moon shines across his face and his ocean eyes glimmer back at me. "You are a very beautiful man, you know that?" His laughter is sweet when it leaves his lips and floats through the night air, weightless and free.

He rubs his thumb against the back of my hand and leads me away from the wedding, down to his end of the street. His giant, godly beach house looming at the end of the street. It's much more daunting in the dark, all the horrible things that happened there casting haunting shadows on the endangered good memories I want to hold onto so desperately.

I stop him before he opens the door, leaning against it with my back, "Just wait." I say pressing my hand to his chest, he touches my cheek so soft and afraid. "I just need a moment."

He says nothing, wrapping his four fingers against the side of my face, grazing around to the back of my head. He looks at me, searching my eyes for a trace of regret or hesitation. He moves closer, just a touch and his free hands move to cup the other side of my face. He's holding me like I am made of glass.

His hands shake, enough for me to feel the nervous tremble against my face. He leans in, so slowly and carefully, breathing so lightly but in the silence that hangs between us, it's so loud and surrounding. His lips are the softest thing I have ever known. Like brushing cotton candy to my lips, sweet and weightless against my own. It's so careful at first, delicate and wavering until it isn't. He kisses me again, his time deeper and desperate. I pull him in, dying to memorize every inch of his lips. It's heat, pure desire and he tastes like mint, it tingles my lips.

He turns the knob, the door giving way as he moves us into the dark, quiet house. Deep and urgent he keeps himself attached to me as we move through. I'm going to split at the seams. In the dark of the foray, he's kissing me like he's lost me and he's found me. I'm slipping away but he'll never let me go, not again. Not ever. I want to scream and cry, and collapse. Now that I've known what it is like to live and love with his kiss, this heart I would never need anything ever again. I could go without water or food, all I need to survive is him.

This makes me ache in every way possible. My entire body is throbbing for more. He pulls away, his breathing hard, his hand slipping down the zipper of my dress. The cool air hit my bare rib cage, the dress falling open slightly.

His hands gripped my waist, lifting me with ease until my legs circle his hips. He starts the stairs slowly, one at a time. I think at first it may be too much but he takes them with ease. His breathing is only hard as he uses the rest of his strength to kiss me roughly at the top. He doesn't set me down, carrying me down the hall to his room; he kicks the door closed behind him and takes me to the bed.

The black silk sheets are soft against my back as he drops me down onto it. Climbing between my legs, fingers teasing around the edges of my neckline, slowly he strips me of each piece of fabric. Dress, bra, underwear.

My spine arches with a gasp as his teeth nip at my thigh, his tongue licking the sore spot and soothing the quick prick of tantalizing pain. Searing desperation tore through me, a toxic mix of desire and need. I rip the buttons off his dress shirt not caring if I wreck it, his mouth comes to mine with ferocious intentions. I unbutton the top of his pants, yanking them down his hips. My palm finds him easily and I take it firmly between my fingers.

He grunts, tempting me to move faster. Deep growl forms on his lips, "Fuck, baby."

216

I feel powerful, and in control, while he loses all of his. His hips push against my hand wildly, wanting it all and more. A cry buckles out from my lips as the warm feeling of his tongue drives deeply, his lips sucking at my clit. He hits every sensitive spot inside, ripping the breath from my lungs.

Every inch of my body, the tender skin feels him, inside and out. For the first time in a long time, it was just us. My mind may not have caught up with my memories completely, but my body certainly has. It moved with him as if I had been trained to do so. I had been. My hands knew each curve of his body intimately, the dip in his hips and the subtle round of his ass. The thick, pressuring shapes of his thighs as they held me in place on the bed. His hardened hands run over my body, as his teeth drag through me. He rises, kissing up my stomach, licking the sweat-dripping space between my breasts. He sucks on the nipple, his tongue doing agonizing slow laps against the aroused skin.

My body burns with pleasure, "Bishop," his name leaves my lips as a plea, a begging moan. I need him closer. He's never close enough, always just out of reach. I could feel my hips lifting wanting him closer, inside me and around me for the rest of time. I could sink into this feeling and forget the world around me as long as I had him.

He answers, lifting off me his gaze heavy he stands over me, yanking his shoes off and kicking his pants fully to the ground. He climbs back over me, pulling my leg over his shoulder. He stares into me, a fiery glare that sets me on fire as he plunges inside me. I almost come undone from the feeling alone, my body breaking from the continuous waves of pleasure. I squeeze around him, drinking in the slight pain of his size as he fills me over and over again with deep, penetrating strokes.

"I have thought about how you feel since the day I left you," he groans, his jaw straining as his tongue licks over his bottom lip. "You feel even more unbelievable than I could have ever remembered." He slams into me, driving deeper. "This is mine. It's always been mine." He slams again. "Say it, Nora. Out loud."

I don't answer right away, letting it sink in around us. The silence that he feared that I had ever been anyone else's. We both knew the lie there. There had been other people for him, Sean for me. But nothing as intoxicating as this, nothing that shook us both down to our very cores. So intoxicating it felt like I was floating and drowning all at the same time. "It's always been yours, Bishop," I moan as he sits back, pulling me up with him.

He's fucking me so deep, that my vision blurs and I can feel my spin curving as I fall back against his sturdy hands. Leaning over and letting the blood rush through me as he rails into me again. He leans in pressing his teeth to my neck allowing me to wrap my arms around his back, dragging my nails in a raking motion leaving long red abrasions. He growls, thrusting harder into me. The extreme bliss of mixing pleasure and pain is getting to us both.

I grab his chin roughly, pressing my mouth to his. I pull his lip through my teeth, causing a deep noise to vibrate through his throat. His blue eyes bore into me, wild like an animal as he threw me back against the back. My legs wrapping around him, hips pressing up into him as much as they could my breast bouncing against my chest and sweat drips between us both as he rams into me as hard, and as fast as he can.

"Fuck," he seethes, I wrap my legs tighter pulling him deeper, and buck against him without remorse. "Nora," my name drips off his lips like honey. My orgasm slams into me, drowning me in nothing but pleasure and I would gladly die here like this. I scream out as he empties himself, his body swaying from the waves of euphoria that raked through him.

29

I prop my head up on my elbow, watching the way the sun tangles in his soft bed hair. The strands of his brunette hair shades of dark auburn, copper and black in the warm morning sun. I lightly pushed a strand from his face, his eyelids still gently closed over and peacefully asleep. I trail my eyes over him, taking in every small detail of his face.

I feel like I'm home.

I can't remember the years we spent together but my heart does and it beats rapidly in my chest when I realize that I'm falling in love all over again. We had been given a chance to get to know each other, but not who we were back then. The us that we are now.

He stirs beside me, the black sheet falling from his shoulder to expose his chest. Uninterrupted I study the scars that riddle his perfect skin and grimace at the sheer amount of them. Years of abuse from his father, fighting against a grown man. So scared he would become him that he didn't notice he already had been pushed down that exact path. Bishop was broken, but it was nothing that scared me. I didn't care. I just wanted to spend the rest of my days engulfed by him.

His arms tangled around my body.

His laugh and smile.

His kiss, the shape of his mouth pressed against mine.

His heart, safe with mine.

"You're staring at me, baby doll." He mumbles, a groggy yawn leaves his lips and he stretches his arms above his head causing the blanket to expose more of his skin. The hair trailing down, the way his pelvic muscles harden and disappear under the fabric.

"Who wouldn't," I say, leaning in, pressing a kiss to his neck. He's warm, I nuzzle into him and rest there against his body. "Natalie is going to kill me."

"Why?" Bishop brushes his fingers over my bare back gently in small comforting circles.

"I may or may not have promised her I would take this slow, and what we did last night was not…" I giggle against his chest, kissing the skin under my lips.

"What we did last night, for us, was slow Nora." His fingers gripped the underside of my ass and squeezed. "That was tame," he growls in my ear and my whole body feels the vibration.

I sit up against his chest and meet his gaze. "I appreciate your restraint, Mr. Bartley," he kisses me softly, slowly with patience that makes my heart flutter.

"If you keep calling me that we aren't leaving this bed today," he whispers against my mouth. I can feel him pressing, already hard against the leg I've hooked around his hips.

"I don't think they'd miss us just yet," I giggle.

"Sadly, they're probably already looking for you. It's twelve in the afternoon, Nora." My head snaps to the clock on the side table. Everything there is scattered as if someone had kicked it. The lamp teetered on the edge of the table precariously and the drawer was half open to expose its naughty contents.

"How did we sleep that long?" I gasp.

"It's easy to lose track of time when you don't care about anything but what's right in front of you." He cups the side of my face. "We should get up before Roberts breaks down my front door."

"I imagine Sean is sleeping off a nasty hangover," I sigh rolling away from Bishop. The mood is mute. Crushed by the thoughts of dealing with everyone else's emotions today. I'm happy, and content with everything. Wishing for more memories, or all of it to come back but happy. "I have a feeling I'm going to have to do damage control with more than one person today."

He nods softly, his hair falling on his face. "You don't have to do it alone, we made this decision together."

"Unfortunately Bishop, I don't think that's going to make much of a difference. You have mom on your side but everyone else is walking on eggshells around me about everything. This is going to be a storm," I shake my head. He slides out from under me and sits with the blanket draped over his leg.

"A storm that we weather, together." He winks at me, placing a quick kiss on my nose. "Let's take a shower, I bet that will help calm you down."

"You need a cold shower," I slide from the bed, turning away from me and he whistles from where he still sits. I turn and point to him. "Are you waiting for an invitation Mr. Bartley?"

That does it, he flies from the bed and chases me into the bathroom. I click the lock shut behind me and hear his grunt of frustration.

"If you can get in, you can help me wash my hair but you better hurry," I yell through the door, more grunts and growls come from him.

I turn on the shower, waiting for the warm water to flow. I close my eyes and let the spray fall over my chest, rubbing my face with my hands. I wash off the grime, makeup, and sweat from the night before. Letting my hands slide down my neck, my arms, breast, and belly. Cleaning in slow motion. I can hear Bishop just outside the door to figure out how to unlock the door.

I pause at my thighs, moving in slow circles, and stop at my pubic bone listening to his panicked movements. Without hurry I slip my hands between my thighs, parting myself and stroking. The door swings open, his shadow casting on the shower curtain as he slips his hand around it. He steps into the shower and trails his eyes down my body.

"So wet already," he jokes, his voice husky and low. He rests his hands on my waist, sliding them up against my side.

"Your turn," I smile at him, running my hands over his sculpted chest.

The water is so warm but the air around us nips at my skin, he presses a padded thumb against one of my erect nipples. Squeezing it gently, teasing my nerves.

"We haven't done this in a very long time," he growls, leaning forward. I tilt my head to meet his gaze, lips parting wanting more of him. He brushes his lips against my cheekbone, next to my ear, and along the edge of my jaw slowly returning to position his lips with mine.

"We haven't done anything for a very long time Bishop," I whisper, his breath tickling my skin as he lets a choked sigh leave his lips. Bishop isn't in a hurry, his hands exploring the small of my back and the round of my ass.

"We have fifteen minutes, tops. I can't get into any more

trouble."

"Plenty of time," he gives me a soft shrug. "Let me remind you how much I can do in fifteen minutes."

I smirk. My hands drift downwards, fingers curling to dig my nails in against his hard skin. He pulls roughly against my backside, slamming his body against mine. "You seemed to enjoy my head between your legs last night, should I start there?"

He all but growls the question and I can feel my insides curl up at the wild look in his eyes. A small nod of my head. "Say it," he grumbles, pressing a kiss to my lips.

"My legs, I want your head," I pause to steal another kiss, "between my legs Bartley. Now."

My hands trace the lean muscles of his lower stomach, his own hands clenching around my body. "Your mouth, your tongue," I whisper over the running water into his ear.

"Let's see what I can do about that," he kisses me, hungry and impatient. The buildup is too much, and my mouth opens eagerly. It does nothing to relieve the pulsing between my legs, rather it drives it up to one hundred.

Bishop turns himself away from the faucet so my back is pressed against one of the walls the cold tile at my back sending a shiver down my spine as he pulls back to stare at me.

Lust filled his vision. The blues of his eyes were like a hot, burning fire.

He dips his head down to lick at one of the water drops still clinging to my breast, my head falls back against the wall as he roughly sucks at the skin before he moves on. Torturing me with every painfully slow movement.

My hands thread through his hair, gently tugging on the

strands as his mouth follows the contour of my pelvis. He stops, turning his head up to meet my face and smiles, "that feels good." He growls leaning into the pain of having his hair pulled.

Mm, good to know.

He kneels, nudging my legs open before kissing a path up the inside of my thighs.

He alternates slowly, his hands gripping the back of my thighs to hold me in place as he works. Bishop rubs his nose against my thought, sucking on the flesh before pressing a final kiss an inch too far from where my body needed him to be.

"I will remember this sight for the rest of my life. Worship it until the day I die." He kneels in front of her, his hands touching my skin reverently, the tension building between us. I'm ready to accept his worship.

A simple nod, a tiny smirk, and the reddening of my cheek have him moving again. His tongue swept over my lips, grazing my clit just enough for me to suck in a harsh breath of air between my teeth. I drape one of my legs over his shoulder, pulling him closer and he obliges. Holding my knee with one hand and the other still cupping my ass he kisses me, edging my lips, sucking at them, and dipping his tongue into the delicate skin of my entrance. He mercilessly teases me before leaving it again, building me even closer to the edge.

I'm reading to beg for release.

His mouth finally covers my clit, I buckle out, shutting my eyes tightly with a gasp. My hand still gripped into his hair, I reached the other up to the facet and held on tightly riding against his tongue. "Bishop," I call his name, urging him on with shallow, breathless gasps until I can't take it anymore.

I let out a sigh as my body relaxed and let go of the faucet. Bishop slides out from under my leg, slowly standing he wipes his mouth and grins at me wildly, an uncontrollable satisfaction sweeping across his features.

"Glad to be of service," he winks. He bends down to kiss me and I wrap my arms around his neck pulling him in as close as I can get him. My leg hooking around his hip, he lifts me up. He is hard and eager for me. Unlike him, I didn't intend to make him wait. I tuck my second leg up, wrapping around as tightly as I can. Both legs wrap around him, supported by the wall behind me and his hands below me.

I dip my hand between our wet skin, grabbing his shaft to stroke him from base to tip before I guide him inside. I move with him as he lifts and thrusts. I rake my nails through his hair again, pulling at the base of his neck to expose his neck to me. He obliges, tilting back into the pain with his eyes closed as I lick along his collarbone and up his neck. Nibbling at his jaw, he hisses but a long growl leaves his lips as he starts to move faster inside me.

Between last night, and the orgasm I had just experienced I didn't think it was possible to have another so soon until the sound of my name rolled off his lips in a long husky moan, "Nora, baby," his mouth pressed against my throat and the arousal overtakes me again.

I lean in, my muscles contracting out of control as I let his rough thrust rub against my clit over and over. The only sound leaving my lip is a whimper of encouragement. He presses tightly against me, my back firm against the wall for support as he trembles against her in pleasure. He kisses my neck furiously as he pulls out, coming into the shower and letting the water properly clean us.

"Do you mind washing my hair for me?" I tease as he braces his arm against the wall behind me. I press a firm, long kiss to the inside of his bicep, keeping my eyes on his.

"Only if you wash mine," he kisses my nose, still holy out of breath.

The next few minutes are spent in silence, but it's not tense. It's just the two of us, rubbing shampoo through each other's hair. I massage the top of his scalp down to his head and he closes his eyes leaning his head back into my hands. I wish I could stay here.

I want to watch him do mundane things for the rest of our lives.

To see him wash the dishes, mow the lawn and watch bad movies.

I want to watch him braid our daughters' hair, and teach our son to cook.

I want everything with him.

"What?" he says, cupping the sides of my face. A sudden sense of dread fills me. I don't want my memories back, not if they do something to sway my mind. Not if they're going to take all of this away from me.

"Nothing," I lied.

"We should get dressed before we get distracted again," I say and he nods but there's hesitation on his face like he can read my thoughts. I press a kiss to his lips in hopes the look is gone when I pull away but it's not.

30

"Some restraint you have," Natalie looks up from her salad, she pushes wilted dressing-covered leaves around the plate with disgust. "You harlot!"

"Natalie," my mother scolds as she pours me a cup of coffee, sliding it across the counter to me. "Where's Bishop?"

"He'll be here in a bit, he has some work things to take care of. Where is everyone else?" I ask, mom nods out to the back door. Ben and my dad fold tables down, while Curtis collects any left behind garbage. I turn to ask her if Sean has surfaced but before I open my mouth to say anything she shakes her head.

"I send Nick back to the house with some Advil, sandwiches and water but he hasn't returned. Give him some space sweetheart," She presses a kiss to my forehead and heads outside to help clean up. I bite my lip nervously and sit across the table from Natalie.

"Am I an absolute jackass?" I ask and she almost spits the water she's sipping on out. Coughing the water up she raises an eyebrow. "Don't answer that."

"There are too many puzzle pieces you don't have. Too many missing moments. The last couple of years have been torture but you've had Sean." She slides her salad away from

228

her and leans across the table to take my hand. "Not a single person in this house has the right to tell you what to do, your body is your body. Your mind is a black hole. I can tell you that even if they made some misogynistic alpha asshole pact that turned into a game of tug of war and horrible insults. Neither of them ever intended to hurt you," she says, her green eyes sad even though a smile stretches across her face.

"It hurts the same," I whisper, looking down at the reflection in my coffee cup.

"Hey Nora," Sean kisses the side of my head and slides into the booth across from me. "What's wrong?" he asks when I don't respond or look up. He gets up and slides in next to me, his face concerned and searching for a reaction.

"I got this today," I slid a small envelope across the table into his open hand. "I don't want it, so you can have it."

I watch him open it, with furrowed brows and careful fingers. Out slides a cheque, no note, no explanation. Just a cheque. "It's from him, and I don't want it."

"Alright, I'll shred it when I get home." he tucks it into his back pocket and pushes my hair back off my shoulder. Leaning on the table he angles so his chest is against my shoulder and wraps his arms around me. The light blue sweater he has on is soft against my arms and I lean into the hug. It's warm and has the exact right amount of pressure to make the world stop spinning for a second.

"Why does he think I want his money?" I ask.

He had been gone for six months, I hadn't left my room for four of those. Mom had forced me to get up, to start moving. Take dad to his treatments and get fresh air. Once a week, I drop him off at the hospital, then join Sean for pancakes at the diner. This cheque was the first I had heard from him since he left. It had been in the mailbox, addressed to me. His handwriting had cleaved through my chest like an ax. Hands shaky, I had torn it open.

I had expected a letter, an apology, or an explanation. But there was nothing. Just a cheque with his father's signature at the bottom. I threw up outside the post office before returning to the car where my dad sat waiting. His thinning, tired face concerned me as I cleaned my face and handed him the mail.

"I just want him to come home," I barely get the words out, they get caught in my throat like nails and I want to cry. Sean just holds me tighter, my chest begging for release, to let all the aching pain-free.

"Nora," Sean says softly, his breath warm on the top of my head where he rests his chin. "He's not coming home."

"He will Sean, I know he will." I hold back a sob.

"Not this time, he made a choice Nora. Let him go." He runs a hand against my cheek.

"That's easy for you to say, you've wanted him gone this whole time." I snap at him, even though I don't mean to be cruel. He deserves none of my wrath, but I'm so angry and sad that the words just flow from me. "You're as much to blame for this pain."

"That's not fair," he sighs. "I didn't want him to leave, I didn't want him to break your heart. I've been spending the last nine months babysitting him so he doesn't hurt anyone, so he doesn't hurt you. This whole time trying to convince him that..." Sean stops talking. "It doesn't matter Nora, he's gone. You have to get up every morning, you need to shower, you need to live your life. Go to school in Atlanta, get a job, and make new friends. One step at a time, say the word and I will help you. This isn't healthy, waiting for him to come home."

I shove away from him.

The embrace had become suffocating.

"I have to go get dad," I say, pushing my way out of the booth. I

walk out of the restaurant towards my car. I go to grab my keys from my back pocket but they aren't there. I must have left them on the table. As I make my way back to the diner, Sean stands against the entrance to the alley, looking frustrated on his phone.

"Why the hell would you send her that?" His voice has changed from soft and friendly, to harsh and demanding. "I know you're trying to help, but for fuck sake Bishop. Address it to me, to her dad, anyone but her. You didn't want her to know the reasons you left, so stop leaving her with so many damn questions if you aren't going to answer them like a man." I swallow hard, listening to him. He hangs up and I press myself against the brick wall so he can't see me.

I watch from my spot as he climbs into his car and throws the cheque on his dashboard. He slams his hands against the wheel, his eyes full of rage as he pulls out of his parking spot in his ugly pickup truck. Sean knew more about why Bishop had left, and he refused to tell me. I'll get the answers one way or another.

"I know it does," Nat snaps my memory away and her soft smile brings me back to reality. "This is uncharted territory for us all."

"It's my emotions at stake, you all get to walk away again. To continue to hide things from me until I remember, if I ever remember!" I raise my voice but she just waits for me to finish. "I just want answers, straight and clear ones. None of this *'he'll tell you when he's ready'* crap. That's a bullshit excuse for both of them. I hate that when I get around Bishop, all I want to do is love him but when he's gone everyone is constantly reminding me that I don't know him."

"I'm so tired of these mind games," I say quietly.

"Ben was saying something about you going back to your apartment for the weekend? Just to see if it will help knock things loose? We can drive you into Atlanta if you'd like, we're leaving on Friday." Nat suggests, *knocking things loose*, the problem is things are too loose up there, to begin with.

"I'll think about it, I don't know if I'm ready to meet the adult side of my personality just yet." I sigh and run my fingers through my hair.

"Ha, I think you already met her last night," Natalie stands from her chair and puts her dishes away before disappearing outside.

The house is so quiet. I can hear all my thoughts rolling around inside my head like fog horns. It makes me want to scream but instead, I pad upstairs in my socks and start to pack my bags. If Ben was right and going somewhere familiar may help, going back to Atlanta and getting back to work may be a great idea.

I'm coming home

I text Nick, I figure he's returning to Atlanta anyways today. Maybe he would take me. I didn't want to be stuck in a car with Nat and Ben for four hours. That sounds like a lot of judgment and a lot of unsolicited advice.

I'm leaving in twenty, would you like a ride?

He messages back almost immediately and I tuck my phone back into my pocket after answering a short yes. Most of my belongings fit into my duffle bag, I sling it over my shoulder and turn to see Bishop standing at the door.

"You're leaving already?" His voice cracks and he looks from the bag to my face.

Heartbroken.

"I'm coming back," I say to reassure him. "I need some time to figure out my head, I'm just going to Atlanta."

"I'm not running away, I promise. Ben thinks it will be good

232

for me to see the apartment." I try to explain to him.

"It seems like running away when you're up here packing your bags in secret Nora," he grumbles.

"You can come to see me in a couple of days at my apartment if you want." I smile, it's soft and hopefully quells his nervous fear.

"I won't," he says, short with me. Darkness creeps in. His jaw tenses and he shoves his hands in his pockets. "I can't go in there, it's…" he stops. It's where I and Sean spent most of our time. He doesn't feel welcome there.

"Do you have a home in Atlanta?" I ask, cautious. I didn't realize how wrong I went about this, the sudden leaving has spooked him.

"I'll call my Realtor and find a permanent place if you wish to go back there," he says coldly, he pulls the cell from his pocket and dials a number disappearing into the hall.

He returns with the same cold look on his face. I touch it softly with my palm, "You didn't have to do that, you could have just stayed here. Visited me. Stayed in a hotel for the weekend. That's a lot of money to just buy a place."

"It's worth it to be close, I never want to be four hours away from you ever again. I don't even want to be five minutes but I'll pick my battles." He leans in and kisses me slowly, it's warm and comforting.

"I'll bring the car around," he says, removing his hand from my waist.

"I'm going to go back with Nick," I say simply and he turns back to look at me. "I want to discuss work things with him. It'll give me a chance to do that. You can follow behind us," I say with a chuckle.

"Mm," he groans and his lips press into a straight line. "Just nick?" he asks.

"Just Nick," I pressed another kiss to his lips. "I meant what I said. I want this to work but it won't be easy."

"It never has been, doll," he whispers in my ear, grazing the lobe with his teeth. A shiver rolls through me. "Off you go. Don't want to make you late to meet Nick," he kisses my neck, licking up and nibbling my jawline.

Nick waits by his car, watching Bishop with chocolate brown eyes as he saunters back to his house. "How did that go?" he asks, taking my bag.

"As well as can be expected, everyone got a goodbye, we should head out," I smile as he walks to my door, his hand covering the handle.

"Not everyone," he looks to the front window of Sean's house. "At least tell him what's going on," I look back at Nick and sigh.

I wander up to the house and Sean opens the door for me. "Nick says you're going back to the city with him. That's good," he's uncomfortable and making small talk.

"We'll figure it out Sean, I just need some time to remember everything. This isn't me forgiving you, but—" I stop. "I will. Eventually. Just give me time to think it through properly."

"Alright. For what it's worth. I am sorry. I should have never said those things to you or him. That's not who I am. I was just angry," he smiles at me but it's sad and nervous.

"I love you, I'll see you soon okay?" I say backing out of the house.

31

The apartment was dark and chilly. I flick on the light next to the front door and set my bag on the counter. There are dishes in the sink and an empty bottle of whiskey on the counter. A harsh reminding shiver runs the length of my spine.

"Call me if you need anything," Nick had said as he walked her up the steps and gave her the keys. I needed something I just couldn't figure out what that was.

Coming here is supposed to knock something loose, a memory that could domino everything.

I wander through the house, turning on lights and exploring a home I didn't even know I had. My mind was stuck somewhere between fifteen and twenty-three. A frame lay face down on the table beside the couch and I flip it up to see it properly.

It's Bishop.

It's a side profile of his face, a long strand of hair hanging down, loose from the bun at the nape of his neck; it tickles his sharp jaw. There's more, in the bedroom tucked neatly under the soft, beige pillows there's a notebook. One of the only ones that didn't burn. I sit and slip my finger under the cover flipping it over in my lap.

Charcoal dusts the paper pages with tones of blacks and greys. Heavy smudges and thin jagged lines make up face after face. This was my therapy. Drawing my pain over and over. I see it now, I see the agony that seeps through the drawn eyes, staring up at me like a ghost. Haunting.

These drawings are nothing like the ones Natalie had kept tucked into her books. That was happy, free, and unfinished. These were dark, heavy, and soulful. So much emotion riding on these pages. Old me begging to feel better with each stroke of my pencil. The last picture was number four hundred and five. Had I really drawn that many? If I had, why was I still so stuck? If this was meant to help, why didn't it stop? Over and over the pain spilled onto the pages.

Over

And

Over

I swallow hard. Even in my grief, I loved him. I carry the note book around the house with me, taking in the dead plants and musty smell. There were more empty bottles tucked behind the couch. I thought I had stopped drinking. Maybe it was a lie, I hadn't stopped. I had just gotten better at hiding it.

Everything feels so wrong here.

A sudden rush of pain came over me and it forced my knees to buckle. I kneel in the center of the apartment, the notebook sprawled open on the floor. I am overwhelmed. The person I was spiraling around me like a hurricane.

I press my hands to the floor, attempting to center myself. My heart pounds in my chest, it's hard to swallow and my head spins. I let myself fall fully to the ground, settling against the cold wooden floor. The frigid temperature seeps into my veins and dulls the burning sensation. Slowing my panic attack the best I can without help or counting.

One, I loved him.

Two, he loved me.

Three, he left me.

Four, everything was different.

Five, but so painfully the same.

Six, who am I supposed to be?

Seven, who was I?

Eight, everything feels so unfamiliar.

Nine, so far away.

Ten, except Bishop, he is real, I can feel him.

"Hey," his eyes meet mine, frantic and worried, "are you okay?"

Shock overwhelms me, he's here. Standing in the living room he told me he couldn't be in. I reach out and touch his face to be sure and he smiles at me. "I've been calling you for an hour," he says.

"No, I just got here," I say, confused.

"I just spoke to Nick on the phone, it's the only reason I'm standing here." He cups my chin with his hand and tilts my face to look at him but something catches his eye. I follow his gaze to the photo of him. Then on the floor, the notebook lays open and an image of him stares back. Sad and lost. His face changes then, it's no longer soft or worried. It's full of conflict and anger.

"I need to meet my Realtor. I just wanted to make sure you were okay," He stands, letting go of me. He backs up until his whole body is just outside the front door. Frozen in place with a harsh look on his face.

"I'm sorry," I say behind a clenched jaw. "I know you don't want to be here, but I need to do this. Even if it's painful, I need to remember."

"I'm trying to be more open with you but some moments are best forgotten, Nora. This apartment was yours, the Nora I never really knew." His hand grips the door frame tightly.

"I'm being forced to get to know the Bishop I never knew, all my cards on the table and you're saying you won't even try?" I ask.

"This wasn't ours, that's because it was yours and," he stops taking a deep breath in.

"Sean's," I finished for him. "So why can't we make it ours?"

"I have to remember this place, I didn't get the chance to forget what it meant to you. I don't get a free pass," he says it but regrets it instantly, his tongue rolling out over his bottom lip in frustration. "That's not what I meant," he sighs. "I just," he scrunches his nose and takes another step back from the door. "I just can't be in here, it smells like him even. He's all over everything, your furniture, your bathroom, even your clothes. He's ingrained here."

"You can't blame me for that," I say. He shakes his head. "You left me here with him, remember?"

"I did," he runs a hand through his hair, "and I don't blame you, Nora, for anything. It's just going to take some time." With that, he turns and leaves. I can hear his heavy boots on the stairs as he disappears.

I so badly want him to stay.

My phone rings from the couch. I must have dropped it there. How long had I been on the floor?

"Hey," I answered.

"Did you get home alright?" Ben's voice is a welcome tone.

"I did, is it possible to have a session? I know you said that you weren't my therapist anymore but I'm feeling a bit weird here and something happened." My voice sounds ashamed but I'm just nervous and tired, confused about what's going on.

"Are you okay?" He asks and I can hear Natalie trying to get the phone from him but he shushes her and waits for my answer.

"I'm fine I just need to talk to you, to anyone I guess, but you always say the smart stuff. I think I need the smart stuff before I do something stupid," I play with the hem of my shirt nervously.

"I'll be there in twenty minutes, we just pulled into our driveway. Let me get Nat settled, will you be okay?" He sounds so worried.

"I'm not going to hurt myself," I say, knowing that's where his concern lies.

"Good, good..." he trails off. I hear the car door slam. "I'll be right there okay."

......

It feels like an eternity sitting with my own thoughts when he finally knocks on the door. I've found all the hidden empty bottles. Eight in total, some still had nasty liquor swirling in the bottoms, I drained them in the sink and lined them up on the island. I lean against the counter across from them with my arms crossed and face in scowl when Ben lets himself in.

"You didn't...." he stops setting his jacket on a hook.

"No, I found them. They were stashed all over the house," I say with a groan.

"Seems you didn't cut out the booze like you said you

did," He scowls now, picking up the bottle on the far left and reading the label. "This is expensive whiskey you were drinking," he shakes his head and sets it back down. "So what happened?"

I sigh, explaining to him that I had the weirdest panic attack I've had to date. "It was like I lost all sense of time. It felt like it was only five minutes but I was laying there freaking out for over an hour. Completely out of control of myself."

"Do you remember the 333 rule?" he asks, taking a seat at the stool around the opposite side of the island. I shake my head no, "You look around and find three real things, then you listen, name three things you can hear and finally you move three parts of yourself. I know counting has been helpful, it was a good way for Sean to ground you during an attack. The 333 rule will help you ground yourself, no need for anyone to help. You can stop them on your own."

"Would have been helpful two hours ago," I groaned and let my eyes fall to the floor. "Bishop had to snap me out of it."

"He came in here?" Ben sounds shocked. "Completely inside the apartment?"

"Yeah he was the one who found me on the floor," I responded.

"He calls this place purgatory. When he speaks of it, he describes it like an endless loop of hell for lack of better words. If he was willing to step inside," he pauses.

"What?" I wait for more information.

"Then perhaps he is growing. It's just not as obvious to the rest of us. The Bishop I know, the one who wouldn't even say your name for a whole year. The guy who moved across the world to stop himself from all but stalking you would have never stepped foot in here. It's painful to him, like electric shock therapy. When we talk about overcoming our fears, phobias we tend to have a patient live through those fears. Push themselves into doing the one thing they believe they can't. I was never once able to get him to come in here. I used to house sit the plants while you were on event trips, and I always asked him to come but he never would." Ben fixes his glasses and rubs the back of his neck.

"He ran away," I say. "He saw these and something changed in him." I handed him the notebook.

"These are hard for me to look at, I can't imagine how he feels when he sees them. These are a representation of the darkest, loneliest part of your soul. It was most likely painful for him." Ben hands me the book back and smiles sympathetically. "I didn't come here to talk about him, what triggered the panic attack?"

"Everything," I say honestly. "The smells, the fabric, the unfamiliarity of a place that I see but don't remember in my mind. But when I smell the air and touch the fabric my body remembers. It's unfair and cruel." I run my finger over the leather cover of the notebook.

"The human brain is horrible but it's magnificent. Being here is going to be hard but it's important that you do this. Much like facing a fear, it's a trial." Ben stands from his chair and comes around to hug me. "This isn't the first panic attack you've had and it won't be the last. It's going to open doors, our brains work in mysterious ways, and if you're lucky one of these attacks might help you remember something." He pulls back to smile at me.

"I don't remember having them when I was younger," I say, trying to think about if I ever had one.

"You didn't, these started after the accident." He says it so plainly, a night that I don't remember a single moment from. A night that they speak about but are careful to never explain themselves or tell me too much.

Fear.

The unknown causes fear. Secrets cause fear.

"Will you tell me about the accident?" I ask him already knowing his response.

"Not yet," he responds simply, "I will though. There are some things you need to remember first before we have that conversation. But if you don't remember, and he refuses to tell you. I will, I promise."

"Really?" I am hopeful for the first time in a long time.

"Absolutely, you deserve to know. I just don't want to put that on you right now, so stay here this week and next week on Friday we'll go surfing you and me. And I will tell you, out on the water where you can release everything without judgment." He taps my nose with his finger and gives me one last squeeze.

"Thank you, for everything," I say with a smile.

32

BISHOP

"Can you get these to Diana, she needs them by Friday and I have two meetings this afternoon that need my attention." I don't look up from my papers but I extend the folder to Scott. He doesn't take it, he just sits there staring at me. "What?"

"Are you really going to buy a condo in Atlanta for her?" He asks plainly. I appreciate his personality. He never bullshitted me, never babied me. He started working for my father to keep an eye on me but our relationship had budded into a tense and honest friendship.

"Yes Scott, I am. What's it to you? I can do my work from anywhere." I snap still not looking up.

"And you think all will be happily ever after when she regains all of her memory?" He questions, always questioning me and my actions, my choices, and my sanity.

"If," I say, finally looking up to him, he sits in the crappy hotel chair across from me. Judging by my every move, his brown eyes follow mine. "If she regains the memories then I will own up to my shortcomings and handle it. I won't lose her again."

"We aren't talking about a small secret Bishop, we're talking about something that destroyed her and you emotionally when you were children. You were eighteen, and it forced you to grow up too fast. You've never dealt with those feelings." He raises an eyebrow at me.

"I don't pay you to give me life advice Wilson," I growl.

"You don't pay me at all, your father does." He responds. "Or did you forget that you lied about that too?"

"It's better if we pretend he's already dead Scott, we haven't heard from him in over eight months," I say, a sudden sense of anxiousness creeping through my bones. "He left in the middle of the night and hasn't said a word to anyone since. He's all but dead to me and to this company."

"Kate doesn't agree," Scott responds, finally taking the folder.

"Her opinion matters very little to me, just because she was exempt from the psychical abuse does not mean she didn't suffer emotionally. She just doesn't realize that her sadness is a pang of misplaced guilt that he beat into her brain to be daddy's little girl." I set my pen down and turn to him fully. "She won't say anything. She's finally happy and has found a corner of the world for her and Curtis. Leave her out of this," I say, it comes out an order.

"All I'm saying is stuff like this will come back and bite you in the ass," he tilts his head. "I haven't seen you this animated, ever. An entire lifetime being your babysitter and not once have you ever hinted at even being a living human being. You fuck and drink away your feelings, come to work, act like a grouchy monster, and then do it all again the next day. I'm just worried this isn't going to go the way you want it to."

"Not everything is planned Scott," I say in return, "I can't control this, for the first time in a long time, this is a situation that is completely out of my hands. It's all up to Nora, if she remembers or not I have to trust that the last month of conversations and time spent together will be enough to remind her who I am." I scowl.

"And who exactly are you Bishop?" The question catches me off guard, I furrow my eyebrows at him. I want to shove him out of the chair he leans back in, watching me so carefully. Making me question myself now.

"I'm pretty sick of your shit," I say pointing at him, "I don't know who I am without her."

"That's the problem," he says so simply, so calm and directly it pierces through me like a spear to the chest. "I'll get these to Diane, here's the address your realtor sent."

He tosses a piece of paper on the table and leaves the hotel room. Leaves me sitting in my own pitiful existence to think about what he said. I sweep my arms across my desk and throw the papers everywhere, the anger overwhelming all my senses.

"Fuck!" I scream at the top of my lungs but nothing helps. I grab my keys off my desk along with the address and leave. The drive will help me think, hopefully. If not the feelings could rot, just like they always had done before. I didn't care anymore. I only wanted to make Nora happy. That's all that matters.

The drive to the condo is quiet, I blast music over the sound system and drown in it so my thoughts don't suffocate me. Charles stands in the lobby on his phone, hanging up abruptly on whoever he's speaking with; he shoves it into the pocket of his expensive suit.

"Mr. Bartley," he extends his hand for a quick shake.

He's a thin man, with hollow cheeks and stark blond hair that reaches up off his head in soft waves. His brown eyes nervously flicker around, his confidence has cracks in it but I pay it no mind. We all have issues we're dealing with. Charles had worked for my father for years, that was his first problem. I was not my father, the temper was there but I never berated my employees, that was beneath me.

"The listing then?" I ask, holding my hand out, he slides papers into it. The condo was a decent size, with four rooms, a huge kitchen, and a reasonably sized office. The living room was encased in dark blue shelving. The bedrooms were all painted a dark gray, with white carpeting and dark accents. "Does it come furnished? I don't have time to shop for everything."

"I can arrange that, yes," he says, taking notes.

"The second bedroom I want will be transformed into a closet. I'll be bringing most of my belongings over from Japan in the next couple of weeks. And the office needs to be soundproofed," I continue. "I would like to move in next week, please have the house stocked with food."

"That's not my job sir," he says but I stare at him until he feels uncomfortable enough to just nod. "I'll find someone."

"Good, I'll have the bank send the money. Forward the contract to Wilson, he'll get it to me." I say turning to walk away.

"You don't want to actually see the property, Mr. Bartley?" His voice is faint from behind me.

"It doesn't matter, it's just a house Charles. Get it done." I leave the lobby and get back into my car. I check my phone, three missed calls in under ten minutes. One from Ben.

I dial back, "What's wrong?" I ask when I hear the line

connect.

"She's fine, I need to see you." He says, his voice stern. "My office. In an hour and don't act like you can't make it. You run that company, move some shit around and get your ass here."

The line clicks dead without another word.

His office building is located only twenty minutes from where I am. I sat in my car for twenty more. Nervous? I think that's what this is, I'm nervous. I have no idea what he wants. Our usual conversations take place on the phone, once a week. I've never been summoned to his office, and I always call him first.

"Am I in trouble?" I say walking into the office and shutting the door behind me. Ben looks up at me over his glasses and sets his pen down. He points at the beige uncomfortable-looking couch to sit on. I listen and fall into, staring across at him. The wall behind him is covered in shelves, and books of all sizes and colors. A few degrees and some photos of his family. One of them, Natalie and Nora, stands out. I had taken it. I recognized the light leak from the top corner. The double exposure creates a ghost effect on their faces.

"No," Ben says, as he walks around to sit in front of his dark wooden desk. His arms crossed and his face judgmental. "You went inside the apartment."

My stomach drops. I hate that place. The smell haunts me, a lingering mix of whiskey and Sean's cologne. Every inch of it was his, including Nora when she was inside of it. The walls close in on me and I swallow hard.

"How are you feeling?" He asks.

"Fine," I respond and he scoffs at me. "You know I could beat the crap out of you for scoffing at me like that."

"Do it then," he opens his arms as an invitation. "Would that make you feel better?"

"Don't 'therapy' me, Lotley." I shake my head and grind my jaw together.

"That's my job Bishop," he laughs at me. "Try again, how do you feel?"

"Like an asshole," I say honestly. "Like I don't have control anymore and it's scaring the shit out of me. She could remember everything at the drop of a pin, a smell, a touch, a look. And I just have to wait. I have to wait for her to hate me again."

"Control has never been your problem," he sighs. "You let others take control all the time. When you hand important matters to Scott when you come to see me for therapy when you order a sandwich at a restaurant. Your problem is the unknown."

"You say this a lot and it still makes no sense to me," I lean my head back against the couch and stare at the ceiling.

"Unknown, not known, or unfamiliar. You spent most of your childhood had a life planned for you, and now you're an adult and you plan everything down to the second. No variables, no unknowns. Nora was an unexpected variable. She was never a part of your father's plan, you could never control anything she was going to do. She's wild, free, uncontrollable. And now she's an unknown, you never know when she might remember. She's the two things in life that scare you the most." Ben pauses, thinking. "You've never understood what I meant by that because you didn't have a tangible feeling to hang on to. You don't experience fear like I do, like a normal person. It's been beaten out of you. Leaving you unafraid of what happens to you, there's no room for fear.

248

She scares you."

"I'm afraid of Nora?" I'm still confused.

"Not of Nora, that would be silly. You're afraid of all of the unknown things she brings into your life. All the things you can't plan for." He explains.

"I can plan, I've spent the last months doing damage control. Planning on when she remembers and I have had the conversation with myself a thousand times. I know what I need to say to make it better." He laughs at me, a full-body laugh that makes me angry. "Are you allowed to laugh at me? You're my therapist!"

"Bishop, at this point you are my brother. So yes I can laugh at you. How have these plans been going for you lately? These talks you have with yourself, when you use them on a panicked and confused Nora, do they go the way you want them to?" He asks and I roll my eyes because he's right, they never go as planned. I always mess it up. "Exactly, stop planning. Stop panicking, just use this time with her to form a new bond, one that is stronger than the old one. Go to her, stop being such a pussy."

"Wow," I say, shocked at his word choice. "Harsh words for such an old, brittle man. What am I supposed to do?"

"Words are nothing, Bishop, actions are everything. She's experiencing extreme panic attacks, when you found her the other night she had been on the floor for almost an hour without even a thought of how much time had passed. With her memory returning more and more she's going to need you there for her. Not just periodically, she's going to need you there day and night. Can you handle that?"

"You want me to go back there?" I ask him, scared of the answer he'll give me.

"You have to." He says and my body turns to ice. "You have to," he repeats himself with a nod.

33

A knock at the door startles me from my trance. I've been sitting, so still, I might be a statue, just staring at the walls of my apartment. I feel small here, like nothing I say or do matters when I'm inside. It feels like a black hole. I wanted information but I haven't found the courage to look through my belongings. Not my clothes, or the trunks in my closet. Not the photo albums, or the books on the shelves.

I had stopped looking when I found the case under my bed. It contained a dark cherry wood violin that I don't even know if I can play. That was enough for me, I slid it back under the bed and sat on the couch for hours, just staring.

I open the door, surprised to see Bishop with bags in his hands. "Are you going to let me in?" He says, one eyebrow raised playfully but his eyes and jaws were tense.

"Do you actually want to be here?" I ask, I know my tone is cold and harsh but I can't help it. I'm so emotionally exhausted I have nothing left to pretend with, even for him.

"I do," he says, he doesn't sound wholly sure but I suspect he also has no time for pretending either. "Are you hungry?"

I give a small nod and step to the side, letting him into the apartment. He sets the bags down and strips them from his suit jacket. Leaving him standing in a navy blue dress shirt, he rolls the sleeves up exposing a fancy silver watch with a black face and two thin silver bracelets. He starts to pull vegetables out of the bags, setting them on the counter.

I sit across from him, watching him intently until finally, he turns to me. "What?"

"What are you doing?" I ask him, genuinely curious why he's here.

"Making dinner?" he leans across the counter, his face so close to mine. His glassy eyes are bright, but there's a tired look to them. His face has a thin layer of scruff on it, and his jaw is still wired tightly as if he was forcing himself to talk.

"I mean," I start but he stops me with a light kiss. It tingles my lips as he pulls away.

"I know what you meant, let's eat first, and then we can talk." He turns away, sets a pan on the stove, and starts chopping carrots carefully. I watch him intently, his movements slow and calculated as he prepares the meat, and then seers it off in the pan. The smell in the house is amazing, like nothing I've ever smelled before.

I'm suddenly so much more hungry than I thought I was. He poured me a glass of wine, "It's nonalcoholic, promise." I sip on the sweet and bitter drink.

"Did Ben talk to you?" I ask and he sighs, his shoulders heaving over the pan.

He turns back to me and with a stern look on his face, he says, "I said after dinner," he grimaces and goes back to plating the food he's made.

Spring carrots and green beans, potatoes, and chicken. It all looks amazing as he pours the sauce over the crispy skin of the chicken. He sets the meal in front of me, withholding my fork, and scoops a bit of potato onto it. I open my mouth

252

for him and let him slide the fork against my tongue and lips. It's creamy, soft, and deliciously warm.

"That's amazing, when did you learn to cook so well?" I ask, waiting for another bite, he grabs a carrot this time to offer to me.

"When I moved to Japan, I didn't want to be around people so I fired most of the staff my father had hired to look after me. I didn't realize that meant I had to cook for myself, I ate takeout for almost an entire year. Mixed with insomnia I found myself sitting up most nights, and don't you dare laugh at me, but I watched the cooking channel." He gives me a piece of chicken and takes one for himself. He watches my face for a reaction.

"You secluded yourself?" That is what I ask, concerned that he lived such a closed-up life after we separated.

"I did," he responds. "Everything just made me so sad and angry after I left home, I was screaming at maids that didn't deserve my wrath and trying to fight body guards. Scott is the only person who ever told me to get a grip. He treated me like a friend." He smiles a little, a small one that he tries to hide. "Scott reminds me of your dad, honest and fair but never holds back. He always knows exactly what I need to hear. Maybe that's why I clung to him the way I did, he felt like a piece of home."

"I like Scott," I say, stealing a carrot because he's taking too long to feed me. "He cares about you a lot. I'm happy that you had him in your corner all these years." I smile. We finish dinner and he lets me lead him to the couch. "Are you sure you're okay here?"

He nods, setting into the old cushions. He takes off the belt he's wearing and lays it on the table. He adjusts so he's comfortable and stares at me for a moment. It's a soft look. His blue eyes glimmer off the lit candles, like ocean waves.

"Are you going to tell me why you're here now?" I ask and the look fades, replaced by something harsher. "Ben sent you, didn't he?"

"I spoke to him, yes," he clears his throat. "It was not just about you. It was about my own problems too," he stops talking again, nervous.

"We can talk anywhere you want Bishop, it doesn't have to be here," I say reaching out to him and he takes my hand in his own, gripping it firmly.

"It does have to be here." He says through clenched teeth, "I need to be able to be here with you, without getting angry or upset."

"This place hurts you," I said tugging at his hand, forcing him to look at me.

"I did this to myself, Nora, it's not your fault. Roberts," he takes a deep breath and looks around as if saying Sean's name would make him appear out of thin air. "Was here for you when I couldn't be. As much as I want to hold that against him. I can't. Everything in this apartment is his, it's yours. This will sound selfish of me, but none of it is mine."

"Wrong," I say immediately, bringing his gaze back to mine. "I'm yours, remember?"

"We're supposed to be a team! Why do I feel like the only person in the room lately?" I say the following after him. He had been kissing some girl in the bathroom, I dragged him off of her but he just walked away from me.

"Bishop you can't do this!" I scream from the top of my lungs, he stops in his tracks. "Don't you dare walk away from me?"

He doesn't turn but I can feel the anger pouring off of him, the rain creates a thin layer between us. Standing here, so torn apart from one another. How had we gotten here, two people so sure of themselves now lost under a sea of stars in the pouring rain?

"Talk to me," I plead, the words but a mere whisper off my lips. "Just talk to me."

"You want me to talk?" He turns around, his face dripping with water. His sharp jaw clenched so tightly together it hurts him to speak. His hair is cropped so short to his scalp I want to cry, he looks so angry and detached. This is not my Bishop.

"What's happening to us?" I ask. Throwing my arms in the air, the wet sleeves of my sweater slapped against the side of my jean shorts on the way back down.

"You lied to me," he says, it's short and cold.

"I've never lied to you Bishop, not once," I responded confidently.

"You have feelings for him, for Sean. I know you do, why would you just admit it?" He barks, I jump, and his face shifts for a moment, aware of how tense I've gotten.

"Sean is my best friend Bishop, of course, I love him. But not the same way I love you, where is this coming from?" I shake off the nervous feeling and step forward but he narrows his eyes at me bringing me to a halt.

"I see how he looks at you Nora, how he touches your arm when I'm not looking. You have so much in common and I can't compete with him." He runs his hands over his head causing the excess water to spray everywhere.

"There's no competition," I argue. "I don't love him, the way I love you."

"But you still love him?" He growls. "You don't deny it! You like when he looks at you when he touches you! You like that you can talk about surfing and school with him, about your childhoods and families. I'm sorry I haven't known you as long as him."

"You're twisting my words," I sigh. "What do you want to hear?"

"I don't know," he snaps.

"What do you want?" I ask.

"I don't know!" He yells now, letting all the rage leave his body. He moves quickly and is in my face within secrets. Angry and breathing heavily in my face.

I close my eyes over, not afraid to think for a moment without his judgmental eyes boring into me. "Bishop," I say pressing my hand to his chest, I feel him flinch at my cold hand on the exposed skin under his shirt. "Why does it feel like you're starting fights?"

He doesn't answer me, the words hang in the air. "Do you not love me anymore, is that what's happening? You're pushing me away so I'll end things for you, make it easier on you?"

My eyes are still closed, I'm tempted to press my head against him just to hear his heart beating. The rain muffles everything around us, but even still I can hear when his breathing disappears. I shut my eyes tighter, and pray that when I open them he hasn't walked away from me again.

Tears are pooling in my eyes but Bishop holds me tightly against him, "You okay?" he asks and I shake my head.

"You were so cruel," I mumble and I know it's mean to say that it's a jab he doesn't deserve but I can't help it. The anger is rolling through my body and I can't stop it.

"I know," is all he says, rubbing the top of my head with his palm. "I know."

34

"Y ou ready?" Ben zips up his wet suit and grabs his board. The sun has barely risen in the sky. It turns the horizon a pretty mix of blues, purples, pinks, and orange. It's beautiful.

"I think so," I say. The wind is a bit intense this morning, this late in the season the cold sets it and makes the waves a little choppier than I would like but I can manage. I haven't forgotten how to surf, I tell myself. Now that my wrist guard is waterproof and my stitches are all out I can finally get back in the water. Where I belong. My body and mind are connected this time. Knowing how long it has been since I've been in the ocean. I needed this.

"Take it slow. I'll be here." Sean and Bishop stand on the deck staring out at us. Sean looks grim, a dark and hollow look on his face. It's disappointing that he's still so upset about everything. It had been almost a month. "At least they aren't killing each other," Ben says gaining my attention once again.

Bishop looks hopeful. He wears a dark red sweater and his hat is pushed under a black ball cap. He had driven us both up yesterday evening to spend the weekend. We had been spending time at both apartments. Some days the memories of the past were too much for either of us and we chose to live in the future instead. Hiding from the past in the luxury of Bishop's new house. His bed was deliciously soft and made it hard to leave it most mornings. It didn't help when I woke up with him snuggled against my back, warm and ready for me. I was getting used to the idea of that life, but the memories kept surfacing. Not all the memories were terrible, some brought gentle reminders that our life had been full of love and laughter. The others were harsh and mostly unwelcome. The pain of each one reminded me of how flawed everything was.

"Tie this on tight just in case a memory surfaces and I lose you in a wave. The board will drag you back up," Ben tugged on the tie at my ankle to check it wouldn't budge.

We waste no time wading out into the water, it's chilly even with my wet suit on. The chill is biting at my hands and feet. The waves bob us up and down as we sit on our boards waiting for the perfect timing.

"Go now," Ben says nodding to the incoming rush. I paddle out and wait. It's like second nature. My memory kicks in and rides the wave through. The rush of moving across the water fills me with adrenaline and I want to do it again. The saltwater hitting my face wakes me up completely and I'm ready for another go. I watch Ben catch a huge wave, Sean hollering from the beach in excitement.

It's my turn again next, a large swell comes forward and I catch it but it's too unstable. My board tilted. Unbalanced. I can't steady myself in time as the tunnel collapses on me. The rolling tide drags me under, twisting me around and around. I can't find the right way up, the water is too dark and rough. I've flipped over again, the waves pushing me deeper and further from the surface. I am drowning. I can't breathe.

I can't breathe.

I can't breathe.

The burning in my lungs ceases only from the impact of my head on the surface floor. Pain vibrates through my body and the world goes black.

I stare at the drink in my hand.

"What's wrong?" Bishop smiles at me. He's wearing the leather jacket I bought him for his birthday. He looks so

Handsome and I'm standing here so nervous to tell him.

"Can we talk?" He smiles at my request and nods his head.

"Always. Lead the way," he stumbles over the edge of the deck, barely having anything to drink. He's just happy and distracted as he follows me down the stairs. We had thrown him a proper birthday, a blazing fire on the beach. All of our friends laugh and drink with each other. Mom and dad watch from the deck like parents would. Sean sits with his arm around a girl, their smiles warm and friendly. Natalie is cradled in Ben's lap, a bottle of wine to her lips. Who needs a glass on the beach, that's where we're free to be teenagers entering adulthood.

Bishop takes my hand and we walk towards the tree house. Once inside he pulls me down onto the couch and wraps his arm around me to hold me against him. He smiles at me. It's soft and light. He's so different from the normal dark and quiet Bishop he is around everyone. So warm and friendly.

"I love you," I say and he chuckles.

"What did I do now?" He jokes rubbing a finger along my jaw.

"Nothing. I just like the look on your face when I say it." I smile and lean into his touch.

"Are you sure?" He asks, his expression softening.

"I have to tell you something," I swallow hard and I feel him go rigid under my touch. "I think I'm pregnant Bishop," I say it so

fast I'm not even sure I said it out loud. But his hand drops from my face and his brows furrow at me.

"Are you sure?" He asks. His tone is hesitant. His eyes flickered back and forth nervously.

"Yes. I'm two weeks late and it lines up with graduation," I bite my lip. His face changes again, it's worried and scared.

"You can't—" his words are jumbled and clumsy. "You can't be. I can't be, Nora. I can't be a dad."

"Bishop," I say softly, I'm not scared of this. Not worried. I know we're young but it feels like a gift. Feels like we're being told that we're meant to be together. A binding piece in our lives. But he is scared. I can't hear it in his voice.

"No you don't understand, I can't be a dad. I'll be like him. I am like him." He mumbles the last part and swallows hard. He pulls back from me, shifting uncomfortably on the couch. "I'll only wreck this. Poison the child. The baby,—" he stops and his gaze is drawn to my still flat stomach.

"Our baby," I say. He meets my gaze with disgust. I can't tell if it's disgust at my words or his own for liking them. Just for a moment, he felt hopeful that it could be alright and he feels gross for feeling so. "You aren't like him, Bishop," I say but I can see he doesn't believe me.

"I am. It was beaten into me, Nora. I was groomed to be like him. And if anything ever happened to you? Would I take it out on them? Like he does to me? You can't guarantee I won't be like my father." He rants. Slipping into a tense stance. He paces the tree house, his boots heavy on the creaking wood.

"So you never want children because of a what if?" I am frustrated now. Gripping the light blue fabric of my shirt near my stomach. I'm going to be sick. I thought he would be happy about this.

260

"No. No, I can't ever do this. I don't ever want to be him. I don't ever want my children to be afraid of me. Scared of their father. It's a what-if to you, but it's a certain fate for me if we have children," he's yelling now. Upset and out of control.

"Alright," I say. I can't figure out what else to say to him. I'm saddened and confused but I'm not ready for this fight. I expected him to be happy at the least. Maybe excited. But he's furious.

"Let's go to the pier," I say. He turns to me, his movements sharp and sudden. He sighs and rubs his jaw. *"Please. I wanna see the ships."*

"Fine," he's being short with me but it means he's processing and thinking. I'm stupidly hopeful.

He helps me down from the tree house, his strong hands on my hips to lift me off the last few rungs of the ladder. We walk up the back way, away from the beach house to his home. Where his motorcycle sits, shiny and black in the moonlight. He hands me my helmet and sits on the bike waiting for me to join him.

The bike is cold against my thighs, but he's so warm. I rest my head on his neck as the bike rattles to life beneath us. He pulls from the curb and starts down the long highway towards the pier. The trees curl in making the highway darker than normal. The light of the bike is the only thing visible against the pitched pavement.

The bike shakes a touch but he steadies it.

He had only one drink, one beer. He's fine to drive. I'm just nervous and emotional.

The bike shakes again.

"Is the road wet?" I yell over the engine but he doesn't hear me. I see the headlights of a truck over his shoulder. Coming right for us but he doesn't steer away, doesn't move the bike out of the path of destruction. He aims for the collision.

"BISHOP!" Last minute he swerves my scream echoing over the

sound of the bike. It shakes violently as he tries to gain control but the bike doesn't correct this time. The wheels slide out from under us and we collide with the pavement. The bike crushes against my leg, a scream tearing from my lips as my head bounces violently against the pavement. I roll for what feels like hours until I slide to a stop against the edge of the road. The bike was in pieces against the highway just meters from me. I can't see or hear Bishop.

My eyes draw so heavily.

Each blink is longer.

My eyes are so heavy.

Blinding lights.

White-hot.

Annoying beeping.

I try to open my eyes but nothing works.

Nothing is okay.

Open your eyes.

"Nora, open your eyes." A voice calls to me. It's not my own now. It's distant and faint but I can hear it. "Baby, open your eyes for me."

I blink and see the young face of Bishop. Tears streamed down his face, hair cropped and sweaty from his helmet.

Red and blue lights flash against the darkness.

I blink again and see the weathered face of Bishop. Hardened and older. His hair is long and wet against his forehead. Sand sticks to his neck and chest. The sky is bright blue.

My eyes are so heavy.

"Nora, baby!" His voice shocks me awake. He's scratched up. His face was bruised and his shoulder was limp. "I'm so sorry." He pleads. Sean throws him backwards. Cocks a fist and slams his face against the wall behind his head. Bishop doesn't defend himself. He just lets Sean beat the shit out of him. "I couldn't," he

swallows a mouth full of blood, "*I couldn't do it. I couldn't let her do it.*"

My eyes are so heavy.

"Hey," the hospital lights are violently bright. Bile rises in my throat, I sit up too fast and puke into the bucket beside me. "Get it up," Bishop rubs my back, the vomit tastes like saltwater and sand.

"Back up," I bark. He stares at me for a moment and as if he can read my mind. He knows.

"You remember," he says.

35

"Nora," his voice is tense but nervous. I can feel his fear. I remember everything. Every moment. Every memory. The good with the bad. It's all there trapped inside my pounding head. Muddled with the images of the good memories of the last three months. His voice, his touch, his lips, and his hands.

It's overwhelming.

"Shut up," I snapped. "Just stop for a minute. Please."

He listens but a huff leaves his perfectly shaped lips. I'm frustrated. Even thinking about his lips makes my heart rate pick up. And the hospital monitor tattles on me like a school kid. Picking up in pace with its obnoxious beeping. I close my eyes.

Everything.

"Nora," he says my name again. It sounds like agony when it leaves his lips. A small sniffle echoes before he asks, "do you want me to leave?"

I'm not expecting his question. It catches me off guard but still, I can't look at him. Not yet. My heart is thumping in my chest too fast to say something smart and controlled. I want to tear him to shreds and curl into his lap to cry all at once. I knew it would be hard to remember everything and retain every memory we had recently made but this is agony.

He's different now. *Remember that.* Hold on to that. He's not that boy, he's a grown man. He's dealing with his issues the same way I am. I can't hate him for that. All these years I've hated him because I thought he hated me. I thought he didn't want *me*. But it was only about saving me. But does that forgive him of his sins? Does that mean everything he did was worth it? Dad would have survived, debt would have been bad but manageable. The beach house wasn't my only home. It was just a place we lived. My home was my parents, Sean, Natalie, and Ben. It was Bishop. *Was.*

Remember.

"Do you have my notebooks?" I ask, my head pounding. "Or some paper?"

"I'll see if there's one in your backpack," he says shifting from the chair. He comes into view and he's still wearing the casual clothes from the beach. His shoulders are tense and his hair is a mess, he's still covered in the sand all up his back and the hem of his pants is wet. I must have just gotten here. He pulls a notebook from the bag on the chair as he turns I look to the left, away from him.

His eyes will break any wall I have created.

"Thank you," I say as the notebook weighs on my leg. I pull the pencil from the binding and start writing.

I hear him sit back into the chair, silently and he shifts his boots against the ground roughly before he settles. I scribble against the paper, trying to remember everything. Writing it all day. All the good and all the bad. The clock ticks by, the monitors beep and Bishop sits wordlessly, so still, I don't even know if he's there anymore.

You love him.

I write it over and over. As though I am trying to convince myself that it's true even though I know it is. I do love him, or I wouldn't feel so heartbroken right now.

Remember his words, all the things he whispers in the dark. When we are alone and in love. The two of us curled into a ball of one person, just so madly in love nothing else matters. Remember his promises, the boat. He bought a boat for me. The cottage. He created a life for us.

Was it for us? Or was it for him?

If he wanted a life, true life for us. He would have told me. He would have confided in me, all his fears and worries. Instead, he tried to kill us. He tried to kill us.

How could I have forgotten the accident?

The baby.

"We never talked about it," I finally say. "We never," I stop trying to sit up, but pain shoots through my head again. He shifts in his chair but doesn't move to touch me. "I blocked it out Bishop, I blocked it all out because I just wanted you."

He doesn't speak.

Please speak.

"All I ever wanted was you. I was heartbroken that you didn't care enough to talk to me. I felt inferior like I didn't matter because I made the wrong decision." I stop, swallowing the fear creeping up my throat. My heart protests against my mind, begging me to stop talking.

He still doesn't stop me, he just lets me get it out. He just takes it.

He's so quiet I can hear his heart beating.

"You treated me like your father would have treated you. I didn't hold it against you because you were scared. I tried to show you that I loved you still and how did you repay me? You kept secrets, you cheated on me, you drank and you left. You didn't include me in the decisions about our lives anymore." I throw the notebook, all the words of affirmation that I had just written across the room. The pencil bounces off the floor and I sigh.

"It took you years to realize that you made a mistake. I almost drank myself to death waiting. Thinking stupidly one day that you would come home. Now, I don't even know. You've been so different these last weeks, a version of yourself that seems so mature and loving. You've proven that you love me over and over but it was built on the same secret that tore us to shreds the first time. Did you expect me to be like this forever, to never remember and you could live your life in bliss again? Were you completely unaffected by the last years?" I ask and I get no answer. I just want him to talk to me. It's all I ever wanted.

"I tried to kill myself, Bishop," I whisper. One last attempt. "I tried to kill myself because I thought you didn't want me."

He shifts in his chair now, I hear his boots make solid contact with the ground and he's walking. I turn to see him standing by the door. "Don't walk away from me," I say. "If you love me like I think you do, don't walk away from me again."

My head throbs, the image of Bishop standing by the hospital door violently flashing between young and old.

Young Bishop turns to look at me. His eyes are red and sore from crying. His lip busted from Sean's fist and a look of despair on his face. His shirt is ripped and his jeans are torn, he has bruises all over his skin. The normally beautifully tan flesh has ugly hues of purple and blue. His jaw is so tense I can see the tick from my hospital bed. His hand is white-knuckled on the knob of the door, fighting with himself to stay. A single tear runs down his cheek and he pushes it away with the back of his free hand. "I love you, Nora."

"Don't lie to me" I say back. The Bishop I know now turns sharply to look at me, confused by what I've said. "The first time you left this room, that night. You said to me, with tears in your eyes. I love you, Nora and my response was 'don't lie to me.'"

His eyes are just as red now as they were that day. His lip is healed but pressed into a thin line making his jaw flex under the pressure. The blue in his eyes is like an impending storm. It hurts to look at them, just as I knew it would be.

"Don't walk away from me again," I say. "Please. It'll only be a lie, I know you love me, Bishop."

He turns the knob and leaves the room.

My heart shatters into a million pieces.

36

BISHOP

"Calm the fuck down," Sean puts his hand in my face and I almost break it.

"Back off Roberts," I shove him backward. He snarls at me and steps in my face again.

"I warned you that this was a bad idea, I told you that she would remember and this could happen, she almost fucking drowned Bishop," he pushes a finger against my chest. "All because you wanted to make sure she never remembered that night."

"Her surfing wasn't even my idea, how about you go push around Ben inside? He's a small opponent, maybe you'd actually win a fight for once." People are stopping and staring at us outside the hospital. Sean hovers over me, his fist balled at his side.

"How do I know you didn't cause the first accident? That this wasn't the plan all along?" Sean is accusing me of stupid things now, he's out of control and could use a tug on his leash.

"Do you know how stupid you sound? Even if I did start that fire, how could I be sure she'd hit her head?" He's trying

269

to detective me, using his bad cop routine only works if the good cop, Ben, is around to help.

"The rung was broken," Sean says confidently.

"How did you know that?" I snapped at him. "She was the first and last person to go up in that tree house, you couldn't have known the rung was broken. The ladder was completely ashed after the fire, I know because I cleaned it myself." It's my turn to get in his face. "What the fuck did you do Sean?"

He's caught, he has a look on his face that I know is a guilty one. He's made it before, caught red-handed. "What the fuck is wrong with you? You could have killed her!" I shove him back just as Natalie runs out with Ben hot on her tail. I think about punching him in the face, but I stop myself. I am not my father. "Don't" I put my hand up to her, stopping her from getting too close to us, "back up I don't want you hurt."

"Bishop," she looks me up and down. "What the fuck?" She backs up though, her hand on her swollen stomach.

The baby.

Nora had been mumbling in her catatonic state about the baby. Every day since the accident I thought about that. I never told her that it was the reason I don't sleep anymore. Every time I shut my eyes, laying in the cold, empty room in Japan all I could see was the flashing lights of the ambulance. I could hear the haunting cries of a baby in the silence. That's why I called her. Her breathing drowned out the sound of my nightmares.

"You want to tell them or should I?" I snap, pushing him again. He doesn't fight back but he barely moves under my shove. His whole body is tense. He doesn't speak, "Cat got your tongue? Sean here is the reason Nora fell the night of the fire, he was just about to tell me why he did it?"

"What?" Ben sounds shocked, he moves to cover Natalie. "Is that true?"

Sean nods.

"Are you fucking serious?" Natalie tries to get around Ben but she's stopped by his arm. "What is wrong with you?"

"I just wanted her to break her ankle or something," he said. "She's been so good lately, between work and her friends. I don't get phone calls to come to get her or texts to talk. I just," he stops. He was desperate, she had pushed him away because it wasn't what she wanted but she didn't have the heart to tell him. He could have any girl he wanted, flash a smile and a wink and they always came running. But he had always been stuck to her.

"You wanted her to need you," I say, shaking my head. "Why didn't you just talk to her? Tell her how you felt?"

"That rich coming from you Bartley," he snarls. I ignored his jab, "she wasn't answering my calls."

"You wanted to immobilize her because she wasn't dependent on you anymore? You're supposed to protect her, Sean, not be someone she needs protection from!" I shake my head in disbelief. "Funny how you've been letting me walk around like the bad guy this whole summer. My entire life. Now we find out you're just as bad."

"Don't compare me to you," he scoffs. "She got gun shy after we slept together, I just wanted it to go back to how we used to be."

"So you're telling me your feelings are hurt because she was feeling better and didn't want to sleep with you again?" Natalie steps forward again, her tone is venomous. "We aren't fifteen anymore Sean, pulling pigtails isn't fucking cute. She lost everything because of this! I had to tell her twice about the wedding, about the baby. All because you wanted your girlfriend back? Grow up!"

Ben sighs, "she's not wrong. You have to tell Nora."

"Are you serious?" Sean scoffs, "You don't think she's dealing with enough right now? She just remembered the last missing years of her life? All of it. The doctor says the impact from the ocean floor gave her a small internal brain bleed and you want me to burden her more? No. Let her blame Bishop for this, just for a little longer. He can handle it, he's a piece of shit regardless."

This time I don't hold back, I slam my fist into his face.

It feels amazing.

He stumbles back, his lip instantly bloody but he doesn't fall. He collects himself and charges toward me.

"Enough," a voice booms through both of us, causing Sean to freeze. Nora's father stands a couple of feet from us. "Do you two never learn?"

He walks over to us, Nora's mom not far behind him. "You're grown-ass men." He says, "start acting like it. Sean, you deserved that, and if you ever do anything to endanger Nora again. I'll hit you myself. Bishop, what happened?"

"Nora bailed on a wave this morning when Ben took her out," I explained. "She hit her head pretty badly but I guess the impact was enough to help her memory out the rest of the way. She remembers everything," I nod, grim because I'm not sure what that means for us.

I walked away from her.

I shouldn't have done that.

But if I hadn't I would have told her everything. Everything. That I regretted that night my entire life. That I wished I could have held our child in my arms. That she didn't deserve to suffer alone in the pain that I caused and ran away from.

She woke that morning so heartbroken, gripping herself in tears when the doctor told her what happened. And I did nothing.

I was so young, so stupid, and scared.

"She'll be okay son," Nora's mother says with a smile and wraps her arm around me.

"Yeah I know," I nod, letting her give me a hug.

"You both need to leave, cool off, and don't come back until I call you or Ben does," her dad points at the both of us and walks away into the hospital.

"You're going to tell her everything Sean because if you don't I will and I won't sugar coat it for your benefit." Natalie snaps at him and follows her father.

Sean turns back to me, his eyes full of rage. "You aren't blameless here, you brought us to this point. Remember that."

"I can't forget it," I say honestly.

37

I t's been weeks.
The doctor cleared me to go home on the day of the surfing accident.

I guess he couldn't tell my heart was broken. There's no medication for that, my mom said as she hugged me closely on the couch that night. Bishop hadn't come home, not to the apartment, not to his condo, and not even the cabin. I couldn't find him anywhere.

I called him, over and over again. The sound of the ringing started to drive me nuts. I could hear it in my sleep, as I ate breakfast and read my books on the back deck. I called Scott, trying to get a hold of him that way but was given no in. He was a brick wall.

Sean was just as bad, he hadn't even come to see me in the hospital that day. Ben explained that he and Bishop had an argument and that my dad sent them both home. I wasn't surprised. The fact that he still hadn't called worried me. The weeks went on and I received nothing from him. Late in October I finally decided to get back to work. Josh welcomed me back to work with open arms. It felt good to have a purpose again. All those weeks of not understanding myself were hard.

Now I sit in my apartment, November is coming to an end and I'm going through event items for the week of work. I stare at my coffee cup, drifting in and out of my thoughts. I'm supposed to hate him. I know I am, but all I can think about is him. My bed feels empty and cold when I climb into it every night and I hope to roll over and feel him there but he never is.

We've fallen back into our old ways.

My coffee has gotten cold. I groan and slide off the island stool and dump it down the sink.

My phone has been going off all morning but focusing on work felt good. I finally flip it over and I have three missed calls, two voice messages, and like thirteen texts. The calls are from my mother, I don't bother to call her back, the voice messages are from her as well. The texts are from a slew of people, mostly Ben and Nat.

Answer your phone, Nora!

Natalie was panicking, so I called her, "What's going on?"

"The baby is coming," Ben answers, he sounds even more panicked than Natalie had in her texts.

"Isn't it early?" I ask, setting my phone on speaker so I can slip into my jacket. I look around frantically for my keys.

"Yes, just get down here." He hangs up on me, the click abrupt over the speaker. I slip on clean boots and my scarf, fumbling with my bag and the door lock.

"Hey," I drop my keys to the floor, Sean stands on the perch of my stairwell. He's wearing a dark blue pea coat and his beard is grown out. He looks tired. "Can we talk?"

"Not right now," I say, my tone short with him. He's been ghosting me just as badly as Bishop. I don't have the energy for this today. "Natalie just went into labor and I need to get to the hospital. You can come or go home," I say but he doesn't move out of my way.

"I wanna talk," he says, he stops me from locking my door and opens it instead. "Won't take long. She'll be in labor for a while Nora," he tilts his head and I consider my options. Argue with him out in the cold for the next hour or let him say his piece and get to Nat faster.

"Fine," I walked back into the apartment and set my bag down. "What's going on?"

He steps into my space and wraps his hands around my face. Pressing a fast and hungry kiss to my lips, his weight is too heavy but I manage to shove him backward. "What are you doing?"

"Ben said you remembered?" He seems shocked, taken aback that I shoved him away.

"I do," I say, confused and rattled that he would try something like this. "Sean, you need to fill in some blanks for me please?"

"I just assumed that we would go back to the way things were, now that you remember everything?" He shrugs his shoulders.

"Back to the way things were? Sean, you haven't spoken to me in months?" I scoff at him. Why is he acting like this? "You aren't entitled to a make-out session because I remember some stuff? What the hell."

"I was just giving you your space, Natalie said you were back to the real world I figured you needed some time to adjust." He leans against the counter, a soft smile on his face. "I'm sorry I didn't call, I should have. That was stupid of me. We can go back to our date nights, movies, and cuddles now that you're home. Maybe we can talk about you moving closer to me so I can see you more often?"

I smiled back at him, "before the accident, we were due for a conversation I was too nervous to have with you."

"I know, that's why you stopped answering my calls. It's okay, I get it. It was a huge step for us, and you needed to take the time to think about it. I don't blame you. I'll wait forever for you to make the right decision," He says, shifting his weight and standing back up.

"I," I pause, not sure how to say this to him. I check the time on my phone, sigh, and look back at him. "Sean, I still love Bishop. I always have and I always will. I think that night, I was just confused and so sad after seeing him with that girl. I used you and that was unfair of me."

"No, no," he says, his tone becoming cold. "You said you weren't sure, that you needed time to think about things. You told me you loved me, Nora. We spent the last couple of years being together and now what?"

"You said we were never really together, I remember everything Sean. I remember the night we spent here and the days that followed. The guilt that ate at me." I shake my head.

"No you called me, I came over and we talked about taking the next step." He sounds unsure, his lie unraveling in his lap.

"I don't remember that," I say, I can feel the pinching at the base of my skull as I try to remember the days after the night he came over. The night Bishop showed up at my event with the other woman. Did we speak the next day?

"Maybe your memory isn't completely back? We can go see the doctor this week, and find out what's happening to you?" He suggests, his hand touches my shoulder but I'm too focused on trying to remember everything.

"No Sean," I say, putting my hand out, and pushing him away.

"It's been months, you should have this figured out by now." He snaps, angry that I pushed him away.

"I have thought about things, the last six months have left me nothing but time to think. We were always meant to be friends, not lovers Sean. Sometimes the world has different plans for us. You can make some girl so happy," I say softly, but his face hardens.

"I've been trying to make *you* happy, Nora. Just you. That's all I want. Why don't you see that? Bishop is a deplorable human being, he strings you along like a puppy dog and you let him tug your leash? And for what? For him to leave you every time things get too hard for him? That's not love, it's manipulation."

"You are guilty of trying to manipulate me as well. How do I know you're telling the truth about my memory, I just can't trust my mind just yet." I say, and I'm confident with that decision. "I need to go Sean. Nat needs me more than your ego does right now."

"Maybe you shouldn't be driving," he says. His face changes again, the anger releases and he's smiling at me. "If you're still having trouble remembering everything. Let me. I know the way to the hospital."

I nod, only because he's right. He knows the way and I would get lost. "No more talk about us though, just for today. I want to go meet the new baby," I say and he winks at me.

"Deal," he nods. He opens the door for me, taking my keys from my hand and locking the door before leading me to his truck. I slip my phone into my back pocket and climb into the passenger side of his truck. He starts the engine and turns towards the hospital. "How has work been?" he asks casually, turning the music down so I can answer him.

"Good actually, It's been really nice to get back into the swing of things," I say.

"Have you heard from Bishop?' He doesn't wait until I'm finished talking to ask. I look at him, a fleeting glance but his eyes are focused on the road.

"No, not since the surfing accident," I say. I slide my phone out from my back pocket and set it under my thigh on the seat. "He won't answer my calls."

Sean mumbles something under his breath that I don't catch because I'm too busy looking at the street signs. "Hey you missed the turn for the hospital," I say.

"Yeah I did," he answers, not stopping the truck he turns onto the pass for the beach house. My heart squeezes nervously in my chest. "We aren't finished with our conversation, Nora. We can talk until you make the right decision."

"And what would that be Sean?" I say, turning in my seat to glare at him. Fear is creeping up my spine, I've never seen him so cold before.

"Well me, of course. Once you realize I'm the better man, we can go meet the baby as a couple." He sounds so sure of himself. I contained my nervous sigh and put a smile on my face.

"You can't hold me hostage, Sean. I already told you my decision," I say again. This time he doesn't speak, he slaps. My cheek stings, and I press my flat palm to it, soothing the burning sensation that rolls across my face. "What is wrong with you?" I yell.

"There's nothing wrong with me, you're the one who's sick,

Nora. You can't trust your mind until you know all the facts. So I'm going to show you everything." Sean nods, putting his hand over the one covering my cheek in a soothing motion. "I promise you'll see things differently soon."

I plaster on a fake smile again and nod. Letting him have this. I turn in my seat again to stare out the window, taking a glance down at my cell phone. The call had gone through.

Bishop's name flashed across the open call screen.

My only hope was that he had heard everything.

38

Sean pulls up to the beach house and turns off the truck. "There's a storm coming so don't be stupid. We have to get inside before it hits. Stay here."

The rain beat against the windshield of the truck, it came down in sheets and made it impossible to see through. He climbs from the truck, pulling a hat down over his head. He opens the back door, sliding a large police evidence box from the back seat, and disappears beyond the sheets of rain towards the front door of the beach house.

I watch carefully and raise the phone to my ear, "Bishop," I whisper, my own voice catching in my throat.

"Nora," he responds almost instantly. "Are you okay?"

"Sean has lost his mind, I don't know what's wrong with him," I mumble, nervously watching for him to return through the rain. "He took us to the beach house."

"I'll be there as soon as I can, don't do anything to upset him until I get there. Just go along with whatever he says," he talks and my heart flutters in my chest. I'm so scared but I can't help but close my eyes and just listen to him speak. I missed him so much.

"There's a hurricane coming Bishop," I say remembering the storm. I hear a door slam.

"He's coming back. Be careful." I can see his shape through the rain coming back towards the truck.

"Leave the line open for as long as you can," he pauses, I can hear the fear in his voice. "I love you," he says quietly. "I should have said it that day, but I love you. I'm coming." I hear the car door slam on the other end of the phone.

Without responding I slide the phone back into my pocket as quickly as I can. Sean throws my door open, grabbing my wrist he pulls me from the truck and leads me towards the beach house. It's dark inside, the windows have been completely boarded up and the lights are out.

"Find some candles, I'll light a fire." He pushes me further into the house. I walk toward the kitchen and start looking for where mom would keep the candles. It doesn't take me long to find them, piled under the sink, with a few lamps and first aid kits.

I set them on the counter in a line before going to find a lighter. Sean moves around the house casually, with no urgency in his steps. Not tense or nervous. He seems completely calm. My hands shake as I open the drawers to find the lighter. The first drawer I open is full of knives.

I stare at the sharp weapons questioning myself. I've known Sean since we were kids, is he really dangerous? Or just confused and hurt. I watch him stack firewood, his shoulders relaxed and his attention on making it perfect. How had I missed all his anger? It had been staring me in the face for so long and now he had snapped. I look back to the knives, do I really need this? I wrap my fingers around the handle of the paring knife, small enough to fit in my back pocket just in case.

"What are you doing?" His voice is abrupt and he's standing

a few feet from me on the other side of the island. He's looking at my hand in the drawer but I don't think he can see what I have a hold on.

"Looking for the lighter," I grab it from the side organizer and hold it while slipping the paring knife into my back pocket. "Found it!"

"Excellent, get those lit and we can talk." He turns his back on me again, removing his weighted gaze from my body. I let a breath of relief leave my lips as I start to light the candles one by one. The storm outside rages violently against the beach house. Rain pelts the house in heavy droplets creating a white noise within. The hurricane was getting worse.

I want to check my phone and check on Natalie but I'm scared he'll take it away from me if I remove it from my pocket. Then I would be without communication with Bishop and ghost to the world if anything happened. I leave my phone where it is and wander around the island with two candles in my hands. I set them on the coffee table and position two more on the side table. I settle in on the couch and watch as he brings the fire to a roar.

"Are you hungry? Thirsty?" He asks, the Sean I know plowing through the possessive, violent version he's projecting otherwise. He smiles at me, the dimple popping and his eyes shining in the firelight. My handsome Sean. "Are you cold?"

He grabs a blanket from the back of the couch and lays it over my legs and feet, tucking me in comfortably. I tense as his hand comes around my thighs and back pockets, fully aware he could feel the knife in my pocket. He smiles at me and sits on the coffee table across from me.

"The next part of this won't be easy, I have a lot of disturbing things to tell you about Bishop. I just need you to listen, you can ask questions but don't make a decision until I'm finished." He puts his hand on my knee. "Promise me that?"

I nod, "I'll listen, Sean. I've always been here to listen."

"Good," he stands up walking over to the box he had hauled inside from earlier, he sets it on the coffee table and opens the lid. "Fifteen years of criminal activity in this box, all done by your precious lover boy."

"Sean," I shake my head as he slides the box towards me. I don't take it though. I nervously run my tongue over my lip and look up at him.

"I'm done being polite. I'm so sick of playing the role of the boy next door. I can't stand by and watch him destroy you again. I won't, Nora. I said I would let you figure things out but I can't do it," he nudges the box again until I take it in my lap.

I run my hands over the papers inside, tugging at the first one in the box. I pull it out and it's a police record sheet. A mugshot of Bishop was clipped to it. His features are so dark, and hollow that almost his eyes stare through me. I shudder. He's so young in it, younger than before I met him.

"This should be sealed," I say coldly, "you shouldn't have this. He was just a kid," I look up over the paper and Sean is staring at me blankly. He truly thought throwing this at me would change my mind. Would sway me? To what side?

"You knew about that?" He scoffs. "You knew he killed a girl and never said a word to anyone."

"Why would I? I know the real story about what happened that night and it was never my story to tell," I snap at him and he lunges forward. His hands resting on the box he pushes his weight into it, into me. He searches my eyes and shakes his head.

"It's not the only person he's killed, Nora." His voice is a whisper through the noise of the raging storm outside. It's a chill down my spine, a nauseous feeling in my stomach, and a spark of pain at the base of my head. "Think," he says. "Think you were there."

The doctor had said it was possible to be missing certain parts of memories. That I may have regained a solid eighty percent but some still may be stuck but I can't imagine what he's talking about. "Nora, think!" He yells and I jump from the noise.

"What did you do?" There was blood on my hands, so much blood. Bishop sits against the wood pillar, and Toby the kid from science class lays in the sand under the boardwalk. "Bishop!" I yell, I hold my fingers to the kid's neck. He's alive.

"Bishop, I need you to tell me what happened!" I yell again, Kate is pulling her jacket over her ripped tank top. Her makeup smudged and her hands shook violently. Bishop rubs the blood off his hand and pushes himself off the ground. He's got a bruised eye and split lip. When I had shown up he was on top of Toby in the sand, beating him over and over with his fists. Toby choked on his own blood and was unable to fight back.

I pull my cell phone from my back pocket and dial 911.

"He was attacking Kate," his voice startles me, he stands over us now as I try to listen for Toby's breathing. "He wouldn't stop, he thought it was funny."

Kate shakes, her eyes glass over as she stares at the kid laying half dead in the sand. The operator picks up, I explain to her what happened and she reassures me that the ambulance will be there as soon as possible.

"Bishop," I say sliding my phone back into my pocket, I grab his hand and turn his focus towards me. "I need you to take Kate

home," I say quietly, "you can't be here when the police show up. They won't care that you were protecting her."

He looks at me, shock crossing his features. "You have to go, take Kate," I repeat myself and he shakes his head. "Let me catch you," I say. After the day on the pier it had become our, I love you. We said it to one another when the I love you was too hard, too difficult to say out loud. When we were scared of loving too hard or too soft. When the fear took over and we couldn't think of a better way to promise that everything was going to be okay. "Let me catch you," I say it again and he nods, just once. His blue eyes caught the moon and shone brightly back at me.

"Take her home, get her in the bath. Don't ask her stupid questions, just let her cry. I'll be there soon to help." I instruct him. "And don't say a word to anyone, you were never here. Either of you." I look over at Kate and she nods in understanding.

He presses his forehead to mine and turns suddenly, moving towards Kate and helping her walk back to the path. I move back to where he lies, the red and blue flashing lights appearing from the parking lot. I wait until Kate and Bishop become part of the shadows and I stand to wave the paramedics over.

"I remember Toby," I say, my eyes coming up from the mug shot again. I see Sean's dark blue gaze and swallow hard. "I was there that day, you were right. I showed up just after Bishop pulled him off, Kate. He assaulted her. God knows how long before Bishop showed up."

"So he deserved to die for that? He died two days later in the hospital from a brain bleed; his attacker was never caught. But we all knew that Kate walked around nervously for a month. Like a scared cat, she jumped at the smallest noises and no one could touch her. Bishop broke his hand and never had it cast, but he wouldn't surf or skateboard. He just hung around with you, taking his photos with his good hand. We all knew." Sean growls at me and grabs my chin in his hand harshly, his grip too strong for me to pull away. "You helped him murder a seventeen-year-old kid, is that who you want to be?"

"Says the guy who kidnapped me. You brought me here to what? Tell me things about Bishop and myself that I already know. Yeah, I helped him that day. It wasn't for him though, and that's where you get confused. I did that for Kate, so she never had to be scared that she would see him again. Maybe that makes me as bad as him, but I don't regret it, Sean." I say sitting up into his grip with a stubborn force that makes him scowl.

"There's more," he starts to panic, his eyes flashing back and forth wildly, "there are over a dozen assault charges."

He throws papers at me from the box, Bishop's pictures all over them. Photos of him at parties, with girls, and in bars. Mugshots and hospital photos. Crime scene photos. All more gruesome than the one before. I look at them all, my stomach turning. I knew his anger was bad but I had no idea how bad.

"He's been going to therapy, making amends for these things," I defend him regardless.

"Has he made amends for killing your baby?" Sean's comment is a blow to the face. It hurts more than if he had actually hit me.

"No," I say softly, whispering into the night. "You can't use that to justify your actions right now," I shake my head.

He comes back to meet my gaze, leaning in closely and wrapping his hand around my neck. "It doesn't matter, does it? No matter how badly he hurts you..." he squeezes and I can feel myself panicking for air. "You will always go back to him. Is this what you want? Someone who constantly risks your life?"

"I can't," I stop because my lungs are gasping for air. "I can't breathe," I claw at his hand but he doesn't let go. I feel around with my free hand, searching for the paring knife, my fingers wrapping around the handle.

I shove the knife to his neck, pressing into the skin. He stops suddenly and looks down at it, I expect to see fear, anger, maybe even disappointment in his eyes. But there is a fire there, he's amused.

"How long has that been there?" He lets up on my throat with his palm and I take a huge gasp of air. "Should have known you were smarter than that."

"I'm learning today. You know very little about me." I shove him backward with the kick of my foot, I catch him in the groin and slide off the couch. I hop over the back to create space between us. The lamp on the table crashes to the floor, glass flying across the room. I step back and a piece cuts into the base of my foot, I hiss in pain but don't take my eyes off of him.

"Why do you have to make this so damn hard?" He stands, adjusting himself, and hops over the couch closing the gap. I'm suddenly regretting not grabbing a larger knife. "Don't," he says, seeing me look to the kitchen. "You wouldn't have the strength to hurt me anyways, you've always done the clean-up. He treats you like a secretary."

"Really? That's the best insult you can come up with?" I snap. "Don't come near me."

"His dad is alive," Sean laughs now, "did he tell you that? That excuse he used, that he couldn't see you while his father was alive. It was bullshit. He could have come home anytime he wanted."

"You're lying," I say, my hand shaking slightly.

"You can ask him when he gets here," Sean scoffs, and I look to the floor. The phone had fallen out when I knocked the lamp over, it sits face up. The open call is still blinking at us.

39

Sean had cornered me, I was pushed up against the fridge with the knife pointed out in front of me. My feet were cut up from the glass lamp that had shattered and I had a bruise forming on my neck and collar from his hand. He had retrieved the splitting hatchet from beside the fireplace and it said ominously on the counter, staring me in the face.

His eyes were savage.

This wasn't any form of Sean I knew.

"This is foolish," I say, trying to steady my hands. "Just let me leave."

"Where are you going to go? There's a hurricane going on outside," Sean chuckles, tears running down his face. His emotions are cagey, he can't decide how he wants to feel.

"What did you expect to happen? Truly, did you think I would come here and believe everything you say and just fall in love with you?" I shake my head trying to make sense of things.

"No," he slams his hand against the fridge beside my head and I jump again. "Put the knife down," he presses up against the tip of it, his face inches from mine.

I don't release the knife, "No," I say. "Not until you calm

down."

He grabs my arm, twisting it hard in the wrong direction and my grip fails. The knife clatters to the ground at our feet. I drive my knee up into his stomach and slide out of this grip. I clamber to the table and stand on the other side of it.

He throws a chair out of his way and storms over to me. "Stop fucking—-" I hit him across the face before he has a chance to finish his sentence. He turns back to me, a hard slap cracks across my face. It echoes through the empty house and stings my face worse than the first time.

"He's a murderer Nora, he doesn't care who he hurts, who he lives to and he does it all under the guise of protecting you. It's bullshit. Everything that comes out of his mouth is a tool to manipulate you." Sean starts to yell now. "You think he's some broken little thing you can fix! He's not! How long before his anger gets the best of him and he hurts you?"

"Like this?" I whisper, I brush my thumb against my bottom lip. Blood smudges against the pad and I show it to him. My throat is sore and swollen making it hard to speak anymore.

"This is a speed bump." Sean shakes his head. "Just like when he crashed his motorcycle on purpose, you forgave him for that."

"I didn't, I never forgave him for that." I groan and shift trying to release the weight on my cut feet.

"You crawled right back into his bed." Sean lunged for me, and I flinched as he threw his hands against the wall behind my head. Trapping me between his arms he stared at me. "You fucked him anyways, so I think if he can do the worst possible thing and still get some action, so can I.

"Back the fuck up," I didn't even hear him enter the house. Bishop stands soaking wet by the living room entrance. His black shirt is soaked through gripping to his heaving chest. His face is tense and his eyes are locked on Sean. "I won't ask you twice."

Sean drops his forehead against mine, his blue eyes are vibrant against the light from the candles and lamps. I want to pull away, flinch and twist from his touch but he looks so sad, defeat imminent. He is a wild animal backed into a corner.

He starts to laugh, a deep routed crazed laughter that bubbles from his lips.

"Are you alright?" Bishop's eyes bore into me, I can see him standing rigidly just over Sean's tense shoulder. I nod softly and turn my attention back. "Sean, this is between you and me, let Nora go."

"No, no," he waves an arm out at Bishop, shaking his head. "It's not. It never has been. You've pushed her out so she doesn't see the real you. How you treat everyone else around you!" Sean turns finally and I take a deep breath. My eyes flash to Bishop and he grinds his jaw together.

"I don't want to do this with you, Sean. Not today, Natalie is in the hospital. There's something wrong, Ben said she's having trouble. If anything happens to her and Nora is here, she'll never forgive you." I can't tell if he's lying, my heart jumps and I start to panic. He shifts, his head dropping and he sighs deeply.

"You think you're smooth," Sean shakes his head, running a hand through his hair. The bloody knuckles leave streaks of blood through the blonde ends. "I spoke to Marianne before I showed up at the apartment. The baby is fine, Nat is fine."

Who is telling the truth? My stomach turns over, I'm going to be sick.

"What do you want, Sean?" Bishop asks and Sean smiles, it's wide and proud like he's finally trapped his prey.

"I want you to tell her everything." He says, "everything."

Bishop moves slowly, coming around to the back of the couch. Sean still stands between us watching his every move. My heart stops, I didn't see it before but tucked into Sean's jean waist is his gun. I stutter, the words almost coming out of my mouth involuntary but I stop short. I try not to cry, tears welling in my eyes as I look up to Bishop. He knows. He just nods at me and gives me a weak smile.

My fear just became one hundred times more real.

Love is fickle, funny, and heartbreaking but I had never stopped loving him. I never would.

"I'll catch you," I say loudly enough that Sean turns and scowls at me but I'm not looking at him, I'm looking at Bishop.

"You want me to tell you everything?" He says recollecting the attention in the room. "Fine," He runs a hand through his wet hair and starts. "But Sean, know that after this whatever happens between me and Nora. I'm going to beat the shit out of you," he growls.

"You've never won the physical fights, Bishop, I'm too big. Always have been," Sean turns back to me and smirks, "Nora put up more of a fight than you ever have."

Bishop steps forward, Sean slides his hand around the handle of the hatchet on the counter. "Don't even think about it."

"You won't even fight fair then? You'll drag Nora here against her will, leave bruises all over her body," Bishop snarls, and looks from me to Sean. "Force some confession out of me. You'll never win Sean, don't you see that? I might lose her today, but you will lose her forever."

"If that's what you believe then you'll have no problem telling her everything right now," Sean smirks, waving the hatchet in the air and then pointing it at Bishop. "Go on."

"When I was ten years old my mother died," Bishop swallows hard. "She was the only person who ever loved me. I have been punished for that by my father for my entire life. Punished for having her blue eyes, nose, and smile. I was beaten every day of my life until we moved here," He leans back against the couch.

"The day I met Nora," He stops to look at me finally, "was the first time someone saw me."

"I don't want your life story, we were there. I want you to tell her what you've been doing in Japan." Sean sneers. Breaking the moment into thousands of tiny glass shards.

"Patience," Bishop puts a hand up. "I came over to your house, do you remember?" I nod at him, I remember perfectly, my heart skips a beat remembering how I felt when I opened the door and saw him. "I was nursing two broken ribs, I went home and my father reminded me that clothes cost money and I needed to be punished for wrecking my shirt."

I shut my eyes. I remember now, how stiff he was and quiet. He sat two spaces too far away for my curious heart to reach him on the couch and he kept looking over at the front door like he was waiting for someone. He had been terrified his father would show up, and find him.

"Your beach house was a safe haven," he gives me a pitiful smile. "I killed that girl Nora," he drops his eyes. "It wasn't my father. I told you that because I didn't think you could forgive me. I was running away the night it happened. The whiskey part is true, dad was forcing me to drink but it's because he found a stolen bottle under my bed. I was driving without a license and drunk."

My stomach sinks, "you lied to me?"

He nods. "See I told you, not everything is perfect. He's a dangerous criminal. Keep going," Sean snaps.

"What about Toby?" I question, not ready for the answer. If that had been a lie. I couldn't take that, I watched that boy die because I thought I was doing the right thing.

"Toby deserved it, *he did exactly what you think he did.*" Bishop's voice is steady. He's not lying.

I step forward, limping on my cut feet but still on guard, "keep going." I give him permission to say what he needs to. Anything to show Sean that he's just a man trying to be a better person.

"Before Japan, I have to confess something else. I just need you to listen," he looks at me with sad eyes and I know whatever he's about to say will break me. "The night you told me that you were pregnant, I got scared."

He's shaking, he's hiding it well but I can see the twitch of his jaw and the fidgeting of his hand against the back of the couch. His hand is gripping so tightly the knuckles are white in color. "I wasn't drunk, it wasn't an accident. I crashed the bike on purpose, I was disgusted with myself for feeling proud that I had hurt you so badly. There was no way the baby survived. You were in pieces and I didn't feel guilty or bad for doing it. Not until you woke up, you looked through me. All of a sudden you didn't see me anymore. Not like you had before." Tears flood his beautiful ocean eyes and I'm not mad, I thought I would be so angry but I'm not. I'm relieved.

"I couldn't let you bring a child into a world that I didn't feel safe in. I thought if I could never feel safe, then how could I keep our child safe? And then I realized that all this time I thought I was safe with you, I felt protected and secure but a baby made me realize it was just a show. That I didn't really feel anything but fear. I'm not even sure I knew what love was Nora, I don't even know if I'm capable of that emotion. Or I wasn't, at one point but now," he doesn't take his eyes off me. "Now I do. It's not about controlling all my emotions, or the emotions of the people that can hurt us. It's just about how we make each other feel. Everything else is just background noise."

"That's touching but there's more," Sean tilts his head, "this is the best part."

Bishop rolls his tongue across his bottom lip, "the first year I was in Japan, I got a girl pregnant. I have a son, Nora. That's why I couldn't come home."

40

"Guess you didn't get a chance to kill this one hey Bishop," Sean's voice is like a knife through the tension that is floating between Bishop and me. "I found out when I was looking for his dad. He kept it a very, very good secret. He sees him twice a week, pays the mother a shit load of money to keep her mouth shut and no one's the wiser."

Sean turns to me, "He tried to bury it when I went to look earlier this summer, even had Scott come to threaten me but once I found out the truth it was game over." That's what the phone call was about. The day I had walked up on him on the phone, speaking in Romanian. He had been trying to push this all under the rug.

"You said," I stop talking to think but my thoughts are so scrambled. "You said to me, even after all that. The accident, the aftermath that happened. That you didn't want kids?"

"I didn't," he stumbles with his words and stands up. He wants to get close but Sean hovers, blocking the path and I'm almost grateful. Just for a moment. Space to breathe and think about what he had just said to me. "I didn't want them. And then somewhere along the line, I didn't want them with anyone but you."

With you.

"But you did," I say quietly, my voice cracking.

"I did." He responds, his tone cold and sad.

My heart swells and I think for a second it might be broken but that's not it. Bishop stands across from me, limp and guilty. Would he ever have told me? Was this why he wouldn't return my calls because he was hiding this from me? Was I mad or jealous?

"I didn't know," he says suddenly, "I know it's an excuse you don't want to hear right now baby, but I didn't know she was pregnant until she showed up on my doorstep with him."

I don't look up from the table, I focus on the wood grain knots and try to think without their voices digging into my brain with their little hooks. A dull throb formed at the base of my neck, I steadied my breath trying not to cry. I wouldn't, not here trapped like a bird in a cage with no way out.

"You said the only reason you didn't come back to me was that it wasn't safe. That the only reason you came when you did was that he was dead, was any of that true?" I ask, Bishop sighs. His dark hair falls in front of his face and he looks up at me with grief-stricken features.

"He's been missing for months," he explains. "He left one night and no one has had any contact with him since. The business is in complete limbo and Kate is delusional thinking he's going to come back."

"So there was nothing keeping you from coming back to me. Coming home?" my voice breaks, but I stifle my tears.

He shakes his head, "nothing at all, you can't even make up some bullshit excuse to save my feelings?" I yell. Sean smiles, and my anger flashes red hot.

"I'm done lying to you, Nora," Bishop says with a shrug of

his shoulders.

"After ten years it's about time," Sean scoffs and I let a wild laugh leave my lips.

Unbelievable.

"Sean, you knew?" I ask.

"I just confirmed a couple of days ago," he says confidently, thinking he's won this war.

"This doesn't make," I wave my tired arms around, the fear had snapped and was being replaced with anger and adrenaline, "this, any better." I scoff. "Are you two fucking serious?"

Both of them look at me. Sean is not surprised that I am having a meltdown, Bishop is still sullen and quiet.

"So Nora," Sean's voice snaps, loud and in my face. "Do you still love him now?"

My anger was too real at the moment, burning under my skin like wildfire. I didn't care what either of them did. I just wanted to be back home with my sister. Sean turned, walked towards me, and put his heavy hand on my shoulder. I tip from the weight and slide out from under his touch. His face is hurt, he thinks I've forgiven him just because I know everything.

"Nora," Bishop's voice floated across the distance, he wanted an answer just as Sean did but I didn't have one with either of them.

"I know," Sean says, digging the gun out from the waist of his pants, he points it at me first but slowly turns the barrel towards Bishop. "You answer the question or I shoot him."

"You wouldn't," I snarl, snapping from my trance. "It would end your career."

"I would," his eyes are vicious and a scowl forms on his face.

"I can say he attacked me, I fired my gun in self-defense." He rubs the side of my face with his hand. His thumb brushed against my lip, "I'll make the decision for you if you aren't strong enough to do it yourself."

"You're not my Sean," I whisper with a shake of my head. "The Sean I know, the man I grew up with, is selfless and kind. He's strong-willed and has the most intelligent mind. You, whatever version this is, is horrible, it's cruel and selfish. It's ugly." He grabs my throat, I push into it unafraid of what comes next. He pushes the gun to my stomach, his finger on the trigger. "When I was at rock bottom with nothing to lose I almost killed myself just to be free. I'm not afraid of death Sean, so do it because I have nothing else left."

I'm lying. Even with all the rage coursing through me I could never let him hurt Bishop. That would hurt worse than death. This had been my job since the beginning to protect him, not the other way around. I was always meant to catch him, no matter the force of the impact.

"You're lying," Sean whispers, his grip is so tight on my neck I can't respond. My toes scrape against the floor as he lifts just enough to put pressure at the base of my chin. I can hear Bishop's boot shuffle on the ground behind us. "You've never been able to hide your feelings. It was torture, loving you while you loved him. For years, watching you look at him like he was the reason the world spun!"

"I can't change the way I feel Sean," I claw at his hand.

"What's so special about him? What does he do that I don't?" He's losing his grip on the situation, his thoughts are crumbling and he's panicking.

I can't answer him because I can't breathe, I can't get any air to my lungs. My vision starts to blur as he squeezes tighter. I can hear Bishop looking for something behind us, I just need to keep him distracted for a couple more seconds.

"I'm sorry," I whisper, choking and gasping for air.

"Me too," a shot rings out suddenly, my ears ringing loudly as the grip on my neck slips. I can't hear anything as I run my hands down my torso. I grip my stomach in shock, my hands are warm and sticky. Blood seeps through my gray shirt between my fingers.

Bishop attacks him from behind, grabbing the collar of his shirt. He throws Sean backward into the island counter. I stumble back against the table, my head is dizzy and my legs start to feel numb.

"You think this will fix things? She'll never forgive you for this," Bishop slams his fist into Sean's face.

"She's forgiven you for worse!" Sean counters with a shot to the stomach.

"You shot her. She's bleeding out as you fight me!" Bishop tries to push him back, "Look at her, you fucking idiot, I don't want to fight you!" Bishop lands another heavy-handed blow but Sean wraps his arms around him and slams him into the table. His back cracks against the wood and the table shutters under their weight.

"It doesn't matter anymore, my life is over without her!" Sean yells his face red and his eyes wild.

Bishop grunts, throwing his hand up to stop the swing of the hatchet. He catches it just in time but it pulls through the soft skin of his palm. I steady myself and hobble to the back door, the sliding lock is jammed. I push my weight against it but my hands are slippery and I can't get a good grip on the door handle. Bishop turns to see where I am but it's a mistake, Sean catches him in the thigh with the hatchet and throws him backward.

Bishop is faster, he uses a kitchen knife to drive it into Sean's hard abdomen.

"Run," Bishop twists the metal from his leg and throws it across the room. Sliding out from a recovering Sean he slams against the thin glass of the back door and knocks it loose. "Don't stop. Just go," he groans and limps away from me to block another blow from Sean.

"Your leg," I pointed to the puddle of blood around his thigh.

"It'll be fine, go to the pier!" He pushes me out into the raging storm, and rain pelts down against my skin. I start down the stairs to the path as he scrambles back into the house, "Sean stop!" I hear him yell but the gunshot that rings out is louder. My body freezes the moment it happens, I can't leave not knowing who was on the receiving end. I swallow hard and try to see through the rain into the house. My hair presses soaking wet against my face and the wind beats against my body.

Sean steps out onto the deck, looking around frantically. I can barely see him, the silhouette of his body against the dim lights coming from the house. He's holding the gun. I didn't think it was possible to ever feel as hopeless as I do at this moment. I want to cry out, scream and run back to the house but it would do us no good.

I turn on my heel and run. The blood seeping from my stomach hurts but I feel around to my back, thinking of all the stupid medical shows I've binged watched. There was an exit wound, I could only hope the bullet went through me clean, I pressed as hard as I could on my stomach and kept moving.

Navigating the path to the pier was difficult in the dark. Trees cut into my arms and face as I stumbled into them. I could hear him behind me, his shots ringing out over the rain and wind. The trees creak in protest around me, a bullet hits a tree to my left sending splinters flying everywhere.

The pier comes into view, desolate and destroyed. Trees have fallen on the beach and the waves in the ocean are raging against the pier's walls. They lick up the sides of the wood and the pier leans back and forth creaking under the pressure of the water.

"You don't have to run anymore," Sean calls out, I press my back against the far end of the pier. Looking down at the drop into the ocean. I had nowhere to go.

"What did you do?" I yell back, shaking my head. My whole body is freezing and on fire at the same time. My vision was failing, spotty, and fuzzy. Every time I blink he's closer, taking small steps toward me. I don't see his gun but that doesn't mean it's not there.

"I did what you never had the strength to do," he keeps coming closer. I try to hold my arm up to stop him but I don't have the energy.

"I was never the weak one," I say over the howling wind. "It was always you. You never had the courage to just tell me how you felt back then. You never told me through the years, even when you had the chance you never told me anything. You just used me to get back at Bishop, that's all this was ever about." I grip the pier to hold myself up, hooking my feet on the first slat I raise myself up over the top barrier. I can feel my legs starting to buckle. "This was never about me. It was about winning and possession. Guess what you can't have me."

He lunges forward to stop me but I'm already gone.

The water is black.

303

The water is ice.
The water is a sanctuary.

41

"Nora," I can hear my name. It's so faint. It's so far away from me. "Nora," it calls again. I reach my arms out in front of me, through the icy cold water and into the darkness.

Find me.

Everything is so dark.

I can see him. Standing there like a dark angel. In a black suit that slides over his broad shoulders and tucks tightly to his torso. His eyes glimmer like sapphires in the darkness and his smile is bright, warm, and soothes the aching in my chest. He holds out his hand to me, curling his fingers, urging me forward.

I am stuck.

No matter how much I try to move my feet I can't get to him. I groan under the weight pressing down on me. My whole body is freezing and I start to shake violently. My lungs ache for air, clawing for it up my sore and raw throat.

"Come on Nora," something pounds on my chest. Up and down, "fucking breathe. Please breathe." The motions are clumsy and intense. It's painful and there's a slight burn in my chest that slowly rises through my bones and seeps into my skin.

"Nora. I need you to come back to me. You were so brave.

So brave, I've never been more proud of you." His voice is honey, "you have to fight right now for me. I know you're tired, exhausted, and sore but you are not allowed to give up yet. Not until you come back here and fight with me."

Two harsher breaths of air push into my body followed by more thrusting. More pumping.

"You come back to me right now and tell me how stupid I am. How selfish I am and how much I've hurt you. I don't care. Just come back to me. If you don't I will burn this pathetic world down around myself. I can't do this without you. I've never been able to. I need you, Nora. I need you." His hands were slow and became weaker with every sloppy push.

"I'm sorry I never told you, I was stupid and scared. I was terrified the night of the accident. I was so consumed with fear that I would screw up I forgot that beside you I can do anything," he's sobbing, I wish I could find my way back through the darkness.

I'm coming, keep fighting, I want to say but no words come out.

"I can't stay awake much longer, but I love you. I love your bright red hair and your big green eyes. I love every scar on your body, I love the crazy personality that gets you in trouble so often. The risk-taker that lives within your strong, breathtaking body. I love your fearless mind, the one that has no filter, no pause on life. You just do everything you want without thinking of the consequences." He pauses. His voice faded into the heavy rainfall. "I'm so sorry I hurt you, I want you to meet my son. I want to be a family. And I can't do that if you don't wake up. Don't you dare leave me!" He warns in my air as he gives me another two breaths.

I spit up water. Like a plug was pulled on my lungs I gasp

for air.

I feel him fall beside me. His hand curled into the hem of my shirt. His breathing is shallow and barely there anymore. I roll over in the sand, my eyes barely open and he's staring back at me. Dark and sticky blood stains the sand around us the rain making everything dark and wet.

"Bishop," I whisper as he closes his eyes.

One week later

"How do you feel?" Natalie asks from my bedside. She looks healthy, happy, and different. There is a glow to her that motherhood brought. Little Yelena had come into the world the happiest, plumpest baby. Natalie couldn't stop showing me photos, every chance she got.

"Like I was shot," I groan, my stitches pulling roughly against my skin as I sit up.

"Well, you were," Natalie laughs. My mind flashes to Sean. The look in his eyes that night and I start to shake. "He's still locked up," Nat rests her hand on my leg comfortably. "I still can't believe he snapped like that. Do you have a magical vagina or something?"

I laugh but it hurts, a sharp hiss leaves my lips. "I guess so." I groan readjusting myself.

"Bishop?" I ask quietly not sure if I even want the answer.

"Still not awake," she shakes her head sadly. The doctors said he had lost a lot of blood. He had been shot in the shoulder and the cut on his thigh barely missed the major artery. His hand needed fifteen stitches and he had woken up from surgery yet. It had been a week.

"Did you know? About his son," I ask.

"No one did. Not even Ben which is surprising. He kept it

extremely well hidden. You haven't spoken much about it." Nat sits fully forward in her chair now.

"I just," I pause. Letting my thoughts catch up with me. "I just want to talk to him. For real this time. It's my fault he's like this," I say. "He almost died."

"You didn't cause that," she gives me a pathetic smile.

"Didn't I? I should have put an end to this stupid rivalry years ago. I should have never slept with Sean," bile rises in my throat at the thought of him sitting in county jail. "I started this and I couldn't even finish it."

"You almost died Nora, again—" she rolls her eyes at me. "If Bishop was awake he'd be saying the same thing I am. You aren't responsible for Sean or how he acted. You are only responsible for your actions and your heart."

"I just wish I knew what he was thinking," I bite my lip. "He seemed so convinced that I was wrong. That I was crazy for loving Bishop."

"You are." She laughs at me. "Crazy stupid in love. You and Sean would have never worked. He only ever wanted to keep you in a bubble. His whole life mission was about you being safe and secure."

"That doesn't sound so bad," I shrug.

"That's not you. You've been living your entire life second by second. You love the thrill of falling, that's why you love Bishop so much. With him, the thrill never leaves. You are constantly falling in love with him."

I had never thought of it that way. She was right. Every time I saw him my heart jumped like it had been electrified. Even when I'm furious with him my skin feels like it's on fire and my body pulls towards him like a magnet. We had lost so much time this summer, arguing and forgetting who we were that we never got a chance to show each other who we are now.

Did I want that chance?

It meant forgiving him for everything, no, not forgiving but it meant I had to be willing to try. He had saved my life. Proved that even when we are broken, falling apart and angry with one another that we mean more to each other than a stupid fight.

She smiles at me. "Do you want to go visit him?"

I nod. "Am I allowed?"

"I'll sneak you in. Let me find a wheelchair." She giggles and slides from her chair. She leaves the room and all of a sudden I feel very alone.

The dark shadows close in on me and I feel like I can't breathe. One, I say to myself trying to remember all the things I'm grateful for. I am alive. Two, if I close my eyes I can hear the ocean in my memory. I can touch the sand with my toes. Three, I turn slightly to admire the sailboats in my mind and I can hear him *"I'll always catch you, Nora."*

This is what I hold on to. My dreams

I open my eyes when I hear the door click open and the sound of wheels turning on the white linoleum floor come to a stop at my beside.

"Slow," Nat warns me. She puts her hand behind my back bracing the bandages near my hip. Where the bullet had gone clean through my torso. It hurts like a mother as the stitches pull in protest to my movement but I make it to the chair without ripping anything.

The halls are empty this late at night and Nat has no problem getting me to his room. "He looks scary with everything plugged into him," she says as she wheels me in.

She's right. He does. The monitors beside his bed beep soft and his chest rises and falls with the machine. His dark hair is pushed back off his face and his cheeks have no color to them. I reach out and rub my thumb along his jawline. It's scruffy and unkempt, its itches my skin but it's familiar.

Natalie nods, "I'm going to go get some food and check in on Ben. I'll be back."

I want to crawl into bed next to him, just to be closer and feel his warmth. I settle for his hand. It's colder than I expect it to be.

"Hi," I say so quietly I barely hear myself say it. "You look awful," I stifle a painful laugh. "I'm sorry," the tears aren't far behind.

"I should have told you how much I loved you, every chance I got, I should have been telling you. Anger is so stupid, we let it get in the way of how we feel so often. Even Sean, I think he was just so lost and angry at us both for leaving him behind. He felt so alone. I know how it feels to be that alone, when I snapped there was no one around for me to hurt but myself." I press his hand to my face and lean into it.

"This wasn't how things should have gone. You should have never come home, now you're lying here thousands of miles away from your son who needs you. I'm sorry you came home for me and I wasn't ready for you." I swallow hard.

"I'm not," he groans. A cough left his lips.

"Bishop?" I nearly jump from my wheelchair. A sharp pain reminds me I can't move that fast. He's so real and awake now I don't know what to do with myself. His eyes cast down to me from the bed and worrying flickers across them.

"Nora," he moans, "are you okay?" He moves his hand and his fingers trace the ugly bruises on my neck with tender

310

patience. He looks up at me again, the anger behind the worry.

"I should get the doctor," I pull away, suddenly afraid to have this conversation with him.

"What are they going to do? Tell me I'm awake?" he chuckles and a small smile forms on his lips.

"I really should get them, Bishop," I say going to pull my hand away but he squeezes it and holds me in place.

"Don't leave me," he whispers, his jaw is tense and his beautiful blue eyes are rimmed with tears. "I'm sorry I never told you. I didn't have the courage to tell you, so be mad at me. Scream, shout, throw things but just don't leave me."

"I'm not going anywhere. I have my entire life to be mad at you for this...thanks to you. You saved my life, Bishop. The doctors said if you hadn't pulled me out of the water when you did I would have died. You did CPR with a bullet wound in your shoulder." I shake my head in disbelief. "You saved me."

"I owed you a debt for all the times you saved me," he leans his head to the side. His eyes flicker from mine to my bruised and cut lip, "I wish I could kiss you right now."

He scowls. I slide from his grip and use both hands to push myself up from the chair and brace myself on the bed. "Scoot over," I say but it comes out a groan. My whole body screams at me as I climb into the bed next to him.

"You're going to hurt yourself," he mumbles moving his arm to wrap around me.

"Worth it," I lean in and pull his face towards mine. Savoring the warm taste of his mouth. His lips part slightly and he presses into the motion until a hiss leaves his throat and he lays back.

"Worth it," he smiles.

"I love you," I say softly, "So much. I know I get angry when you choose to be quiet and I know that talking isn't your strong suit. But I love you for that because you've always been the best listener. I just feel like I should be telling you every single thing that I love about you but the list is-" I pause.

"Long?" He laughs pressing his head against mine with a huff of air. "On the beach, you were so cold. Your lips were blue and your chest was sick and pale. I just started talking, it was like I needed you to hear everything."

"Did you mean it? What you said about me meeting your son or was that a near-death hallucination?" I ask nuzzling into his shoulder. He groans, "I'm sorry," I say forgetting his bandages and trying to pull away.

"No, come back. It's fine. It's nothing compared to the sheer agony I felt when I found out you jumped into that water. I thought you were gone. Sean was just standing there. I got the jump on him and knocked him out cold. But you were gone." He shudders. I run my hand over his cheek and sigh.

"I thought you were dead," I say quietly. "I heard the gunshots and when Sean came after me—I thought the worst. I didn't care anymore, death seemed easier than dealing with the grief of losing you all over again." Tears stream down my face.

"Promise me you'll never do anything like that again?" He says looking down at me.

"I thought you were dead," I grimace.

"I wasn't. I would never leave you so easily," he says.

"You have before," I remind him.

"A mistake I will regret my entire life but will never make again. Death himself tried to rip me apart from you and didn't succeed. I'm not going anywhere. Ever again." He kisses me again, "and yes I meant it. I want you to meet him, for us to be a family. If you're okay with that. I know that's not what you wanted."

"I only ever wanted to be with you Bishop," I smile.

42

The sun is low in the sky, creating soft and warm colors along the horizon. The world looks so peaceful and calm on the water. Bishop appears from below deck dressed in navy blue and lays a fuzzy blanket over my shoulders. He's still limping from the wound on his leg but it gets better every day we're on the water.

It's been six months since it all happened, and two weeks on the boat with Bishop.

"I don't think I've ever been happier," he nuzzles into my shoulder, wrapping his arms around me and leaning against my back.

"This is exactly what we needed," I snuggle back into him and let him warm me from the early morning chill. He smells like spice and seawater. I turn to him and hold his face between my hands.

His hair is long again, tucked into a messy bun at the back of his head. The loose pieces fly around his face and he smiles at me, the twinkle back in his ocean blue eyes.

"You know sometimes I think you can't be real," I whisper and press a light kiss to his perfect pouty lips. "I look at you and I can't believe someone as beautiful as you can exist for normal people to see."

"Normal people? Really?" He throws his head back in laughter, it's sweet and his eyes squish together tighter the larger his smile grows. "You are far past normal, baby. You are an angel."

"Have you heard anything from Ben?" I ask and the mood drops. Sean had been convicted of assault with a weapon, intent to murder, and kidnapping. Bishop pulls back and takes a seat against the left side of the deck, he pulls his phone out. Service isn't great on the water, we can usually only get it when we dock for refuels.

As expected he has none, he sets the useless phone beside him on the bench seating. "On Monday when we refueled I called. He said Sean is having a hard time in prison, he's a cop so the other prisoners don't take to that well."

"We didn't put him there Bishop," I say, the guilt was visibly seeping from him and he sighs looking up at me.

"I know, Nora. I know. I just wish we could have seen it coming, stopped it before he spiraled so far out of control." I walk towards him and slide into his lap, wrapping my arms around his shoulders.

"He tried to kill you. How do you still have so much compassion for him?" I ask.

"I spent my entire life in Sean's position, being the guy that no one wants to forgive. He was just lost and unfortunately, he doesn't have a lighthouse." He rubs the skin on my cheek. "You're the only reason I didn't wind up in jail right next to him."

"And you are the only reason I'm alive." I muse, pressing my forehead to his and breathing him in I close my eyes.

"If I hadn't seen you go over the edge, I would have killed him. Not knowing if he hurt you..." he pauses.

"Hey," I say, pulling his chin up to meet my gaze. "We're alive and we're free."

"Finally." He smiles and looks out to the ocean surrounding us. "It took a long time but you finally got your wish. You're one of the sailboats now," He leans against me, tightly hugging me to him, and smiles.

"I love you," I say, letting him hug me. I feel so warm and safe here like nothing can touch us ever again.

He touches his lips to mine, full and warm they press down against me and I feel like I am in the clouds. His tongue slowly touches my bottom lip, tasting me carefully he waits for me to open my mouth. His hand cups the slim curve of my neck, trailing down over the shape of my breasts. His thumb brushes over the already hard nipples, he pushes himself against me and I settle back against him just the same.

I tuck my hand around his neck, pulling him deeper into the kiss. I run my fingers through his hair, releasing it from the elastic and letting it tangle in my fingers as he moves further down. His hand grips my thigh with a teasing squeeze before tucking between my legs.

"mm," he moans against my lips, he holds his hand against me as I long for him to touch me more. He laughs into the kiss and his whole body twitches in response to my body. "Seems once this morning already wasn't enough to satisfy either of us."

"We do have a lot of catching up to do," I tease. His tongue juts out over his bottom lip and his eyes are dark and full of desire.

He wastes no time pulling me back to him, his lips on mine again as he pushes the silk fabric of my shorts aside. I groan against him as his fingers slide further down and dip into the

316

wetness that is between my legs.

"So ready," he laughs, "what is going on inside your mind, dirty, dirty, Nora." He smiles against my lips and drags his tongue against my lip before placing a trail of kisses against my jaw and neck.

"Well, you know how badly I want you, what are you going to do about it?" I tease, he shakes his head and chuckles against my skin.

He strokes a finger over my clit, rubbing slowly at first and I begin to involuntarily circle my hips into his movements. He picks up the pace making me gasp. I lose my grip and almost slide off his lap, gripping tighter I lean back into his arms.

"Bishop," moans escape my lips as he pushes one in, and then another fucking me on the deck in the open air in a steady rhythm while his thumb still circles my clit. Harder and faster, I feel the heat rise in my stomach. I buck, tangling my fingers in his loose hair, pressing my face into his shoulder to muffle my screams as I come.

He smirks in triumph, very clearly proud of himself.

"You want more?" He chuckles, sliding his fingers out, and wraps his arms around my waist, lifting us off the bench he carefully walks towards the stairs to the lower deck.

"I'm nowhere near done," he growls into my ear as he lays me against the bed in the back of the cabin. "Come here," he pulls me close to him, our bodies entangled, his hard length moves against my groin. It had been only an hour since they were first in this position, yet I ache more for him.

He rolls us over on the bed, pulling my pajama shirt up and over my head as part of my legs, and settles against him. I can feel the heat between as he begins to tremble from the want of it all.

I arch my back, tightening around him as he thrusts upward and into me even deeper than before. He wiggles out of his shirt, exposing the hard and tanned muscles beneath the fabric. I run my fingers along the scar on his shoulder, it's awful. The skin twists and puckers together unevenly. I grimace but he pushes my hand down against it.

"Not right now," he moans, sweat beads at his navel and across his collarbone. It's so damn hot in the cabin the temperature rises with the sun and it doesn't help when we are this close, moving this much. I moan as he pushes his hips up and around in a circle.

I run my hands along his chest, digging my nails in just a little. He groans and pushes against the bed as I squeeze my thighs against his. For a second my mind betrays me and Sean lays beneath me. His blonde hair was messy against the bed and his ice-blue eyes were cold and murderous. *That feels good baby, keep going,* he grins. I shudder but Bishop puts his hand against my waist.

"It's me," he whispers. Ben had been treating my PTSD, we hadn't found a solution for the lapses in my memory yet. I went weeks without seeing him, feeling him, and hearing him. Bishop had been too good about it. I had hidden it for weeks after everything happened. I had to sell the apartment because he found me in the bathtub, fully clothed having a panic attack.

The walls had closed in on me. So I told him everything. Sometimes he even materializes when it was supposed to be Bishop.

"Come back to me," he sits up against me, still connected and tangled in one another. He wraps my legs around his back and presses his head to my chest. I find purchase by running

318

my fingers through his hair and breathing him in heavily.

"I'm sorry," I whisper, "I'm so sorry."

"Look at me," he pulls back and looks at me. His eyes are so blue, his soft smile pulls at the corners of his lips. "It's you and me."

I nod, returning the smile, and kiss him. It's slow at first, but as we start to feel each other again he becomes hungry against my lips. He pulls away and sucks a nipple into his mouth causing me to shudder against him in pleasure.

"Bishop," I moan into his neck.

Changing pace he adjusts the angle of his hips, I cry out but he keeps going. Harder this time, he pushes into me. Making me forget everything and everyone but him.

I reach between us and touch myself, begging him not to stop. He understands what I'm doing, rolling us back to the bed to give me more room while he thrusts his cock deeper inside of me.

My gasps and quick breaths fill the cabin as I come to a second finish, pushing back against him as he grips my thighs and holds me in place. He cries out, quaking under my body. His body goes slack against me as he pulls out and lies back.

"That was good," he groans and rolls against me, tracing small circles on my bare stomach. His fingers trace over my scar, just as ugly as his but maimed the soft skin of my stomach.

"Is it getting worse?" He asks me softly, his voice traitorous to his true feelings. He's scared.

"I've never had an episode in bed like that," I admit and he sighs, running his hand against my stomach. "He just won't go away," I tuck my head against his shoulder.

"We'll handle it like we handle everything, together." Bishop leans close and presses a kiss to my temple. "The ghost of Sean

Roberts isn't going to scare me away. I think you should up your meetings with Ben when we're done on the boat. These are only going to get worse."

"I hate that you're right," I sigh. "I'll call him next time we make land."

"I love you, Nora Quinn," he smiles against my forehead. I can feel the upturns of his lips as he hums into my hair.

"I love you, Bishop Bartley." I smile to myself, pushing away all my fears and doubts. I was finally home.

Made in the USA
Las Vegas, NV
20 September 2022

55691551R00194